Paradox in Paris

Paradox in Paris

C.R. Page

Turn The Page Creations

Also by C.R. Page

Bedside in Berlin
The Ride to Work

Coming Soon

Hurdles in Hobart
Survival in Saint Petersburg
Festive in Finland

This book is published by Turn the Page Creations.

Fullarton SA 5063 Australia

Copyright © 2023 C.R. Page

Cover designed and created by Alison Page Photography

ISBN 978-0-6454757-8-4

A catalogue copy of this novel is held by the National Library of Australia

First published 2023

To Mum. Not only did you teach me the magic of travel, but that much of the joy came from documenting the experiences and telling the stories afterwards. This book would never exist without these lessons.

9 March 2023

ELLIOT

Claudia had always insisted that the first mouthful be treated with the sanctity of a religious ceremony. It didn't matter if it was dinner, a glass of wine or a piece of chocolate, she believed that the moment the flavour hit the cleansed palate should be close to bliss. Consuming the remainder was merely a way to fill the stomach and be reminded of the glorious moment that preceded it.

It isn't only our tastebuds where the initial impression is everything. Claudia's influence was vindicated with the satisfaction of every first moment. Whatever it is, the first moment is always special and generally defines the progress of everything that follows. In most respects sex with Claudia may have gotten better with time, but never did my heart beat faster than through the trepidation and excitement that accompanied our first night together. We never would have had that experience if we didn't make the right first impression when we met. It was surprising that I had achieved this. Claudia had an air of mystery that intrigued me, and anytime I was interested enough it usually resulted in me turning into a babbling idiot. Actually, that tended to be a best-case scenario. More frequently I chose to run away.

Experience teaches us how to live, and it had taught me that running away was a legitimate approach. Once I had done this enough, the updated experience proved that running away was rarely the best option. By then it was so entrenched in my approach to life, that I knew little else. I had to change, and my trip to Europe was central to that. I understand the irony; I was running away to learn how to stop running away. That over-simplifies both my movements and my objectives.

Organising my first overseas trip so soon after Claudia broke up with me was not designed to run away from a reality but to run towards one. I had started with the security of the English-speaking world with a week in London and another touring the rest of Britain. Now I was raising the stakes as I moved to the challenge of somewhere that was in equal parts daunting and exciting. Not only was Paris my first foray on to the continent, I was set for my first encounter in fifteen years with a man I equally admired and feared. My Uncle John.

The first sight of suburban Paris is, as Claudia had instilled so deeply in me, a recollection that I'll never lose. I wanted to take in every high-light and every flaw the way I had savoured every piece of her when that relationship began. A city and a person. The similarities are far greater than people often realise. Both have a public persona, but stripped away, they reveal a deep inner unique set of qualities. In every case, how-ever blinded we may be by a choice of admiration or disdain, there is a set of both positive and negative characteristics within. I feel Paris, like Claudia, may change my life through her stunning allure before cutting through me with her dark side.

How could anyone not be excited by the prospect of this magnifi-cent city? No city in the world attracts more overseas visitors. No city has such an array of books written about it or is the source of as much storytelling, painting and other art as the City of Light. For the resident and tourist alike, Paris is more than a city. Its name automatically con-jures a powerful array of images that tell a story more complex, diverse and beautiful than anywhere in the world. Perhaps, once I experience it for myself, mystique will be replaced by disappointment as it has for a proportion of those who hate the city. For each of them, there are many who maintain that this is the most wonderous place on the planet.

After the photos and maps I had studied in the months since planning my trip, I felt that I knew the city well. Looking out the window from the outer suburbs, I realised that the highlights of a city were no great preparation. There was no Eiffel Tower or Notre Dame outside, just the standard outer suburbia that you'd expect in any city. It is the best side of every city that gets exposed, so it is not a surprise that the less appealing features I've been seeing seem a world away from all I've looked forward to seeing in the flesh.

That the city has been home to one of my closest blood relatives highlights the unorthodox family ties that supposedly bind us. More, I would suggest, it emphasises the unfortunate consequences of people too stubborn to yield fractionally when complete agreement is not forthcoming.

I was eight when I last saw Uncle John. He came home when his mother, my grandmother, passed away. He bonded with my brothers and I, but even at that young age I could see the strain in his relationship with my father. When Dad died three years ago, I knew John wouldn't be back again. I wasn't sure that he'd want to see me now, but he was not the purpose of my trip, merely a possible bonus.

Uncle John is a writer. Or maybe he *was* a writer. He wrote a book in the 1980's called *Of Virtue and Vice*, which became a global best seller and set him up for life. Nothing he ever did after that point had remotely the same success, and though he did release other novels nothing else ever gained traction. If a person writes words that nobody reads, are they still called a writer? Perhaps I will have a better idea of what tense to use for his career after I see him.

He certainly doesn't believe in using too many words through electronic communication. I have sent him a couple of emails in advance of my arrival, seeking to organise meeting with him. The responses have ranged from '*Sure,*' to the more expansive '*Whatever suits you,*' of his last reply. I didn't expect overwhelming enthusiasm, for the relationship within our family is strained, but I am not the source of any issues. I had hoped he may show a little more interest in seeing what he'd hopefully consider untainted flesh and blood.

It should come as no surprise that I look to John as a hero. Imagine being so closely related to a man so famous and admired around the globe. It doesn't matter how prolific or otherwise he may have been since, if you produce one work of such magnitude, you have an eternal legacy. How can I not be in awe of that?

Naturally the pride I feel was the same view that all of my family shared at one point in time, but that changed over the years. Dad always maintained that there is a level of success that people can have which changes their outlook on where they belong in the world.

'Humility is one of life's essential qualities. Once people reach a certain level of success and fame, they lose the ability to be humble. Where that line sits is different for each person, and it also tends to be different based on how quickly their successes comes. Your Uncle John went to Europe with a dream of writing a novel. Everyone's perception of his ability was that he'd be lucky to write a letter that would be worth reading. Within two years he'd gone from untalented nobody to releasing one of the most admired novels any Australian had ever written. It's hardly surprising that he thought the world revolved around him. Sadly, the people who made him were the ones who copped this arrogance.'

Dad was five years younger than John and struggled to have any impact in the many careers he tried his hand at. Was living in John's shadow an excuse or a reason? As much as I heard similar views of John from my grandparents and Aunt Julie, I was never willing to be talked against him. He was my family, and he was a recognised genius. At worst, he was also an arsehole, but who isn't in some ways? I never tried to suggest he was an example of what I would want to be as a person, but I was equally sure that he was a perfect example of what I'd yearn to achieve in a career. Respect, admiration and success. Thanks to my father, I would do everything in my capacity to make sure that I retained humility if these results surfaced.

I've spotted the first great landmark through the window. Sacre-Coeur, the stunning white church at the top of the hill above Montmartre is distant but proves we're getting close. It is only a couple of kilometres between Sacre Coeur and our terminus. I only get the occasional sighting of the basilica as gaps between buildings briefly allow a more panoramic view. We must be only minutes away.

The train starts to decelerate and the most enthusiastic are getting ready to alight. I may be more excited about what's awaiting me than anyone, but jumping a place or two in the queue for passport control isn't going to achieve much. I deliberately booked a hotel close to Gare du Nord so that it should be easy to get to. As it is the first time I've ever arrived in a place where I don't speak the language, I'm taking nothing for granted about the speed with which I will find it.

There is the platform. A feeling from deep within forces me to take a deeper breath as I take in the magnitude of the moment. As insignificant as it seems to the flurry of activity around me, it is an unbelievable landmark moment in the scheme of my life. I am in Paris.

9 March 2023

JOHN

There is no city in the world so famed and fabled in book, song and on film. Paris. The name triggers thoughts to people the world over. More international tourists visit Paris than any other city, but to billions of people who have never been here, the thoughts are just as clear. From the Eiffel Tower to the famed cuisine, the world has a pre-conceived view of this city. On arrival, there is so much of the city that plays to the stereotypes that are normally expected, but it is only those who stay long enough to dig deeper that get to understand all that Paris truly is.

The City of Light or the City of Love, to me Paris is home. I grew up in Australia, but after coming here for a short time at the end of my first trip to Europe, I found myself unwilling to leave. I've never been the type to feel so connected to a place, but everything about this city told me I belonged here. I'd always been an outsider, and I felt this way in Paris too, but in a very different way to what I'd been at home.

Paris is a city of rebellion. Perhaps that resonated with me more than anything. Growing up, I was constantly rebelling, whatever there was to justify such behaviour. Here you can rest assured that strikes and protests are never far away. Since the time of the French Revolution, Parisians have never been content to accept what they consider to be wrong. In Paris, you fight for what is right. Always. Like everywhere else, things are never right for everyone, and as a result, there is rarely a time when strikes and protests aren't taking place across the city. The King of England was meant to visit us recently, but his trip was abandoned such were the demands on the security services with the recent wave of unrest.

Paris is a city that prides itself on individuality, despite the role that fashion plays here. Fitting in with fashion is stereotypically Parisian, but there is great scope here for people to put very individual twists on this. Parisians admire style, and the more individual that style was, the more it was appreciated. Fashion in Paris didn't mean following others, it meant twisting the established templates on show and adding your own persona to it. I never looked fashionable, yet I never looked out of style. I would have in many places, but I knew how to dress Parisian. I knew how to live Parisian, and it was all inter-connected.

Paris has always been one of the world's greatest cultural capitals. Artists, writers, and performers have flocked here, seeking the inspiration that had drawn the greats of previous generations. That is what brought me here. My grandfather was a writer, and it was the time that he spent in Paris that led to his most successful period. He spent a couple of years here before returning Down Under. I have now been here for nearly forty years. There is no other home for me, and never will be.

I came here in my early twenties with little idea of where I was headed in life. Now in my sixties, I am equally as uncertain about my direction. I guess at this point, I understand how damned insignificant that is. You don't need a place to be going. Days meld together and however well planned your future may be, it can all get taken away from you in an instant. Living for tomorrow is a recipe for disappointment. The best laid plans get shattered all too often and you're left picking up the pieces of broken dreams. I've lived dreams and I've lived nightmares. I have learned that life is best served just staying awake and rolling with whatever life throws at me in the moment.

Paris has more that keeps me awake than anywhere else. It's a big enough pond that no fish can outgrow it. There was a time when I was a somebody, but I could retain the level of anonymity that made me just like everyone else. A stranger in my hometown, able to escape the unwanted attention that turns a normal person into a public identity. Sure, there are public figures here that command the same sort of adulation as anywhere else, but in Paris the melting pot of global success stories diminishes the level to which anyone is accorded overwhelming reverence.

Paris isn't greater than any other city, nor is it inferior to anywhere else. If the most beautiful woman in the world is also the biggest bitch, would her partner be the most or least fortunate? Such measures are always subjective, and nobody can ever clearly define the score. Paris, to me, is the most beautiful city in the world. Does it have flaws? Of course, but to me the drawbacks anyone could ever point to are merely characteristics that add something to it. I understand that there will be people who hate the place, unimpressed by its strengths and focussed only on its weaknesses. This is true everywhere, and the greatness of any place is thus a matter of opinion.

Imagine a world where we all saw the same beauty and the same flaws. Every person would flock to the same places until they were so overrun that all appeal would disappear. I can walk down the street here in peace, eat in my favourite brasserie where there is always a table for me. I mightn't be able to ascend the Eiffel Tower at any time I wish, but what resident of a city ever wants to go to its main tourist beacons. I see the tower every day. It is a landmark, a defining point of my city, but as it draws in the millions that visit us, it leaves the Paris of the locals free from feeling cramped by all who just pay passing homage to our city.

The Louvre, the D'Orsay, the Rodin, the Picasso, the Pompidou. There are museums spread around this city in every corner, honouring the creativity of those who have called this city home, and which highlight the constant progress of human culture through history. Paris is not the origin of all great art, but like moths to a flame, artists have sought inspiration here and their marks are housed throughout this city to an extent unrivalled anywhere in the world.

For all of the devotion the city shows to the arts, there is an equal reverence that the city shows to sport. We'll soon host the Olympic Games for the third time, something only London had done before us. We've also hosted the football World Cup twice. We host one of the four tennis Grand Slam tournaments each year as well as the final stage of the Tour de France. Parisians may be less renowned for their sporting obsessions than the people of some other cities, but this is merely a reflection on the diversity of society here. The city is not defined by its love of sport, it is merely another component of the multi-layered way of life that makes this city special.

Is there a more famous street on the planet than the Champs-Elysses? A greater cabaret than the Moulin Rouge? A more celebrated structure than the Eiffel Tower? For all of these celebrated symbols of the city, there is another darker side. For everything that is celebrated about Paris, there is a counter. From the Eiffel Tower, look across to the Tour Montparnasse, the ugly black stump that is famous for having the best views of Paris. They say the highlight of the view from here is that it is the only spot in the city where you can't see the eyesore you are standing atop. For all the great cuisine the city is famous for, I've had thousands of awful meals. Though the city is revered for its beauty, there is more filth and grime here than most cities. Every positive has a related negative.

The City of Love is home to more cheating spouses than anywhere in the world. '*Cinq a sept*' is the famous part of Parisian culture where people spend the time between finishing work and dinner time, off on trysts with other people. The lovers visiting the city place their locks on the Pont des Arts to celebrate their exclusivity, while the locals are racing past to head to the apartments of someone new.

Those that visit Paris and leave with a sour taste are not necessarily those who garnish the least enjoyment from their time, but those for whom the city least reached the expectations they had. This usually says more about their expectations than the city itself. If you believe this city will be something more, you are destined for disappointment.

There is a recognised medical condition known as Paris Syndrome, characterised by a variety of psychiatric symptoms. It is most common in Japanese tourists, though people from other Southeast Asian nations are also highly represented in the numbers afflicted. It stems from an acute form of culture shock, the body and mind unable to cope with a reality so removed from their preconceived ideas. Perhaps isolated cases of something similar may have occurred in other places, but here it is a regular ailment. Paris doesn't just evoke wonder and passion in its visitors, it quite literally makes others sick in a way unlike anywhere else.

If life was one-dimensional and we all walked the same road, I'd be a grandfather, living these years with the ultimate celebrations being those with family surrounding me. Basking in the glory of my legacy, I'd be proud of the achievements of my children, excited by the development of my grandchildren, and focussing on my wellbeing so that I could extend my lifespan and continue having moments like these. That wasn't my road. How much of this was choice, and how much circumstance, I can't really say. I never sat down to thoroughly plan a novel, I merely started with an idea, then saw where it took me. I lived how I wrote.

I don't regret anything. For every negative, I've had a positive. How does anyone really measure who got the best of life. Experiences set the curve by which we grade our lives. Those who have experienced the greatest triumphs sink furthest with their failures. Those who have lived with nothing get the greatest appreciation from the smallest wins. At the end of the day, the overall satisfaction with life has little to do with what an outsider sees on the scoreboard. All any of us can seek is to be satisfied within, by what we have and what we have done.

I wrote a best-selling novel when I first came to this city. A generation on, my name is remembered for that one success. Ever since, I have been measured against that success, and to each person who looks at my life after that moment, I've been a failure. It doesn't concern me at all, for everything I've worked on since hasn't needed to make a cent. I have written about life as I have witnessed it, and I have written what I believe to be truth.

Through my eyes, my work has got better with time. If there is not another person alive who shares that view, so be it. I live every moment of my life in my own skin, hearing my own thoughts. I don't need to justify anything to anybody else. I don't need validation. Success for an author is not the number of sales you make, but the satisfaction you have in what you complete.

Every work I've ever started has begun with a thought that I was writing a masterpiece. What I've finished up with has never been as good as that first idea. How I measure a work is how close I've come to the original vision. While *Of Virtue and Vice* may be my only success in the eyes of many, it fell further from my original idea than all the books which have followed. For me, that makes it the greatest failure of my career, not the great success that critics and sales figures suggest.

You can wish things were different without regretting the choices that has led to a point. I wish I did have family beside me. My relationships with my family fell apart many years ago. At the time, it was all my fault in their eyes, and all theirs through mine. With age has come wisdom, and I know that blame is useless. None of it was anyone's fault, for each of us were living according to who we genuinely were. Being true to myself drove a wedge between my family and me. Although those recollections sadden me, there's not an action I ever took that I would change.

I've been in contact with my nephew recently. He is coming to Paris, and it will be the first possibility of me seeing anyone in the family since my mother's funeral fifteen years ago. I'd love to believe that this may be the start of a burgeoning relationship with blood connections, but I keep expectations realistic. He may think he's meeting John Martin, the public figure that he's researched online. He may be very disappointed to meet John Martin, the anonymous Parisian who blends into life in the city like everyone else. Whatever life delivers, the satisfactions only come when they are based around truth. If the ties that bind us turn into something positive, that is ideal, but only if it is genuine.

All of that is irrelevant if he doesn't come and see me. If I was a twenty-year old arriving in the world's liveliest city, the last thing on my list would be seeking out a comparatively lifeless old bastard.

3

9 March 2023

ELLIOT

Within a minute of walking out of the main entrance of the Gare du Nord, I have learned that Paris has a symbol more telling than its famous tower, museums or cathedrals. Car horns. In most places I've ever been, the car horn is a rarely used item, there for the necessity of capturing the attention of another driver before calamity occurs. Here, it is used more like an indicator, just as a reminder to everyone that you are near. Cars barely move as I look at the long line of frustrated drivers on the Rue de Dunkerque and the even more concerned people in vehicles stuck on the Boulevard de Denain hoping to join the main road.

Between me and traffic, the paved forecourt is overflowing with people. Some, with luggage at the side, are recent arrivals or soon to be departing passengers. It seems that we may be the minority. This clearly is the place to be, though not for the elite of Parisian society. Within a minute I have had at least three people ask me for a cigarette, though with my well-rehearsed line of *'Je ne parle pas Francais'* at the ready, I make short shrift of each one.

My initial thought of finding the traffic lights to get across the madness of this road didn't last, as I watched the ease that people had crossing. Ease may have been the wrong word, for the ability cars ever had to move was so limited, that they weren't going to wait for pedestrians.

When a gap came, they'd move, and if a pedestrian was caught in the middle, so be it. Pedestrians played the odds that cars moving was so rare, they'd probably be safe. Probable wasn't my preferred level of safety, but I followed close enough behind a confident looking local that I felt I'd really maximised my chances. Successfully, so it proved.

For all the planning I had in my head of exactly where I needed to go, the reality wasn't quite so simple. 'Walk out the entrance, cross the road and walk two blocks,' was my rehearsed plan. The reality of any train station, particularly one the size of the Gare du Nord, was that there were many entrances, and I'd worked out that the one I had taken was not the one I needed. The street I was on ran perpendicular to the Rue de Dunkerque, while I needed a road running at 45 degrees. I looked up and down and couldn't see where I was meant to be, so for all of my organisation and planning, I was back to looking at my phone. I was following the exact manner that I could have achieved without any advanced preparation.

Eventually I found my way to the Boulevard Magenta, and I knew it was just a short walk to my hotel. I tried to take in every shop I passed, ensuring I knew where I could get anything I may need. I wanted to be sure that at least some small part of this overwhelming city could be managed with confidence. I probably had little reason for apprehension, but most circumstances in life were daunting when we lacked precedents to refer to. London had been an extension of life at home, as conversation could easily be used to manage any scenario I faced. Here, conversation wasn't an option, so trouble would never be so easily overcome.

A small supermarket, a Turkish restaurant, a souvenir shop and a chemist later, I had arrived at Rue des Petits Hotels. As limited as my knowledge of French may be, I knew that this was the Street of Small Hotels, which seemed appropriate. My hotel was indeed a small one, and it was sandwiched between and across from several others. Being so close to both Gare du Nord and Gare de l'Est, it was a convenient location for people to stay on short trips to the city.

I opened the door to my hotel and kept repeating my limited rehearsed spiel of French that I hoped would get me through the check-in process. It may make sense that anyone working in a hotel can speak basic English, but this isn't about sense. This is the reality churning through my head as I encounter a completely new experience.

'*Bonjour monsieur,*' the hotel receptionist greeted me.

'*Bonjour,*' I nervously replied. '*Je ne parle pas Francais. Parlez-vous Anglais?*'

'Yes, of course. Are you checking in?'

'Yes, thank you,' I replied. All these years I have heard stories of the French being rude and arrogant to people who don't speak the language. It had filled me with a nervousness of the reception I would get. None of the people who I know have been here have ever said this, but it is such an oft-repeated story that it becomes as synonymous with Paris as the many genuine attributes of the city.

Check-in was simple, and within a few minutes I was in the elevator with my suitcase, albeit squeezed in tight. Never in Australia had I experienced an elevator so small, but clearly a couple who each had a suitcase would not be able to go upstairs together. I've been in elevators that have listed seemingly impossible maximum capacities back home, but not to this extent. The limit indicated on the sticker was a total of eight people. If they were under the age of four and piled one on top of the other, there still would be no chance of getting that number of people in the lift. My suitcase took the place of a second person, and I could see no chance of anyone else finding space to both enter and breathe.

Paris is filled with many thousands of similar buildings. Many of these are hotels, while more again are apartment buildings providing a more permanent home to residents. These were built across the city in the 1850s and 1860s before the point of time when elevators were installed in such buildings. When the need to add these was determined later, there was only very limited available space. As such, people with a tendency for claustrophobia were always going to dodge them in this city.

My room, like the elevator, was small. It had to be. It was inexpensive, unlike almost everything in Paris. Very few cities have such a significant part of its population living in the centre of the city, and such a balance can only be achieved with a certain level of sacrifice. Here that means dwellings are small by necessity and that land is extremely expensive. A relatively cheap hotel room here may not be cheap in the way I was accustomed to, but retaining affordability means that rooms are no bigger than necessary.

Why would you need a big hotel room in Paris? There couldn't be a city with more to see, so spending too much time in your room rather defeats the purpose of being here. I intended to be out on the streets seeing as much as I could as soon as possible. I filled the kettle to make an instant coffee so I had something to drink while I emptied my suitcase and put it under the desk by the wall, maximising the available floorspace.

I decided to have a shower so I could feel a little refreshed after the days long journey. The London to Paris train takes only a little more than 2 hours, but from my accommodation on the other side of London until I got to the room here was well over double that. I want to cover a lot of territory tonight, so delaying my departure slightly seems reasonable enough.

It is tempting to lay down. The bed looks inviting, but I'm resisting temptation. There is a time for sleeping. When you only have a week in the most exciting city on Earth, that point of time is when you are completely spent. That for me remains a long way off. I don't know how much of my time here will be taken up with my uncle. I hope it will be most of it, so I need to make the most of my free time now.

4

6 April 1984

JOHN

Another day and another arrival in a new European city. For all they say about the beauty of Paris, as the train starts descending on the French capital, the journey through suburbia is of no greater interest to me than it has been anywhere else. For the past six weeks I have traversed Italy, Austria, West Germany, Switzerland, Spain, Portugal and now parts of France in the search of inspiration. Now I'm counting on this city to fill my pot sufficiently to fuel the novel that I hoped this trip would inspire.

This city feels like a line dropped in the sea. Its famous attractions the bait on the hook, and as I sit on the train, I'm like a fish that has been unable to resist the lure and is now being reeled in. I will shortly lie in the city's basket at the Gare de Lyon. Life as I have known it will be replaced by something else.

I know what people back home think. In their eyes, my trip to Europe was purely to run away. I'd been engaged to Beth for only a month when she found out about Debbie. I was only seventeen when that happened, but I admit I should have been open about it from the start. If she couldn't accept the mistakes of my past, then it wasn't meant to be. I certainly didn't need to be running away from her, for I see it as her loss not mine. Paris is not a place you go to escape somewhere else, it is somewhere you seek for its own sense of magic.

I admit, I had run away from Debbie several years earlier. She was pregnant and neither of us were ready for what that involved, only she wasn't able to admit that. She was resolute about keeping the baby. I was steadfast in my opposition, and soon after we split. I ran, starting a new life in Melbourne. A month later, tragedy intervened when Debbie went into labour very prematurely. The baby never made it out of hospital. I felt overwhelming grief and guilt. I hadn't wanted it, but that doesn't change the fact it was my baby. I was mortified that someone I had genuinely loved suffered through that without me. She had made the decision about the baby, and she made the decision to end our relationship, but it took me a couple of years before I returned to Adelaide.

I met Beth a little over two years ago. We got engaged at the start of this year, but that lasted a little over two months before the secret I had kept about Debbie came out. Whether the main source of her anger was the fact I had kept it secret, or the fact I had walked out on a pregnant partner, the result was the same. She ended the engagement immediately. All attempts at reconciliation proved futile. I wasn't the man she thought I was, and she wasn't changing her mind. A month later, I stopped thinking about the future I wanted, and began to pursue what I wanted in the present. Travel. In particular, Paris.

I was eight years old when my grandfather Leonard told me about his first visit to Paris. He had been a writer, and in Paris in the 1920s he met some of literatures most famous names. He never reached the heights of Hemmingway, Fitzgerald and Joyce, but his exposure to such luminaries did feed him with the ideas that would lead to his first novel. Sixty years on, I was seeking the same result, though the mindset I carried within me was demanding more.

My grandfather learned lessons in Paris, but while it helped him grow, it didn't change him. I seek to shed my skin and become a new man. The man I want to be, or at least the writer I want to be, is within.

He is buried deep under the layers I have accumulated in order to cope with life. Stripping them away in the anonymity that is on offer in this great city will allow the writer within to surface.

The southern suburbs of Paris. I may as well be passing through the suburbs of London, New York or Rome. There is nothing romantic I can see outside these windows. Dirt. Grime. People slogging their way through life trying to manage the expense that most of the world won't see until the 1990's, on an income that they should have had in the 1970's. All the big cities are littered with people who struggle to get by. The bigger the city, the more people it draws towards it. Like anything, the supply and demand in a big city means that plenty of people miss out. To anyone who knows me, I'm far too insignificant to make it here. What they don't grasp is that I'm too insignificant for the predators to notice me, so I can lurk and develop until I'm big enough to stand up and fight for my place. I know what lies within, and I know I can make it wherever I choose to be. If Paris can inspire me as it did my grandfather, then it will be here that I stay for the foreseeable future.

To our right I can see the Bois de Vincennes, the massive park that dominates the east of the city and I know the destination is close. However non-plussed I like to believe I am by whatever comes before me, I can't pretend that arriving in Paris doesn't feel like a watershed moment. I might not be someone who will be running to the sights that tourists fall over themselves to see, but as sure as they all arrive on a quest of their own, so too do I. I won't stop strangers and ask them to take holiday snaps of me by the Eiffel Tower but I will be taking far more detailed prints in my mind of every little subtlety in this city that most tourists will never see. I will sit out the front of a café with a glass of wine, a packet of cigarettes and will turn a passer-by into a character that will be read by millions for decades to come. Those are the memories I seek to capture.

The train slows, and our journey from Marseilles is coming to an end at the capital's eastern-most terminus. I have organised a room in a hotel near the Place de la Bastille, which is about a kilometre away.

After sitting so long, the walk will do me good, albeit with an awkward amount of luggage. The place is a little out of where I want to be and also above the price I want to pay, so I will only be there for a night or two before I find a more suitable option. My resources aren't that limited, but with nothing coming in for the foreseeable future and a desire to maximise my stay, I need to economise. God knows I don't want to be cutting out the good times, so something else has to give. I was following in my grandfather's footsteps. As he made the most of his time in Paris, I was intent on living similarly.

The relationships I had with most of my family began to deteriorate in my mid-teens, but it was at that same point that my bond with Grandpa Leonard began to grow stronger. He had said that in his youth he had been something of the black sheep of the family, something that I closely related with. Although at that point I would never have considered writing as a career, I did like telling stories just as he did. In his last years I spent considerable time listening to his stories, many of which were about the times he'd spent in Paris. I had read all of his books, most of which had been out of print for decades and I would never have found if not for his own collection. It had certainly made me view literature differently.

Before we stop, half of the people in the carriage are already lining up for the door. Whatever the coming weeks have in store for me, I calculate the effort of joining the rush would be significant for the most negligible of gains. I remain in my seat and I watch my fellow passengers, just as Grandpa told me he always had. The inspiration for characters came less from the people he knew, and more from the strangers who passed him in situations like these.

The man who'd sat in front of me could have been anyone, but there was a manner to his breathing when we stopped for a missed signal that suggested he was a man in a hurry. That behaviour was repeated at arrival despite the fact we have arrived a few minutes ahead of schedule. If we are early, surely he has no need to rush, but routine impatience in any scenario takes over for some people. I imagine him driving a car, his blood pressure on the rise when stuck behind a slow driver before he gets the opportunity to fly past them, only to be forced to stop half a minute later at traffic lights. The car he passed pulls up alongside him, and through the good fortune of the lane he is in, moves off ahead.

How any of that would fit into any of the ideas I have for my novel is questionable, but it highlights where inspiration can strike. The more you watch people, the more examples like this become evident. Paris is the home of café culture, working in tandem with people watching. Chairs outside faced the road, not each other, as the sight of the world that passes by is always filled with inspiration, whereas similar wonder in a companion is far rarer.

The passengers thinned out, I stand and walk to the door. As I alight, I take a deep breath and step into the Parisian afternoon. My first moments in the city, yet it feels like I have arrived home. Home is less about the place you live, or the place you are from, but the place that feels right. I've never known a true feeling of home, and even if this is a false dawn, the confidence I have in the city has given me belief. It is an unfamiliar feeling, but walking along the platform in the direction of the famous clock-tower, it is one that I'm willing to pursue.

I'm ready for you Paris.

5

9 March 2023

ELLIOT

From the moment of leaving the hotel to explore the city, it has only taken me four minutes to find trouble. Or was it? Maybe I missed an amazing opportunity by reading too much into it?

I was walking along the Boulevard de Magenta, heading away from the Gare du Nord. I don't know Paris enough to know the type of area I was walking in. In most cities it isn't so hard to tell. The size and style of dwellings makes it very hard to be confused between the best, the worst and everything in between. In central Paris, most dwellings look similar enough that it isn't clearcut. The 19th century buildings share a common style wherever you go, so I had no reason for apprehension.

Maybe it wasn't a reflection on the area, but I saw a few groups of people congregating in the street that had me alert. I'd read enough about street crime in Paris to be conscious of worst-case scenarios. There was little to suggest that things were worse here than in any big city, but anywhere I am unfamiliar with has me taking certain precautions. Principally, I carry a wallet in my jeans pocket, filled with a miniscule amount of currency, as well as a range of cards of no value. Of course, buried on an inside pocket was my real wallet, but if any trouble was to come my way, I could give up the decoy wallet. In theory this would have me escaping trouble while losing nothing of value.

On the third block from my hotel, there was a young woman, possibly not eighteen, sitting on the ground. She looked up and smiled at me. Absolutely beautiful. She called out to me in French, and it was the most direct and appealing introduction I had ever received. There was so much I had wanted to spend my first evening seeing, but none of it was going to appeal as much as this angelic looking woman. I stopped, and time briefly stood still as I envisaged how every fantasy I'd ever had, seemed to be coming together in this moment.

In a split-second before it hit me. I had never won the lottery. Surely a stunning looking Parisian woman approaching me in this place and in this manner was about as likely as a lottery win. I didn't have girls throwing themselves at me in any situation. This couldn't be genuine could it? I looked around and saw the group of similarly aged men staring at me, and to the other direction another similar looking group.

The girl called out again, this time speaking broken English.

'Why not come with me? I would like to get to know you better.'

In the best-case scenario, I was going to be paying a financial price for her "getting to know me" service. More likely, I was going to be paying with more than money.

Just seconds after first seeing that smile, I was again moving, albeit a little quicker than before. The men weren't going to launch any sort of attack on me while we were on this busy footpath, but I sensed the young woman's objective had been to lure me along the little laneway she was at the corner of. From there, I would have been gone in no time. The group would now wait for the next man who had a little less capacity than me to allow his brain to overrule his dick. In my case, this was a very close fought battle.

I'd immediately decided that my next expedition from the hotel would see me take the Rue La Fayette instead. I had no idea if that would be any different, but I stuck to the adage that you don't make the same mistake twice. I may be going from bad to worse, but when you know one way is wrong, any other option should be explored before repeating the original mistake.

I didn't come with a clear plan of where I was going, just a general concept of making my way towards the Seine. From there I figured I could walk along and see the majority of the cities most iconic sites. I hadn't planned the best way of getting there, but I'd always had faith in my sense of direction. I knew I'd taken off the right way, but where and when to turn would be another story.

At the end of the Boulevard de Magenta, I reached the Place de la Republique. This was an enormous public square, highlighted by a massive statue of Marianne, the personified symbol of France. It had been in the news recently as one of the central points for protests as the people of the city fought to block reforms to the pension system. I walked across the square, hoping to navigate the best way to turn. There were almost a dozen major roads breaking off from the square, so any choice would be no more than a guess. I took the road closest to the statue and hoped for the best.

From the next street sign I saw, I learned I was walking along the Rue de Turbigo but my stubbornness stopped me looking at my phone to determine quite where it was leading me. I don't have an objection to maps and itineraries in many situations, but tonight was about exploration. I had places I wanted to see, but throughout life I have found the greatest feelings of discovery come when they are not expected. I want to stumble across some of these sights, and better still, discover spots I never knew existed. The statue of Marianne at the Place de la Republique was incredible, but far more so because I hadn't known it was there.

At the end of the Rue de Terbigo I found myself at Les Halles, a giant shopping centre that was not the kind of spot I was in the mood for. I took the next street on the left which led me towards the Seine, but before getting that far I saw one of the few Parisian street names that meant something to me, the Rue de Rivoli. The street runs from Bastille Square to the Place de la Concorde, though I knew it best as part of the course from the final stage of each year's Tour de France. While much of the city's architecture was standardised, though beautiful, on the Rue de Rivoli there was a touch more to the buildings.

After a few blocks I came to a pair of large buildings on either side of the road. On the right was impressive residential and hotel accommodation, while on the left was a far more stunning structure. The Louvre. The enormity of the building should have been no surprise, yet by avoiding maps and signage, I hadn't realised at first this was quite where I was. Halfway along, the Place de Carousel intersected with the Rue de Rivoli, so I turned and walked through the archways and followed the road to the concourse.

There are varied opinions on the Louvre's glass pyramid. It is either one of the most magical structures in the world, or one of its great eyesores. I think it is the greatest highlight of Paris. Alone, it would be mildly impressive, but the connection between the modern glass masterpiece as it stands, surrounded by the regal structure from centuries earlier, highlights the essence of what the museum is about. History and modernity must work together, for that is the essence of progress and evolution. Nowhere, to my mind, achieves this balance in such an extreme yet perfect manner.

I don't care about being a stereotypical tourist. I was happy to wander the forecourt taking selfies with the pyramid as my backdrop. I didn't want to stay too long, as there was so much more to see.

I walked through the Jardins des Tuileries appreciating the integral part of any great city that its parks and gardens play. Paris as an entity needs a clean set of lungs in order to thrive, and Tuileries serves this role.

Following the gardens was the Place de la Concorde, another of the legacies of my years watching the Tour de France. A location once famous for public executions, including Louis XVI and Marie Antoinette, it is now a public square more ceremonial than functional. While spots like the Place de Republique can accommodate vastly greater numbers of people, the Concorde is famous for its Egyptian obelisk and the Fountain of River Commerce. It is a hub for tourists, who can stand in the middle and see the Louvre behind them, and the Arc de

Triomphe at the end of the Champs-Elysees in front of them. That was where I was headed.

The first part of the Champs-Elysees passes through another set of gardens, but after the grumbling of my stomach had started, a small food van captured my attention more than any garden could. I'm not sure whether the roadside creperie was more a symbol of authentic Paris or an overly derivative stereotype, but at this point it was winning me over either way. Although it was dinner time, I always thought savoury was a waste of a crepe, so it was sweet by default for me.

'*Une citron et sucre crepe, s'il vous plait*,' I requested, impressing myself if nobody else of my longest French sentence so far.

'Four euros thanks,' came the reply, putting me in my place. So much for the stereotype that Parisians refuse to acknowledge people not speaking their language. The two attempts I'd made to speak French since my arrival had been met with immediate English responses. Clearly my accent and questionable pronunciation had been as clear as my order. Central Paris is a city that is dependent on tourists and caters accordingly. I think most people appreciate those that make any small effort to respect their language and culture, so these simple attempts with greetings and orders are worthwhile. That said, my crepe man wants to make a living, and I doubt he'll turn business away by refusing customers who don't measure up to his language preferences.

Further along was the essence of what made this street so famous. The Champs-Elysees was often referred to as the most beautiful avenue in the world, and the section near the Arc de Triomphe was filled with high-end shopping, cafes and theatres. It was home to the beautiful elements of Parisian society, though in truth I suspect that these days most of the people here were tourists, or workers servicing the tourist market.

I hadn't planned it but as I saw the crowds at the top of the Arc de Triomphe the temptation was too great to say no. Having already walked for several kilometres, I knew it would be a struggle to make it up there, but I also knew that the promise of the spectacular always managed to allow me to scale the greatest heights.

There were nearly three hundred steps to climb to get to the top. It is amazing how deceptive numbers like this are. My mind told me that this was just a simple thirty steps, repeated ten times over. At this stage of the day, the first thirty steps weren't so simple. Each thirty got progressively tougher, until I knew I was close to the top and the knowledge of the view that awaited me gave me the inspiration to push on. While I'd done it, I felt as though I had climbed nearly three thousand steps rather than three hundred.

It was dusk as I stepped out at the top. The lights of the city were beginning to shine prominently. The views of every angle of Paris were spectacular, none better than along Champs-Elysees to the Louvre. The greatest clamour for space was in the corner looking out towards the Eiffel Tower. The top of the tower had often come into view throughout the day through gaps between buildings, but from the height atop the Arc, most of the structure was visible. Exhausted as I felt, when I watched the tower sparkle for its 9pm light show, I decided I would be making my down there for the same show in an hours' time.

Once back on the ground, I headed towards the tower, which appeared during breaks from the obstructions of buildings. It was a twenty-minute walk before I arrived at the Trocadero gardens, immediately across the river from the Iron Lady, with my first unobstructed view of her from head to toe.

At just after 9.45pm, my stomach was reminding me how little I'd eaten, and the convenience of another food van was the only option. I resisted the temptation of another crepe, choosing the mildly less derivative option of a hot dog. Though satisfying my hunger, it was probably less memorable than my earlier choice. So what if I have twenty crepes while I'm here. This is Paris, so why not!

I was walking across the Pont d'Iena when the tower began its 10pm sparkle. Stopping to get a quick video, I took in not only the spectacular sight, but the unbelievable feeling I had. I was standing right by the Eiffel Tower, a place so deeply entrenched in the human psyche, that even as children we yearn to see it in the flesh.

I hardly consider the decision to travel somewhere as an accomplishment, but in this moment, I feel like something fundamental to my life has been achieved. I am living a dream. Tomorrow, today's dream will be a very strong memory, but it can be more. It can serve as inspiration to pursue more dreams. Dreams that are not just the purchase of a ticket, but the input of blood, sweat and tears in pursuit of goals. Anything we aspire to is achievable. Make choices and pursue them.

This moment wasn't about the Eiffel Tower, but the realisation of a dream. A reminder that so long as we can dream, there is always a direction to head towards.

6

7 April 1984

JOHN

The great thing about buying one-way tickets when you travel is the lack of urgency you feel on arrival in a city. With other cities I have arrived in, I've been out seeing as much as I could immediately. Despite Paris having more to see than just about anywhere else, I've barely left my hotel room since arriving here yesterday. Admittedly much of my afternoon and evening was quite productive, making sense of notes I'd been writing on the train and formulating a little more of the concept for my book. I did pop out to a brasserie around the corner where I had a cheap meal and a few drinks before feeling spent early.

Today I'm a tourist. It isn't my normal role, and I might not play it quite like most do, but I will be making my way around the city to see the sights. Maybe not the same sights as everyone else, but I do have my own set of places to see.

I don't have any great interest in the museums, cathedrals and buildings that capture most people's attention. Plenty of people here would set aside half a day each for the Eiffel Tower, Louvre, Notre Dame and Sacre Coeur. I'm interested in seeing each of them as I walk past, but just to say I've seen it. None of them fascinate me enough to do anything more than stop and look as I go past.

My excitement about Paris stems from stories rather than postcards. The places my grandfather told me about conjure far more interesting images in my head than any structure that happens to appear in television and movies. Sure, when I arrive at the left bank brasserie where Grandpa dined with Hemmingway, it is now going to be a very different place with no sign of the stories I heard. That doesn't matter, for I feel that that the stories in my head will suddenly appear with a whole additional layer of depth. I won't know which table they sat at, but I won't need to. The mind will have enough of the background that it can fill in the additional details however seems most appropriate. From there, I will walk out with a memory that will stay clear forever. Most of the tourists walking out of the Louvre will have very little memory of their experience once time passes.

My grandfather also talked a lot about a couple of English language bookstores in the Latin Quarter. Shakespeare and Company was a famous store run by Sylvia Beach, and offered a home and writing space to aspiring writers. It was here that Grandpa first met Hemmingway, and where he spent a lot of his free time seeking ideas and helping others with theirs. The bookstore closed during the Nazi occupation, and Beach never returned to sufficient health to reopen. The name was later used for the modern-day bookstore on the banks of the Seine, just a few blocks away. I mightn't feel the presence of my grandfather here, but it still is a place of significance for anyone with a love of literature.

While he spent a lot of time in the Latin Quarter, his accommodation was in Montmartre for most of his stay. He was here for six months, and in that time wrote the first draft of his novel *Valour*, the tale of a Parisian labourer who rose to a position of power in the government, bringing down corrupt people above and winning reforms for the working people of France.

In the bars of Montmartre, he met Eric Beeh. Beeh served as the inspiration for his next book, *Rubber Man*, which was released early in the 1930's. Grandpa said he regretted writing it so early, for many of the great stories from Beeh's life came well after this time. Now, fifty years on, I had considered crafting the novel Grandpa would have liked to have written in later years about Beeh's full life story. It wasn't at the top of my list of ideas, but it had made me keen to go and walk the streets of the Montmartre area and retrace the places where Grandpa and him frequented.

I want to go to Pere-la-Chaise, the cemetery that is the resting place of Jim Morrison, the one rock star I really idolised. He died before I knew much of him, but once I became exposed to his music, I became a fan. Ever since, I have felt a level of intrigue about his life and death in Paris. With his quest for recognition as a poet, the affinity has only grown as I have got older. I've never yearned to visit a grave of anyone else, so this is strange for me. I won't be alone. More tourists visit Pere-la-Chaise than any cemetery in the world. It isn't just Morrison pilgrims that visit the cemetery, for it is the resting place of many of the rich and famous of this city.

More than anything I want to experience the Paris that isn't on post-cards and in movies. I want to ride the subway with Parisians as they commute across the city. I want to people watch as I sit with a coffee and cigarette out the front of non-descript cafés. I want to use these experiences to learn the individual feel of the different neighbourhoods. I want to soak in real Paris.

Although I had a wide array of general intentions, I had no clear plan. It was a random decision that had me walking south alongside the Canal St Martin until I reached the Seine. After crossing the Pont d'Austerlitz, I found myself right by the station, so decided it was time to tick one item off the list, by buying a carnet and taking my first trip on the metro.

Both lines 5 and 10 passed through Austerlitz, but as I found the platform for the latter first, my decision was made for me. The 10 went to Boulogne Pont de Saint-Cloud, which meant nothing to me. Without much idea of where I was going, I decided I would stay aboard until the mood told me it was time. As it turned out, that came at Michel Ange-Auteuil.

Coming above ground I found myself in what could easily enough have been a new city. From the east where I was based, I was now in the heart of the 16th Arrondissement. Based on the bends of the river, I was back on the same side as my hotel, yet now in western Paris. I got out my map that I kept with me as a reference that I intended to use sparingly. If I was to continue walking west, I would come across the Roland-Garros tennis centre, the Parc des Princes football stadium and both the Auteuil and Longchamp racecourses. They may all be places for another day, but for now I would focus on the more important task. Lunch.

I settled for the first bistro I found and ordered 'la formule'. This was giving me an entrée and main that would deliver two things I'd been particularly keen to try once I got here; snails and duck. Both were amazing, and whether that said more about the place I was eating at or the overall state of French cuisine, only time would tell.

In Australian cities, the eastern suburbs tend to be the pricier part of town, but unless looks are very deceiving, this section in the west of the city appears to be the more affluent part of Paris. The buildings are ornate. The streets are clean and wide. There are small private galleries and exclusive looking schools. Parks that look like a hairdresser has carefully given the lawn a stylish trim. Dogs appeared to be looking down their noses at me as an uncouth foreigner as their snobbish owners walked them through the upmarket area.

It was beautiful, but it wasn't me. I decided that a day at the tennis would be my next visit out here, but for now it was back to the station. Metro line 9 also ran through Michel Ange-Auteuil, and I took this train half dozen stops to Trocadero, which I remembered from the map was right near the Eiffel Tower. Sure, it was the ultimate in 'touristy' but if not now, when? I had to have a quick admiring look from close by.

I climbed the stairs and found myself by a small park surrounded by bistros that no doubt charged like wounded bulls for the view as much as the food. The tower, in all its pristine glory, stood proudly. From the promenade past the square was arguably the greatest view possible of the tower. Far enough back that you could take it all in far more clearly than was possible from a closer point. That said, I made my way down the stairs, across the Pont d'Iena and began a walk around the base towards the Champ de Mars. I wasn't planning on going up the tower, but I figured while I was here, I would take it in from all ground-based angles.

In keeping with the moment of stereotypical tourist mode, I hopped aboard a river cruise. Taking in the perfect spring day with the spectacle of Paris from the most ideal spot proved a point about the tourist scene. It may be a fake way of seeing the city, dressed up to its finest and made-up to cover its weaknesses, but by God it was stunning. I got off by the Notre-Dame Cathedral and did a quick wander around the Ile-de-Cite before crossing the Pont au Change and walking along the riverbank. I took the stairs up to street level and wandered past the back of the Louvre to the Rue de Rivoli. It is a beautiful boulevard that runs from Bastille to the Place de la Concorde. The facades of the main buildings opposite the Louvre are stunning, creating a look that I think is more Parisian than even the Champs-Elysees.

I walk to the Place de la Concorde and take in the panoramic view of the National Assembly, the Madeleine Church, the Arc de Triomphe and the Louvre in the four directions surrounding me and know that I'm as deep in the heart of the city as can be. As I now want to feel more of the city's soul, I backtrack to Concorde station and get on the 12 train to head to Montmartre.

It's a big area and not one that I can even begin to do justice today. I will be back here regularly, to sit, to eat, to drink, to watch and most importantly to feel. That said, in a couple of hours I managed to experience a hell of a good first taste. From riding the Funicular up the hill, I wandered to the lookout by Sacre Coeur, appreciating the incredible view of the city as well as the basilica behind it that offended so many artists a century ago that they all headed across town to escape it.

I visited the Place du Tertre and watched artists in the square work on portraits of tourists while others competed to sell their paintings of the beauty in the area. Where any of these artists sat in the range of talent level was uncertain, for it seemed to be more an attempt to cash-in on legend. Nevertheless, it provided a unique feel that was entertaining to sit and watch with a glass of wine from a bistro across the road.

I walked down the hill as far as the Boulevard de Clichy, and made my way past the famous Moulin Rouge. I would be back at some point to see the show here, but not tonight. It has been a long day. I've traversed the city and walked possibly more kilometres today than any day of my life. It is time to find a bar near my hotel and settle into recovery mode. Who knows how long I will spend in this city? All the sights in the world wouldn't be enough to hold me, yet a watering hole with cold beer, cheap spirits and interesting people would be enough that I'd never feel the need to leave.

7

10 March 2023

ELLIOT

My brief walk yesterday afternoon ended up taking seven and a half hours, but I'm more than happy it did. It seemed logical to get the most touristy part of Paris done first while the excitement is at its greatest.

I got a taxi back to the hotel from the tower. The driver didn't understand a word of English, but I managed to get enough information across that it seemed like he knew where to take me. He had the radio broadcasting a football match. Paris St Germain were playing Bayern Munich in the European Champions League. I wasn't a big football fan, but arriving in Paris yesterday it was hard to escape the build-up for this clash. Despite not understanding a word coming over the radio, when the noise built at the sound of 'Messi,' I was able to have the most meaningful interaction with the driver.

'Ah Messi.' He shook his head and raised a hand with contempt, indicating his belief of the comparative failings of the city's biggest name recruit. They may have been the top team in the French league but had hoped his arrival would signal European domination. This hadn't occurred and the Parisian method of having the best surrounded by the best wasn't working. Their team was in the process of crashing out yet again. It is not just the sporting field, but all walks of life when the champion team usually conquers the team of champions.

I had sent John an email when I got home before crashing into bed, exhausted. I feared I'd sleep through half of today such was my tiredness, but sure enough I was awake early, the adrenalin of being in such a vibrant city recharging my batteries just as quickly as it had drained them.

While I was eating breakfast downstairs, a reply came from John inviting me around to his place this morning.

'*Looking forward to it Elliot. Get metro line four from Gare du Nord to Bastille and transfer to line one heading to La Defense. Get off this train at Louvre-Rivoli. When you get above ground, you'll see the world's greatest museum one side. Turn 180 degrees and you'll see a small building diagonally opposite with the Café du Musee at the bottom. Text me when you leave Bastille, and I will meet you downstairs. Aim for about 11am, so we can have a bit of a catch-up before lunch.*'

It seemed simple enough, but then walking seemed even easier. It was only two and a half kilometres and would take less time than transferring between multiple trains. More importantly, there was no better way of discovering the city than by travelling on foot. I'd been right outside the Louvre yesterday, so it only meant doing part of yesterday's walk.

After the issues I had on the Boulevard de Magenta, I took off from the other end of my street along the Rue la Fayette. As I suspected, it was a nicer walk with far less cause for anxiety. I knew the quickest way involved turning left part of the way along, but I chose to continue on this road to the end, coming out at Boulevard Hausmann and finding Galleries Lafayette, one of the most exclusive department stores in the world. From there, I continued another block and reached the Paris Opera House, the Palais Garnier, one of the world's most spectacular theatres.

Despite looking at the map this morning, every turn was half-chance. The next one took me to L'eglise de la Madeleine, a spectacular Roman style church that occupied a whole city block. From the front I could see the Place de Concorde and I knew my bearings sufficiently from there to know I'd be at John's in a little over ten minutes. I decided it was safe to text him at this point and let him know when I'd be there.

I took the Rue St Honore and detoured briefly through the Place Vendome, home of the famous Ritz Hotel, before passing the Palais Royal then back down to the Rue de Rivoli. Although he was looking across the road at the train station, expecting to see me come from there, I spotted him right under the Café de Musee as he'd said he'd be. The years had aged him, but he was still unmistakeable.

'John,' I said from a few metres away.

'Well, I'll be damned. Little Elliot. My God, I can't believe it.' I was eight when John last saw me, so I wasn't surprised that he was taking a while to come to terms with me. He looked older than I remembered, but the change in a man between his mid-forties and early sixties is comparatively insignificant alongside a child's transition to manhood.

I let him take the lead, and when he hugged me, I felt relieved, and held him tighter. Love and family were exceptionally strange things. He had an irreconcilable relationship with the rest of the family, yet he wasn't going to take it out on the next generation. His take, I assumed, was that I was flesh and blood and having never wronged him in any way, I should be treated as a loved one. That was how I saw it, though with an additional level of admiration for all he had achieved.

'You probably don't even remember me, it has been so long,' he said.

'Of course I do. My superstar uncle. I was nervous when I met you at the age of eight, and I was nervous again today.'

'Both times for no reason,' he said. 'I was no better in my career than your father was in his. Might have been more high profile, but that doesn't make me any more significant in the scheme of things. Anyways, it is fantastic to see you.'

'You too Uncle John,'

'I'll give you Uncle bloody John. You're not eight anymore. You're my equal, so just call me John, alright.'

'Sure,' I said. My memories of him had been vague, and I'd never been certain of the accuracy in any assessment I heard of him from the rest of the family, but he seemed to fit exactly in line with my expectations. Paris may have been his home for well over half of his life, but he was more of the ocker Aussie in accent and manner than any of my family down under had ever been.

'Come on up,' he said, inviting me upstairs before we headed out. I had no idea what he had planned. I wasn't sure if today would be the only time I'd see him. Possibly he'd decided to be vague, uncertain of how much either of us would want to deal with the other. After the years and the history, we may both consider the other a chore that we wish to escape. I doubted that.

The apartment was small, but the location was such that it still had to be worth an absolute mint. I think there were very few apartments in Paris that weren't both small and expensive. Surely this address had to carry an additional premium on the price.

'Home for more than half my life,' John said. 'I thought it would be a stop-gap solution when I bought it, but things don't always go as you planned. I thought my career would fund something much bigger and better. To be honest, once it became home, I never really wanted anything else. Once you find a place that truly feels like you belong there, nothing is better.'

He offered me a glass of wine. I wasn't used to saying yes when it was still morning, but I figured if he was, I should. As he gave me the glass, I looked around the open planned apartment and wondered where we'd sit. Space was at a premium, and with the homage paid to literature with jam-packed bookshelves the whole way around the apartment, it left little room for what I suppose he considered unnecessary options like furniture. I didn't see a television anywhere which stood out as particularly unusual.

'Here's to connecting when all around us is disconnected,' he said. 'Come outside. There are not too many other places to sit.'

The balcony was narrow but had just enough room to run the whole way along his living area with sufficient space for a small outdoor table and two chairs.

'I spend half my life out here. My efforts on boosting my health have been to restrict my smoking to outdoors. It lasted until we had a very cold day. Now, it's a good intention rather than a resolute commitment. I think the sight of me on my balcony with a cigarette and a glass of wine is almost considered a part of the landscape these days.'

I asked him about the television.

'No. When I moved here, I wanted to live life, read about life and write about life. Watching life on a screen seemed like a distraction from everything I wanted. Every woman that has moved in here has insisted on bringing a television, but once they've gone, the TV has too.'

Every woman who has moved in? It sounded like a production line.

'If there's something important enough to see, it is on in the brasseries where I can see both the event and the people's reactions to it, which is what interests me far more. I watch a lot of Paris Saint Germain football matches even though I couldn't give a shit about the game.'

It took a while, but eventually we got to the inevitable awkwardness of discussing family. It was potentially dangerous territory, though it may have been safer than talking about his wives.

'You know, my father, your grandfather, was an arsehole. I don't mean ultimate shit of the earth abusive bastard type, just fucking impossible and unreasonable. Not uncommon. I always respected him, but I needed to be as far away from him as possible. So yeah, I didn't talk to him more than a few times in his last twenty years.'

'What about Dad?'

'Your father and me never had an issue with each other. We were chalk and cheese, which stopped us being overly close. Family ties matter until they don't. When I went down to your grandmother's funeral, he wasn't too happy to see me. He was angry I didn't come down to see her when she was sick, but her illness was kept hidden to me. I haven't seen him since, but we send each other the occasional email so we know each other is alright, and you guys too. I've told him many times he should come to Paris, but it doesn't seem likely. I'm glad you have. Just wish you'd stayed here instead of that bloody hotel.'

He never had offered accommodation, but I didn't think it wise to bring that up now. I don't think I'd have felt comfortable accepting the offer. Yes, we were connected by blood, but I'd met him only once before this. Every other blood connection he had didn't seem to be part of his life. Was I one difficult conversation away from being the same?

'If you can cancel the hotel, you can stay here,' he offered now. 'At your age you're probably planning to get laid each night, so you go back to their place and won't need a bed anyway, just a place to leave your bags and occasionally drop-in to.

I laughed. 'My strike rate isn't that impressive.'

'You're in Paris now. Anything is possible here.'

8

4 October 1986

JOHN

Thank God I am back in Paris. The past six weeks I have done fifty talks and book-signings across the United States and the United Kingdom on a tour far more relentless than I expected. I shouldn't complain, for that much interest is reflected in the sales of the book and will be paying my way for the long haul. It is more of a chore than spending thousands of hours over notebooks and a typewriter. I am a writer. I want to write. I don't want to speak.

Of Virtue and Vice has sold over a million copies in six months since its release. My publisher had been very optimistic about it and had believed we may be able to sell fifty thousand. I never believed that was possible, so to have sold twenty times that already, seems like a dream.

The book was the story of Jeremy Duncan. Jeremy was inspired to build a better life for his family and to help build a better society around them. He was willing to take any action, however immoral or illegal, to do so. Whether the protagonist was a hero or a villain was open to interpretation. As I started on the book, I pictured a villain with redeeming qualities, but those qualities seemed to become more significant to the arc of the plot as it continued. Living in a city where I barely knew anyone, and didn't speak the language, I was bringing a feeling of the outsider to my work, and I think it showed in the empathy I had for the character.

To what extent can an unethical action be justified by the overall good that comes from its result? If someone knew that a man was molesting children, and acted on this knowledge to kill the paedophile, is the murder justified? On the surface, I think most people would say yes. The danger than stems from accepting such self-appointed vigilantism, is that everyone can take actions based on belief rather than knowledge. How does the vigilante know with absolute certainty what the other person has done? Our legal system is designed to ensure a fair trial before a verdict and a punishment is delivered, but this rarely can be delivered with absolute certainty. It is often only the perpetrator and the victim who can ever be completely certain of all that has happened.

Every person's outlook on the world stems from a combination of belief and knowledge. In theory, we all understand the difference between these, but can we be certain exactly where the line between them falls? Everyone takes a certain amount of belief as knowledge. We all know who the president of the United States is. We can all have a belief in whether the guy is an arsehole or not. If he enacts a policy that is so goddamn evil that the whole world is out to get him, the wrongs of the policy may only be a belief, but the universality of the view will mean it is soon accepted as fact.

A ball on a hill may need a little force applied to start rolling, but if the hill has sufficient gradient, it will then continue to build speed. This is the impact of momentum, something that we see in many elements of human behaviour. The first step takes assistance, but movement from there becomes progressively easier.

I suspect that most people who read *Of Virtue and Vice*, would have a positive attitude towards Jeremy. Like the ball before it is pushed, it took external force when he wrestled with the first great dilemma. From that point on, it didn't matter that each step was a bigger one, it was taken with greater ease. As I wrote, it kept seeming like the character was descending to a lower point and less worthy of any sort of redemption, but when I got to the end and viewed him in his totality, I saw him as being in line with standard human behaviour.

People's weaknesses grow with time. Nobody goes from addiction to casual use. Nobody goes from dementia to mild memory loss. If something is wrong, there are only two pathways forward. Eliminate the problem or see it grow. If you choose not to recognise something as a negative, there is near certainty that you will allow it to fester, build and become a greater issue. Jeremy could only find the ability to continue his choices by excusing his action based on a greater good. From that point, the greater good he needed to justify any action was progressively less. I ensured that the view readers had, indicated the clear grounds for all he did, until finally the other side of the story could be seen.

In fiction there is a tendency to pit good against evil, and to ensure that it is clear which side is which. In life it never works that way. We often see it in exactly that light, but do you really think that the majority of human beings are willingly taking the role of evil? Everyone sees life through their own narrow view, shaped by the events and experiences that have delivered them to this point.

Whenever conflict exists, we always see ourselves on the side of good. Almost always, the person we are in conflict with sees the same picture, but with us cast as the villain.

When I was writing the book, I was living in an apartment building near Bastille. There was a woman next door to me named Ellen, and she had a dog that never shut up. Everyone in the building hated the dog, and courtesy of her indifference to their complaints, Ellen as well.

A man named Patrice lived in the apartment on the other side of her I got along well with Patrice, possibly because he spoke a bit of English with me. It wasn't a friendship as such, but he was the only person in the building that I had any regular interaction with.

After a particularly trying few days, the dog was poisoned. Ellen blamed everyone, including me, though I think she considered Patrice the most likely assailant. I assumed it was him, having long been the most vocal complainant about the dog. Despite the strong dislike I'd had for the dog, I considered the action to be unforgivable. I didn't know what the right approach was, but this certainly was not it.

I asked Patrice if he had done it. He denied it, but admitted he was glad someone had. That he justified the action was enough to consolidate my suspicion. It was unlikely that anyone would admit to being the guilty party, but anyone so quick to focus on the result as it impacted themselves was someone who I felt was capable of doing it.

I couldn't take any action against Patrice, for it was nothing more than a suspicion. However strong, however valid, it was a belief that he was a guilty, not knowledge. Nobody but he can know for sure of his innocence or guilt. All Ellen's attempts at getting justice led nowhere. No charges were ever laid. The police were never able to trace the action back to Patrice or anyone else.

If I was right, Patrice had taken an evil action. Did it make him evil? I don't think he would have taken any pleasure from doing what he did. As I perceived the turn of events, he would have considered that the impact the dog was having and the complete unwillingness of its owner to acknowledge this or remedy the situation. He then fixed it the best way he was able to think of. It was a massive miscalculation for which I would never try to validate, but an example of how the different experiences of people result in contrasting views of wrong or right.

Everyone will have a point where the line between right and wrong gets crossed. What if the dog was attacking a person? What if there was a prospect of such an attack being fatal? I didn't know at what point the murder of the dog would become validated. I was sure it hadn't been in this case, but equally certain that a scenario could exist where such an action was acceptable. At every point along that line, some will argue passionately on both sides between the wrong and the right. Nobody knows, we all believe.

I had many scenarios like this present in front of me in a short space of time, and it directed me to the essence of what the novel became. My focus was less about good versus evil than trying to identify what each of these combatants really were. Nobody could suggest that Jeremy was an upstanding citizen, but rather than the bad guy, he was written with a quality in the tradition of Ned Kelly. A villain, but arguably one with more conscience than the so-called good guys who were after him.

As an English speaker living in Paris, there is far less interest in me here than overseas. There is a French translation on the market, and between that and the original version, we've sold several thousand here, but it's been infinitely more successful in the two regions I've just visited, and even more so in Australia. Despite living here, it has been heavily billed as an Australian novel down there, and it has been one of the more successful books of the year. Thankfully it's a small enough market that I haven't been harassed to go back and promote it there. It isn't that I never want to return to my homeland, but there's a lot of issues I would have to face if I went back, and I am not yet ready for that.

I was last in Australia nearly two years ago. After spending six months here at the end of a European holiday, I had decided I didn't want to return home. I had written *Of Virtue and Vice* in just three months, and I had found a British publisher who was desperately keen to take it on. While the editors worked on it, I went back home to tie up loose ends. Unfortunately, this led to the strained relationships I had with my family becoming even more disharmonious. If anything, half a world separating us is the one thing that may give us a level of salvation, though two years on and I haven't had any contact with any of them.

My publisher has an office in Paris, so it was equally convenient for me to be based here. It seemed right. To have written the book here so quickly told me that it was the home of my creativity. I felt like an outsider here, yet bizarrely there was a level of comfort within this. You don't always need to be in the centre of things to be at home. There are times when sitting on the outside of the circle allows you to see everything more clearly. I drank at brasseries listening into conversations with no ability to understand a word being said. Because I didn't understand the words, I learned to interpret through tone and non-verbal communication. I think it taught me more about what people believed than if I had words to go on.

Although I considered Paris a base, I really had no concept of how long its novelty would last. I was living in the Latin quarter, in a cramped apartment in an equally cramped street. I liked the area. I liked the array of young Parisian women in the area, and particularly the fondness they had for a young Australian writer.

Now, it is time for a new stage. Paris is home, and I want to lay down my roots here with a permanent home. I have an appointment tomorrow to look at an apartment on the Rue de Rivoli. It is small, but that doesn't bother me. A balcony with a view of the Louvre and the city's most appealing street. A space to write. A place to sleep. There isn't too much else I need. I want to be out experiencing the city, not couped indoors. I want the security of ownership now that the big money has come in, but it doesn't mean I want to live like an old man. I want to live like a Parisian. A boulangerie at breakfast, a cafe for lunch and a brasserie for dinner and drinks. Familiarity one day in my neighbourhood and the fascination of somewhere new the next. Learning all the city has to offer by walking all of its streets.

Paris may be part myth. Under the surface it may be no better than anywhere else, but now that what's on the surface has reeled me in, it's where I want to be. After being fed to the sharks in the lands where they speak my language, I am far more comfortable and at home in this thriving metropolis where nobody cares who I am.

9

10 March 2023

ELLIOT

'You know, most bastards want to say that the world is constantly getting better,' John said. 'Others say it's always getting worse. They're all full of shit. The world never gets better, nor worse, it just changes.'

We were seated out the front of a café a few blocks from John's apartment. After an hour together, the social niceties of conversing with a stranger had been dispensed with. It was now family members, speaking as we saw it, without fear of the response from the other. That said, it wasn't on issues too close to home. I knew enough to be certain that when we encroached on delicate topics, I would tread gently.

'Surely it evolves. We don't invent things to go backwards. Everything we do is in the quest to advance society. That inevitably makes life better.'

'Newtons laws of physics apply to far more than just force. He said that every action has an equal and opposite reaction. Applies to everything from economics and business to going down on your girlfriend. Every advancement in history has carried a benefit, but it's also had an associated cost. Most people want to go on forever about the benefit, but no bastard sits around counting all the costs. I'm not just talking about financial, right.

'What else?'

'Look at all these people walking around with headphones in their ear. Can't walk without listening to music or a podcast because they need to do two things at once, right.'

'How is that not an advancement?'

He had an incredibly animated way of screwing up his nose, pursing his lips and narrowing his eyes to give a pulled face that spoke of disdain. I'd seen it several times already, but he held it in place longer this time.

'In some cases you don't hear the car that ends up hitting you, the assailant who mugs you, but more often than not it's the subtle things. You don't hear the birds and the sounds of nature. You don't focus on all that is around you in that unique moment of time. Your attention is split multiple ways. Maybe you can do more things at once, but you end up doing a half-arsed job of all of them.

'There are more people suffering with depression and other mental illness in the world today than ever before. And you know what, they're rarely in fucking Syria or Yemen, where every bastard is ducking and weaving the next round of bombs. It is in your home, my home and the rest of the first world. Everyone is so damned advanced that they feel they can have everything. In chasing everything they do nothing properly, including relax. You're on your fucking phone as soon as there is no other stimulus for a moment. Humans, and every other living creature, needs balance. Every advancement tips life further out of balance.'

'So you think we're going backwards?'

'Fuck no. It's not about better or worse. It is the action and the reaction. The benefit and the cost. I point out the costs because I've got more people around me who only see the benefits.'

I understood his point, but what was of more interest to me was the passion with which he made it. He'd throw his arms around when he spoke, he'd raise his voice and get more animated in tone and would present his view in such a resolute way, that you couldn't help but focus in on the view he presented. It didn't always change others' views, but consideration is the first step to transformation, and he inspired that, if nothing more.

'One thing I don't understand John, is why you moved to Paris to write a novel that was set in Australia? Surely coming to France would have been the option if your book was set here.'

'When I came here, I didn't have a concept to work on. *Of Virtue and Vice* hadn't entered my consciousness yet. I wanted to write, and this was the place to do so, but that didn't mean Paris had to be the setting for anything I wrote. Writing is storytelling. Stories are in front of us every day, but when you write those stories, you don't just regurgitate what happened. You alter the people, the places, the events. Tell me a story. Anything. Just as it happened.'

'Like what?'

'I don't care. The first girl you banged. The best meal you had. Your greatest sporting achievement. Whatever.'

'I won my club tennis tournament last year. I was down match point in the final but came back and won it against the top seed.'

'Is that so? I played tennis. Forty-five years ago. I was no great star, but I was better than your old man, whatever he may tell you. Anyway, your story isn't going to sell a million copies, so we're going to make a few changes. It was an international event, you were American and your opponent was a Russian. You'd finally come to terms with your break-up from your Ukrainian girlfriend Gosia, until you found out that she is now seeing the Russian. After a mishit, he had the chance to nail you in a vulnerable mid-court position, and while players generally wouldn't do this, he did. After being knocked down, he turned the even match in his favour to set up three match-points at 5-1 in the second set. Gosia yells out encouragement to him, and after stopping and staring at her, you crack the first of three straight aces, going on to win that game and begin a Herculean comeback.'

I raised my eyebrows. 'It could work.'

'Monsieur,' he called out to a waiter. 'My friend here would like a café latte. He is the famous American tennis player Elliot Martin.

'Monsieur Martin, I follow tennis, I don't know your friend, but I notice he has the same surname as you. And looks like you. I don't think he is American, no?'

Sebastien, the waiter, was familiar enough with John to know that whatever introduction I got was more likely that of a character. John confirmed the coffee order for both me and him and went back to the point of his discussion.

'If I wrote that tennis story, it would be through watching a tennis match. If I watched it in Australia, France or South America, I would still have set it as a match-up between players from opposite countries. A Russian today is an easy target for the bad guy. That an American would serve as the good guy doesn't sit well with me, but the objective of character is not to go with your personal preferences, but to create the clearest distinctions.'

'Wouldn't that be a Ukrainian?'

'Today perhaps, but literature is timeless. Pitting a Russian against an American always presents the perfectly contrasting opponents. By making the woman at the centre of their battle Ukrainian adds that extra element. Considering her involvement with a Russian at this point of time allows the development of the characters to show another side, where the individual is so far removed from the affairs of the state.'

'I don't recall you ever writing anything like this.'

'No, because I never wanted to demonise Russians or glorify Americans. If you want to sell copies, you play to stereotypes. If you want to enrich your readers, you tell the story that needs to be told. The fact that I had one blockbuster and fuck all else, tells you that I had one story that managed to do both of those things.'

John was only twenty-five when *Of Virtue and Vice* was published and it remains a mystery to me how it happened so fast. He'd arrived in Paris two years earlier without a clue of what he was writing. Somehow, he created a masterpiece, and even more impressively, managed to get a publishing contract. All of this happened in just over a year. Whatever allowed such a miraculous turn of events, it appeared that he utilised all his good fortune on that miracle. He never managed to climb the mountain of success again.

'Everyone has their own way of measuring success. I could have sold millions if that was what I wanted.'

'Why didn't you?'

'When a writer creates a story, they create a world for the story to take place in. God, if you believe it, is the only other entity who ever created a world. That is the feeling we have when we write. If I'm going to be a bloody god and create my own world, then I'm going to do it my way. I don't care if critics or readers don't like what they get. My world, my rules. Nobody else has to deal with it.'

'If the purpose of writing is to tell stories, surely the point is for people to read those stories. Wouldn't the great legacy that *Of Virtue and Vice* gained never have happened without selling so well?'

'For sure, but my pride is in the work, not in the sales. I'd love the world to read my work but in saying that sentence, I am more focused on *'my work'* than *'the world'*. The prospect of selling out my work to get readers sickens me. The prospect of my work not getting readers disappoints me, but substantially less. Always did, always will. That's why I live in a small apartment rather than a stately mansion.'

'On the Rue de Rivoli,' I add, highlighting that he'd managed to do damn well to be living in such a prestigious address, however small the place may be.

'I made a lot of money fast. I pissed most of it away just as fast, but at least I managed to hold on to the apartment. Still, take the location away and there's nothing too special.'

'You don't need space when you have that location,' I said.

'Is that so? You need, or at least want, what you don't have. What the hell do I care about having a view of the city?'

'The most beautiful city in the world,' I said.

'Forget all the crap people sprout. It is just another city, no more special than any other. I've been here long enough to know. I couldn't give a shit about it.'

John had lived in Paris for nearly forty years. He acted as though he hated it, yet clearly he would never leave. I had been here roughly forty hours. I adored it like nowhere else, yet I wouldn't be staying too much longer. It didn't make sense how the feelings for the city could be so inversely proportional with the time spent in it. Or was that the paradox of its appeal? Could the ultimate in beauty really lose all appeal the more you saw of it? If that was truly the case, then wouldn't all the anti-Parisian sentiment exist in those born and bred here. It didn't seem to be that way with most of the people I had heard speak.

'Don't give me words like beautiful. You can use that anywhere and it all comes down to personal preference,' he said. 'Go deeper. Tell me what it is that you think makes Paris so fucking special?'

I paused for a moment. When you are talking with a writer, you are conscious of trying to find the best wording for your point. I knew that I wanted to say that there wasn't one standalone factor, but I was less sure of how to express it.

'I think of a city as an entity. It is made up of millions of characteristics, just like each individual person. Within that are always good qualities and bad, but in some cases the total of all of these features combines to take your breath away. I had that with Claudia, my recent-ex. She was incredible, but, well, I'm here now for a reason. I guess Paris is the Claudia of cities for me.'

'Claudia broke up with you, did she? Well Paris broke up with me. We cohabitate still, but that just gives her more opportunities to piss me off. I get to see the worst of her every fucking day. I bet Claudia looked fantastic even at her worst. But if you had to wake up in the next room while she's sleeping with someone else, she wouldn't look so hot then. That's Paris and me. I know how beautiful it is as a matter of fact, but it no longer resonates in the same way.'

I contemplated Claudia appearing before John at her worst. He'd still be blown away with her. When you don't share a history, you don't make the same judgements. John has a resentment towards Paris. It isn't the city, its art, architecture, cuisine, culture, fashion or literature. It is the unfulfilled nature of his life within the city. Paris has only been a backdrop for his life, not a participant, but it serves as a convenient place to lay the blame for failures in both his professional and personal life.

I'd chosen a person as my scapegoat, while John chose a city. Everyone needs to have a point at which they can lay the blame, otherwise we end up forced to accept the responsibility for our own failings.

'I get it,' John said. 'When I first came here, I talked about the city like you do now. I thought Paris was the answer to everything. The longer you live, the more diverse your questions become. With time, nothing is the answer to everything. I wish it was. I wish I could walk out here and look over the city and see what I did all those years ago. I remember doing an overseas publicity tour for *Of Virtue and Vice*, spending a couple of months away from here. I came back and thought I'd finally returned to an Eden I'd never leave. I didn't leave, but it didn't remain the utopia I had originally thought it was.'

10

22 May 1988

JOHN

The Rue de Rivoli. Hard to believe a boy from the western suburbs of Adelaide could be buying his first home on one of the most famous streets in Paris, but here I am. I want to make this city a home, and the first step is locking in the future with the purchase of this apartment.

My relationship with family back home had disintegrated further. I don't know how they have drawn such conclusions, but they believe that *Of Virtue and Vice* is a slap in their faces. They have decided that all the characters connect to part of our family unit. As such, they believe the book was essentially the airing of our family's dirty laundry. Nothing could be further from the truth. It was written half a world away from them and they were all a world away from my mind at the time. It is a reminder that people will always find ways of interpreting things as they want to.

I've been living in the Latin Quarter and most of the people I spend time with are based in that area, so that is where my search has been centred around. It may be the rebel within that gives me the desire to avoid expectation, but I had a desire to go elsewhere. It is hardly a big move; I am a fifteen-minute walk from Saint-Germain-des-Pres and twenty minutes from my editor's office. I like this side of the river, not necessarily more or less than the left bank, but it has a different set of selling points.

Home is less about location than feeling. For some people, however far they journey in life, home always remains the place they grew up in. I will never feel at home there. I don't know if I will in this part of Paris, but I believe it will suit me, for now at least.

Home is more than community. I had community in the Latin Quarter, but I felt that threatened my own sense of self. When you are at home, you don't need to adjust and conform to what is around you. I want this apartment to be part of the definition of me. The streets surrounding it. The bars I drink at. The cafes I eat at. The grocery stores I shop at. I want all of that to combine in creating the feeling of home. Maybe it is just a stop-gap measure, and home may prove to be much further away, but across the river I was just another foreign artist seeking to follow a tradition. Here, I am not just another person. I am John Martin.

I'm far from fully settled, but after the bulk of the moving process was completed yesterday, it was an amazing feeling to wake up, walk out onto the balcony and survey the scene of a waking city. The area around the Louvre dominates the view from my apartment, and although we are in the heart of the city, it is one part that is slower to move at morning time than others. The same could be said for me as a rule.

Normally I like to work for a couple of hours before I do anything else, but I am taking a little time off at the moment. Inspiration has been hard to come by lately, as too has discipline. Once settled, I intended to get straight back to a routine that may assist my progress better, but day one in the apartment hardly qualifies as settled. Although I've wandered the local area prior to buying the apartment, day one as a resident means it is time to do a better job of assimilation.

It is a brisk morning for this time of year, and the scarf and jacket that I would normally have dispensed with by late March are still a necessity. After descending the two flights of stairs, I survey my options before choosing to head north along the Rue de Louvre. A block away from the Rue St Honore, I can turn right here and head to Les Halles or left and go towards the Palais Royale. This street is home to numerous cafes and boulangeries that I know I will spend time savouring, but for now discovery is a higher focus than satisfying my tastebuds so I continue straight ahead along the less familiar route.

The smells encourage me to stop. Like so many parts of Paris, the omnipresent combination of coffee brewing and fresh baked delicacies wafts out on to the streets to challenge pedestrians to walk past if they can. Although saying no is difficult, I do so with the certainty that I will build up an even stronger desire before relenting to it. Appreciation is greatest when temptation is given the opportunity to build.

I turn right at Rue Etienne-Marcel. A couple of blocks later I arrived at the midpoint of arguably the most beautiful street in Paris, the Rue Montorgueil. For someone with a plan of waiting until later before I ate, this may not be the wisest choice, for the Rue Montorgueil is the ultimate street for food. Fine dining, bakeries, cafes, chocolatiers, green-grocers, the street has something for every taste. Cars are not banned from the street, but pedestrians have right of way, filling the cobble-stones the whole way across, making it virtually impossible for vehicles. At this time of morning, delivery vans make slow progress up to their destinations, the crowds yet to dominate, but the feel of the street is already on display. The overwhelming choice is the one great asset that saves me, for as much as temptation keeps luring me at each doorway, the knowledge that something better may be just metres further away keeps me from stopping.

Rue Montorgueil is more than just temptation for the tastebuds, it is a visual and aural feast too. The sounds of the Parisian morning at full cry, and the sight of the stunning architecture split by just the narrow street filled with locals and tourists alike, offers a spectacle more reflective of the true soul of the city than you will see near the more famed structures that dominate Parisian travel guides. By lunchtime, and through to the evening, the spectacle will be even more complete, though for me, the comparative peace of morning makes this the ultimate time to experience such a special spot.

Turning left at the Rue Reaumur, I realise my short walk has extended further than planned. I continue as far as the Bourse, the home of the Paris Stock Exchange. Just a few hundred metres from the festive Rue Montorgueil, the people I see seem like a different species, suited up and out to make their millions on the rise and fall of share prices. The surrounding cafes are equally as full, but all with men in suits and newspapers open at the business pages. The area is all business, with the coffee and croissants treated as mere necessity rather than the source of appreciation. The building that serves as their hub looks more like a Roman temple than a stock exchange, but I guess for people making a living on the buying and selling of others, there is a level of prayer necessary to their lives. After doing a loop of the block to take it all in, I continue as far as the Rue de Richelieu and its most famous structure, the National Library of France.

I continue down this street, the grounds of the Palais-Royal on my left, taking me to Rue St Honore. Half-way along I decide to stop for breakfast, at a cafe on the left that is just busy enough to fill me with confidence in its quality without being so busy as to make me feel it is overhyped. I have time to try dozens of places before settling on what will be mine. For someone who likes to spend hours people watching in search of inspiration, my world centres on a place to sit and take life in. Good food, good coffee, good wine is essential, but more than anything is the feel of the place and the rapport with the staff. Chez Nous, serves as the first attempt at finding this in my local area.

As I sit outside facing the busy street of people going about their day, I light a cigarette. My coffee arrives, followed by a juice, a tartine served with butter and jam, and a croissant, arguably the greatest symbol of French breakfast. Around the world the croissant is adorned with ham, cheese or condiments, but here the croissant is eaten as is. When fresh and made correctly, it needs nothing atop it, for the humble croissant itself is the delicacy.

The trap for an author is to get so caught up trying to write about life that he can miss out on living it. I moved across town to get out of that lifestyle. It had seemed like there were so many of us sitting and watching that we lost perspective of the life beyond our own realm. Over here, I was the observer, and those around me were filling my head with ideas. I'd intentionally left my notebook at home, wanting to avoid a day of journalling things to add depth to certain characters, yet never finding their way into anything I wrote. I wanted to break free of that, but habits are never broken quickly or easily. Before allowing myself to get too settled after finishing my meal, I knew I had to make a move or else I would spend most of my day here, achieving nothing.

'*Garcon, l'addition, s'il vous plait,*' I uttered as the waiter passed.

With a nod, he disappeared inside before returning soon after. The number of customers had thinned since my arrival, so he had little else to attend to once my request came.

'You are English, no?' he said on his return with the bill.

'Australian,' I replied. However long I spent here, I was never going to sound like a local, and when people here heard my ordinary French, they were always perceiving me as English. I never clung to my nationality as a source of great pride, but I far preferred to be seen as Australian than the usual expectation of English or American. Australian was novel, it was different, and it brought a pleasant curiosity. Many here perceived English and Americans as looking down on the French, but Australians and New Zealanders were those who had risen up to France in the eyes of the locals.

'Ah what a wonderful place. I would truly love to go there, but it is so far.'

'There's good and bad everywhere. I have been here for years and have no desire to go back, so I would say Paris is the wonderful place.'

'You are more local than Australian.'

'I am a citizen of the world. It doesn't matter where you go, the same positives and negatives exist. We all wander through life trying to make the best of it.'

'So why Paris for so long?'

'I'm a writer. Everything here is foreign enough that I continue to see something new every day to inspire me. Not understanding most of what is said forces me to look deeper at the humanity that drives people's actions. Of course, I could say the same thing for most of the world, but Paris just seems to be the perfect combination of familiar yet different. Eventually I may fit in enough here that I need to escape this city as well, but until then, it remains ideal for me.'

'What is your name?'

'John.'

'John Martin?'

'Yes'

'*Mon dieu*. I am sorry I did not recognise you. I read *Of Virtue and Vice*. It was *formidable*!'

The anonymity I had in Paris was one of the things I loved, yet there was still a part of me that thrived on recognition and appreciation of my work. I didn't want celebrity status stifling my day-to-day life, but there was a natural high that came from people showing appreciation for my work that hadn't changed in me.

'Can I get you another coffee. On the house.'

I declined the offer. One coffee each morning was enough for me, and though I was tempted to ask for a glass of wine in its place, I knew I had enough unpacking to do when I got home to keep me busy. Starting with a wine mid-morning would lead to an unproductive day which stood against all I'd planned when moving across town. I paid the bill, tipped Jacques generously and thanked him for the service.

'You come back, anytime. We look after you, monsieur,' he said.

'I will. I've just moved. Right around the corner from here. We'll have a drink together some time when you're not working.'

'*Bon*. You know Benita's, a few blocks up towards Les Halles. Nice spot for a drink and a meal. When I'm not working, that's where you find me most of the time.'

I told him I'd see him here or at Benita's sometime soon, then made my way the remaining few blocks home ready to deal with the chores awaiting me. He may be little more than an over-zealous fan, but every person has a story. Every person also can lead you to others and within them may lie even greater stories. Any opportunity to uncover these was one worth taking at this point of time, my professional direction seeming so lost. For all the ideas that circulated within me, nothing was getting me closer to the follow-up my publishers demanded.

I ended up becoming good friends with Jacques, and it proved to be incredibly beneficial. Not so much for anything about him, but for the fact he introduced me to a singer at a bar one night. A recent arrival in Paris from the Netherlands, Inge was set to shape my life far more than anyone I'd ever known.

11

10 March 2023

ELLIOT

'I have never driven a car in Paris,' John said. 'Haven't driven a car since I was 23 and first left Australia. Here, there is little reason. Traffic here is so stagnant. The city was built for a quarter of the population, so it doesn't cope with 21st century volumes. The metro struggles, but the infrastructure is newer than the roads, so I find it better. Plus, I prefer watching people than roads.'

John had promised to show me his version of Paris over the next few days. He wasn't giving me any sort of thorough itinerary, but after spending several hours talking about Paris and all of the things I was most keen to see, he was bound to know some of the best ways of combining his highlights with my wish list.

We went to Louvre-Rivoli station, the platforms of which paid tribute to the great museum. Copies of artworks held in the museum adorn the walls of the platform, ensuring that the station identifies itself in far more than name. The equivalent spots on most stations are filled with advertising, but here it appears that a more lucrative return can flow from the promotion of the assets above. It reminds me of the stories I've seen on the Moscow Metro, where stations are like museums, and each is reflective of a relevant individual theme. Paris should do this with all of its stations.

We got off at Nation and transferred from line one to line two which began at this station and ran to Port Dauphine in the west of the city. John told me that we were below the Place de la Nation, another city square that honoured the French national pride, though smaller than Republique or Bastille.

'You know Marianne, from the statue at Republique. There is another of her at Nation. The main claim to fame of this square is that it had the most active guillotines during the revolution. Always find myself feeling a tightness around the throat when I pass through.'

We didn't get out of the station, walking through underground to another platform to change across to line 2. I surveyed a metro map that I picked up at Louvre-Rivoli and tried to make comparisons between the city and my hometown of Sydney.

'In Australia everything centres around a small part of the city,' John explained. Doesn't matter which city, they all have massive towers in the CBD where half the population gravitates to work, then they all disappear to big suburban houses many kilometres from the city. Here, we have more people travelling from the city centre to business districts further out, like La Defense. At peak hour in the morning back home, everyone is headed in one direction, right? Here, there are just as many people going in every direction.'

'So all of this is the equivalent of the Sydney CBD,' I asked, circling the outer section of the metro map.

'It's comparing apples and oranges. I ask you where you live and you'd say Sydney, right, even though you're probably thirty kilometres from the city. If you're even half that distance from the city here you would say just out of Paris. Paris means central Paris. Australian cities mean the city or anywhere in the greater metropolitan area.

'It impacts much of how people live,' he continued. 'Street after street dominated by buildings with shops on the ground floor and apartments above. The apartments are too small to keep excess of anything, so people shop and buy fresh. As a result, you have bakeries, butchers, convenience stores, greengrocers and the like on every block.

Then because you can't buy bulk and few people can drive, the need for big supermarkets is diminished. Down under your major supermarket chains dominate peoples purchasing, as it's easy to drive down a wide road to get to a big shopping centre and pack a fortnight's worth of goods into your car, storing it all in your walk-in pantries and oversized freezers. In Paris, so much more of peoples shopping is done at mum and dad shops, buying what you need today or tomorrow, from a shop-keeper who knows you and ninety percent of their customers by name. Whatever shit I say about this city, that is something I love. I don't know how long it will stay that way.'

'Why?'

'Money talks and bullshit walks.' It was the third time I'd heard him use this expression, clearly a favourite saying of his.

'When your old man and I grew up in Adelaide, there were multiple corner stores in every suburb. You knew the shopkeeper, they knew you. We might only be buying 20 cents worth of mixed lollies, but most people in the suburb would be stopping in there and making a few purchases to keep them profitable. You paid a little more than at a supermarket, but nobody minded. Eventually, big business started to mind, as they saw an easy way to become more dominant.

'Half a century ago you'd get a litre of soft drink for a dollar on the corner. Ninety cents at a supermarket wasn't enough of a saving for the effort involved. Now, you'd pay four dollars at the local store, while the big chain gets it cheaper from the manufacturer as they can have massive amounts to delivered to one distribution point. They can sell the same product for less than half the price. Goodwill meant the little guy could get by selling for a little more, but not double. The corner stores died, big business thrived, and then were able to manipulate costs between themselves. The people who think they're saving money end up with less choice and before too long, the savings have disappeared. Nobody is better off except the big companies.'

'So why hasn't the same thing happened here?'

'It is slowly happening now to an extent, but it isn't so easy for them here. Mainly just that issue of space. Plus, its cultural. People like the way things are here. They did at home, but not quite to the same extent. If big business finds a way, they'll screw the little guys here just the same. Or should I say, when they find a way.'

John seemed to gravitate between admiration and contempt for Paris. Whenever he referred to something he loved about the city, he quickly followed with a slap in its face. Once he was on to something that riled him, he'd always then bring up another of its positive features.

'Do you still love Paris?'

'I never loved the city. Perhaps I felt that way in my first few days, but that was more lust than love. Once I lived here, it was a place to go about life, just like anywhere else. Good things, bad things. The more time passes the more shithouse things seem, doesn't matter where you are.'

'Have you considered moving? Maybe going home?'

'I am home. I hate home at times, but I'd never leave it.'

I didn't want to go any further down that line at this point, but I could see no logical reason why anyone would be so willing to stay somewhere they hated. I suspected that though he claimed it was the city he hated, it was probably his life at this point that was the problem. Moving cities wasn't relevant if that was the case.

John motioned for me to get up as we arrived at Philippe Auguste station.

'We're at the doorstep of the worlds liveliest cemetery,' he told me.

'Something of a paradox,' I said.

'Paris is full of these. When going to Pere Lachaise you ignore Pere Lachaise station and get off at Philipe Auguste. Paradoxical in its own way.'

'So, what do you mean by a lively cemetery?'

'I don't mean the residents,' he said dryly, 'but the tourist numbers that come through here are unlike anywhere else you'll ever find. Most cemeteries, the visitors are only loved ones. Here, they are snap-happy tourists. Jim Morrison may be the number one, but there's Edith Piaf,

Oscar Wilde, Sarah Bernhardt, Chopin, Moliere. People aren't mourning, they're here in the same mood and manner that they walk the banks of the Seine.'

John told me that he came here on his second day in Paris, purely to see the grave of Morrison.

'It was less of a deal back then. He died in 1971, and for the next year or two it was the place to go. With time that interest dropped off until it became a pilgrimage for fans, especially after the movie they made about him in the early 1990's. It has been like that ever since.'

As we arrived at the grave, there were about half a dozen other people around it, all with the cameras on their phone busily snapping away selfies at its side. Somehow the concept of 'rest in peace' seems incongruent with this. Not that I was that familiar with him, but I bowed my head, looked around and was ready to move on.

The cemetery had some of the most elaborate tombstones that I had ever seen, but these weren't for the more famous people in here.

'The most famous don't need the attention,' John said. 'Rich bastards who nobody would remember are another story.'

We passed a few of the other famous people buried there but kept our stay short before going back to the station. We got the next train to Anvers. From the busy road at the foot of the hill, we took a very narrow side street and walked a couple of blocks uphill, culminating in the amazing sight of the Sacre-Coeur above us. At the base of the hill was a carousel that entertained the children and a whole lot of seating to allow parents to recharge their batteries. Above them, the stunning basilica was offset by the grassed hill that led to it.

'Don't even think about walking up there,' John said, and he took me to the funicular station. The funicular was a cable car railway that ran a little over 100 metres, but with a gradient of more than 30%, saved us from a very difficult walk.

'I wouldn't live to tell the story if I tried the steps now,' he said.

At the top, we walked over to the Sacre Coeur and took in the view from the lookout at the front. It was often said that this provided the best view of Paris. At the top of the hill, you could see east, west, north and south of Paris from one spot. Even from the amazing Eiffel Tower you had to walk around the tower to see everything. Here, all of the city's highlights fit into the panorama.

Next it was on to the heart of Montmartre.

12

4 May 1990

JOHN

Four fucking years! I have been through hundreds of concepts, expanded them into more than twenty synopses, a dozen extended plans, eight first chapters and three full first drafts. After all of this, I still had only one book on the shelf. Four years old. One and a quarter million copies sold. A dozen major awards. And not a fucking clue about how to follow it.

Nicole Lewis, my literary agent, was coming across from London to meet with me and discuss my progress. She thought she had the perfect meal ticket. The contract she negotiated after *Of Virtue and Vice* meant there was little left for her to do. Sit back and count the commission. Instead, her life has turned into a constant requirement of standing between the publishers, the editor and me. She was constantly trying to convince each of us that she is working on the other ones, bringing their opinions around. I keep trying to get a change in editor but the publisher won't budge. They want me writing a sequel to a story that has no means of continuation. I won't budge. Through it all, Nicole continues to move each of us closer, a little at a time.

Writing a novel is a massive task. The entire process can be done in months, but there are frequent examples of a project taking decades to complete. Once a debut has sufficient success, the expectations, and the royalty advances, put the pressure firmly in place. I had a contract for three books. I had generous time allowances, or so it seemed when agreement was made. *Of Virtue and Vice* was written relatively quickly. With that experience behind me I felt certain that the next book would be quicker and easier. How wrong I was.

My first book was written without any expectation of finding a deal. I wasn't writing for a publisher, an editor, a manager or an agent. I was writing the story I wanted to tell. Whatever anyone else made of it was irrelevant. It was my novel, my way. The fact that an agent loved it was the unexpected bonus. From there, everything fell into place perfectly which made the entire process a dream. Unfortunately it meant that the follow-up was destined to be a nightmare.

An author is inspired to tell a story. The business doesn't care about stories, just sales, and there is a roadmap to follow in order to best achieve these goals. After the success of my first book, the roadmap was quite definitive. John Martin means *Of Virtue and Vice*. The follow-up needed to be as close to that as possible. Better was a nice ideal, but not important. My name now meant something, and from the agent upwards, they weren't interested in anything that didn't align with that meaning. I, on the other hand, had no idea of what this goddamn meaning was. All of these fucking marketing geniuses should write the book and pass it off as mine. They're so damn certain of how it should be. I haven't got a clue.

I have ideas. Many ideas. As artists, half the challenge for a writer should be the idea, with the execution of that idea as the other half. Turns out that the day I signed the contract, I forfeited my claim to being an artist. Now, I was a cog in the wheel of business. I was a link in a chain. However critical my link was, it remained just one link, and one that needed more than ideas and the ability to execute them. More than anything, it needed the ability to sell these ideas to people who weren't willing to yield from where they stood.

***

'In amongst everything else I do, I have written 134 songs in the past four years,' Inge said. 'How is it you haven't written one book in that time?'

Women had come and gone from my life ever since I arrived in Paris. Inge was the first to come without going soon after. We'd been together for three months when her lease expired, and she moved into my apartment. She was predominantly a performer but enjoyed writing her own songs. The best of these made her set-list, for shows in front of an average audience of fifty. Explaining the difference between that and writing a follow-up novel to a million seller was a challenge, when trying to be diplomatic.

'Your 134 songs were each complete when you say they were. When I write a book, it is complete when it is in the bookshops of the world. From my mind to the bookshops involves a hundred steps. Roughly half of those steps are mine to take. The other half are completely beyond my control. If other arseholes refuse to take their steps, then I may well never have another book. How many of your songs can be bought in the CD shops of the world?'

There I go. One question too far, and diplomacy was out the window. She considered this as a knock on her song writing talents. Maybe it was, but from the first time I saw her perform, I liked her music. That said, it was music that worked fine in an intimate venue, not music that had dominated the worlds music charts. She could write a good song in a day, but I could write a good chapter in a day. In a month she could have an album, while I could have a novel. Neither would see the public domain. She continues to work this way. I cannot. I have a contract that sets certain demands. I must provide something that meets those demands. Whether it takes a month or a decade, the only complete novel I produce is one that the world will see.

Since meeting Inge, there has been an obvious impact on my work. Whether she has served as more of an inspiration or a distraction was open to interpretation. It is probably fair to say that both are true to an extent. The structure of my working time is more malleable than before. If she wants to see me, then all else works around that. When that means I don't work for several days, so be it. It also means that when I do work, it is more solidly than ever. I feel more inspired by life, and that leads to a spike in my creativity. I feel less certain of the direction of the novel I am working on, but one definite positive is I have a fucking amazing character built. All that remains is what I do with her.

***

'What do you expect? Once I couldn't have you, I had to find someone who'd have me,' I said.

Nicole looked at me with a subtle smile that indicated she appreciated the compliment despite an understanding that it wasn't the truth. She was in her early forties, and as a man still clinging to the last days of his twenties, I'd always favoured someone who could pull me back to youthful exuberance.

'I've never had concerns about you being alone,' she said. 'Though I've also never known you to stay with someone for more than a month. You're really falling for her?'

'True.' I had paused briefly before getting this out. I knew it was true, but it was the first time I'd indicated that to anyone else. I couldn't imagine Nicole caring about it at all, other than its relevance to my work.

'That may lead to a less cynical outlook in your work,' she said.

'Don't you believe it. Cynicism has a source. It is called life. When one aspect of life builds a level of faith, a hundred other elements can see that destroyed and cynicism takes over. Don't you get more cynical with time?'

'No, I don't think so.'

'Bullshit. You're telling me you have the same belief in humanity you had as a teenager?'

'Maybe not completely.'

'It is inevitable. As children we believe what we're told. From the moment the truth about Santa Claus gets revealed to us, we begin a spiral of learning that all the wonder and amazement of life is not what we hoped. People do what they must to get ahead. Lie, cheat or whatever else, everything is a means to an end. The more you live, it more you see just how darker means they'll pursue for the end they want.'

'There's no good in the world?'

'Of course there is. Without good, there would be no bad. Everything needs an opposite to define it. That was at the heart of my book and fundamental to everything I've tried to put up since. Sure, you call it cynical by saying that everything positive will be offset by something negative but change the order and you can view it as an optimistic approach to life.'

The last two times I'd seen Nicole had been in her London office. It was amazing the power shift that occurred from the choice of meeting places. There, she was the powerful agent who was in charge of me, the hired help, who merely had to nod my head and accept all that she said in order that we would reach the end result we all wanted. Here, in my local café, I was in control. I was the artist. The very industry of John Martin was about a whole group of bit players seeking to share the revenue that was created through my inspiration. Meeting here, she had to work to my cues.

'So where are we?'

I wanted to say the Rue St Honore, but I knew that retaining my control of the meeting meant ensuring she retained her faith in its progress. Smart-arsed remarks may have been my natural forte, but this was one time I needed to reign myself in.

'I've gone back to *The Paris Paradox* as a title, but if they are that fucking determined for something else, it's something I'm flexible with. Paris in a title already stimulates interest, and the paradox gets to the essence of the contradictions between the good and bad which rekindles the themes of the previous book. Unless I remove all pretence of it being a new book. I can write *Of Pleasure and Pain*, just renaming characters and changing places.

'Let them have their way on title. What else?'

'I know they wanted Bill changed to an American, but it just doesn't work. It isn't the language that defines the experience of a foreigner here. English, American and Australian all bring something different. We are loved. You lot, not so much. Americans, even less. I change Bill and we're looking at a different book.'

'Is the love interest Dutch by any chance.'

'Fuck no,' I say indignant that she would think that Bill's story was mine. As aware as I was of the imperfections of any relationship, I was at the stage with Inge where I preferred the ignorance of believing all would stay ideal. Bill's relationship had to die in the book, thus it would be foolish to draw any similarities between her and Inge. 'Jene-Marie is stereotypically Parisian. She is the paradox of Paris. Stunningly beautiful, yet under the surface, as flawed as any place you've ever been. Everyone is attracted to her but get close and the appeal declines. Some of us still are so enamoured with her highlights that we ignore the negatives, but we inevitably pay the price for that.

Nicole still didn't look overly enthused. 'Where are all the twists that *Of Virtue and Vice* had?'

'There weren't twists there really. It was quite linear in Jeremy's descent. Here, we see the same sort of evolution in Bill as each step along his pathway has him more aware of the negative beneath the beauty.'

'That may be how you saw the previous book, but that wasn't the perception of most readers. Nobody saw his descent coming.'

This was rubbish. I'd done enough talks and interviews that everybody knew what the book was about. This wasn't about reader expectations. This was a continuation of the seemingly endless battle that was seeking to destroy my creativity.

***

The constant back and forth continued for close to two more years. It would end up being marketed as 'The long-awaited follow-up to *Of Virtue and Vice*.' In truth, anyone who loved the first book had long since given up on waiting.

The Paris Paradox title was dismissed by the publishers, and after a period of negotiation it was renamed *The Price of Success*. When I say negotiation, it consisted of the publishers suggesting it, me firmly rejecting it, and the process repeating until I eventually gave up. They were insistent. A four-word title linking a positive and negative word. That was the publishers link to the first book which they considered essential.

'But there is no fucking success and no goddamn price,' I argued continually through Nicole.

'Well, Bill ends up emotionally destroyed – that is the price, but he has made a life for himself in Paris which I guess is the success.'

'If that is what anyone has taken from the book, then I will apologise for wasting so much of their time. That isn't what I was saying.'

'This is business. They have a contract for three books. This is one. Get the next two done quicker and we can then look for someone who will allow your creative control to be a little stronger. Though, trust me, it will cost you. It will be your price of success.'

The Price of Success. If only they could have given me the title first, I would've had a brilliant concept. An Australian relocates to Paris and writes an international best seller. He then gets signed to a three-book deal with a bloodsucking international publishing house that wants to fuck him up the arse until he loses all creativity and writes like a robot. Bastards.

In November 1992, *The Price of Success* was finally released. I expected a failure, but I wasn't quite prepared for how badly so. It was slammed by critics and sales were poor. The upside, I hoped, was that the publishers would be less likely to get as involved in what would come next. The failure stemmed as much from the direction they had pushed this book in, as from my work. I wouldn't be given the same marketing budget for the next book, so sales figures were destined not to turn around greatly, but I wouldn't face the same pressures. Nothing could then be a similar disappointment.

'Unless your name is forever mud because of this book,' Inge said.

She may have been right, but it wasn't the supportive remark I was looking for at the time. By this point, it seemed to be all I was ever hearing.

13

10 March 2023

ELLIOT

'The best thing about being a writer is that however old you are, your greatest work may still be ahead of you. Countering that, however young you are, you never know if you have anything of value left within.'

John was talking about the novel that he was currently working on. He said that depending on interpretation this would either be his eleventh or one hundred and forty seventh book.

'Quite different interpretations,' I said.

'I've started 147. Ten have been published. I could say why I believe this will be something special, but I could have said that on everything I've started. You don't start a novel without a belief in the idea. Translating the idea into something more isn't always so easy.'

We were dining at Benita's, a small brasserie just around the corner from John's apartment, and a place where he had spent hundreds of evenings in his years in Paris.

'It is called *Paradoxical*. My follow-up to *Of Virtue and Vice* had touched on the concept of paradoxes, but after it had originally been the heart of the story, the publishers' demands had seen it fade into the background. I find the whole subject fascinating. Facts that are completely counter intuitive. Understanding the great paradoxes is integral to living your best life.'

'Such as?'

'The more available something is the less you want it. The more connected you become, the more isolated you feel. The more choice you have, the more dissatisfied with choice you become.'

'How do you turn that into a novel?'

'It is based around a Parisian named Jean-Luc who is out of step with everyone in the city because he understands all of these paradoxes that plague other people's lives. Eventually he suffers from what gets called the 'Jean-Luc Paradox,' whereby one who is wise enough to understand all the important contradictory truths in life, ends up suffering a from a different set of seemingly more obvious realities.'

He could see the confusion on my face. Whether he was concerned that it may be the reaction that his potential audience may show, or for the principle that I might be a disappointingly unintelligent relative, he realised going deeper may not be the best approach.

'For example, to avoid the paradox of connection, he gets rid of all communication devices. Rather than the isolation from all contact being screen based, he becomes isolated through losing touch with people.'

'Doesn't that prove the paradox is false?'

'No, for the supporting characters carry that narrative. You see, paradoxes isolate certain realities at the expense of everything else. Have you ever heard of the three-door paradox?'

I shook my head, but as he went on to explain, I did recall it. I think there are multiple different versions and explanations, but each is built around the same principle. There is gold behind one door, and feathers behind two others. You are forced to choose one of these and there is a one in three chance of getting the gold. If you are then shown one door that had a feather behind it, then are given the opportunity to change your choice, the paradox suggests that the chances of getting the gold remain one in three if you keep your original choice, but two in three if you change. I never believed it, though when testing it, the proof was there. When this topic was first discussed, PhD's and Nobel laureates argued against it but were all proven wrong. How this related to his idea still confused me.

John was a paradox himself. He had moved here nearly forty years ago, believing that as an outsider looking in, he was best placed to be able to forge his way as a literary force. He couldn't be any further inside Paris now, having lived two-thirds of his life here. The very thing that had made Paris appeal to him had disappeared, yet the prospect of him leaving was long gone.

He had grown as a writer and believed that each step he took was an advancement of his legacy, yet his work was continually less appreciated. He seemed to consider commercial failure to be a badge of honour, for he considered sales to reflect accessibility. In his mind, good writing wasn't accessible to the masses. The more criticism he received, the more he believed he had succeeded in saying what he wanted.

'How often do you see a fat woman in Paris? Pretty rare, right? All of the incredibly rich, fattening but delectable food that is on display, yet everywhere you look you see firm, lithe bodies. The constant exposure to such delicacies means that they take these things for granted. They see the most gorgeous éclair and know that there'll be something just as good on the next block. They don't need to let loose at every oppor- tunity to tantalise their tastebuds because they know that it is always available. When they do, the serves are small, they eat slowly, savouring the flavour, then when they've finished, they follow the local lifestyle by walking it off. Back in Australia, they'd eat something twice as big, with half the flavour and hop back in the car to drive the three blocks home. Another paradox of Paris. The richness of what is here means the indulgence is kept in check.

'The patisseries and boulangeries are such a part of Paris. The smell that emanates from them each morning is so magnificent, yet in most of Paris that is currently being overpowered by the smell of rotting food from piles of uncollected garbage on the streets in front of them.

'One of the greatest things about Paris is that we stand up to the government, fighting against injustices. The price we pay for this is a reminder that such determined opposition made it also one of the worst things about paradoxical Paris.'

As I looked around the brasserie, and outside along the street, all that he said rung true. That said, a book needed to be more than an acknowledgement of a particular foible of humankind. It needed a hook.

'Don't you want to have another success like *Of Virtue and Vice*?

'Everyone wants what they don't have. When the first book became so successful, life changed. In totality, not for better, not for worse. You can isolate the changes, and many of them did make life better, but they were offset by changes for the worse. I lost freedom, anonymity and the ability to live as I wanted. Money was great, but once I had it, it mattered so much less than when I was penniless. Adulation was great, but once I'd banged half the pretty girls in Paris, each one meant less. Respect was great, but once people started seeing me as Jack, the protagonist, I realised there was less respect for me as a man than there was for the public figure. From that point on, I didn't care. I knew then that I was writing for me. I don't care if a million people buy a book I write or if nobody does. What I want, ideally, is for some small number of people to see life differently after they read my work. I'd rather most people say 'what the fuck was that,' while a few others have their world changed by it. But what can really change mindsets is different for each person. You can entertain the masses, or you can genuinely shape a tiny subset of people. That is what I keep aspiring to do.'

He claimed he didn't care what anyone thought, yet he wanted to shape people's lives with his work. The combination of these wishes made no sense, so it was no wonder that he was caught up in a desire to focus on paradoxes. His life was one.

'I tried giving people what they wanted, but I didn't have it in me. Great writers have a way with words that enables them to craft prose that moves people irrespective of the story. I never had that. I was just a bum who'd had a concept that resonated with people, and just enough talent to pull it into a story that they liked.

'Anyways, life takes us in different directions. The more frustrated I got by my career, the more that other aspects of life took over. Eventually I decided that I couldn't give a shit if I never sold another book. I had more important things in my life.'

14

27 November 1991

JOHN

She said yes!

It is completely out of character for me to choose such an obvious approach, but there are times in life when the stereotype exists because it simply is the best way. The Eiffel Tower may be gawked at by every tourist that visits the city, but for those of us who live here it is just part of the skyline. It doesn't demand our attention, it's just part of our backdrop. However derivative it may seem, there are times when the star needs to be brought centre stage. Tonight was that time.

Inge had arrived in Paris at a little over two years ago, from the Dutch city of Rotterdam. She was drawn here by similar dreams that had brought me and so many others here. She was a performer; an actress, singer, dancer who was blessed with the talent to achieve in any of these disciplines. Unfortunately, the less specialised an entertainer is, the harder it can be to reach the zenith of any discipline.

I met Inge after seeing her perform at a club in Saint-Germain-des-Pres soon after she arrived in town. Jacques knew her as another regular at his brasserie and introduced us. I can't pretend my desires were the most noble when I met her. She had the face of an angel and a body designed for sin. I was captivated from the moment she appeared on stage.

'Thank you, that was a fantastic show,' I said, sounding like an over enthusiastic fanboy.

'You think? Not much of a crowd tonight,' Inge replied. She was right, other than me being completely transfixed by her, there was limited other interest from the people in the club. She had a good voice, but I can't deny that had been a secondary factor in winning my attention. She was quite down about the lack of enthusiasm from the audience, which probably played into my favour. She needed a boost, and I was keen to give her that and more.

I walked her home to her place in the 7th Arrondissement. As we turned a corner, the Eiffel Tower came into view. She told me that she had always been infatuated with the tower, and when she arrived in Paris, her one wish when searching for an apartment was having a view of the tower.

'How much money have you got?'

'Not enough,' she said. 'When you are young you have ideals. Dreams seem realistic even when they're not. I thought everyone in Paris had a view of the tower. I thought every decent singer played to big crowds. I play to small and disinterested audiences. I have a view of just the edge of the tower, and only then from outside my building.'

'I can assure you, you had at least one fan tonight who couldn't have been more interested,' I said. It must have been exactly what she needed to hear, and from there we didn't look back.

Our relationship blossomed quickly, and she had moved into my apartment on the Rue de Rivoli within a few months. While the view of the tower was non-existent from home, I managed to convince her that sitting on a balcony overlooking one of the world's most famous streets was a reasonable substitute.

She was intent on focusing her career on music, though with her dancing background, there were more opportunities in theatre and cabaret. I had no real desire to direct her in any way, wanting her to find what she considered her ideal niche. If anything, I probably wanted her to be moderately successful. Too much disappointment would leave her giving up and losing the magic she had. Too much success and I feared that she would outgrow me and the relationship. It was selfish, but at that stage I can't pretend that I wasn't putting my own interests first.

She eventually changed tack when the opportunity to join a European tour of the musical *Cats* came along. Her first professional opportunity was in a Dutch production of the same show. There she was an understudy, and the frustrations associated had turned her off musical theatre. Now she was ready to try again. This was destined to be a challenge for our relationship, with a six-month contract taking her to more than a dozen different cities. While I had the freedom to move around, it wasn't part of my inclination. Paris, though waring on me with time, was now home. The thought of leaving home was getting less appealing each year. I agreed that I would visit her every couple of weeks, but it would only be for two or three days at a time.

By the time Inge returned to Paris we were both happy the season had ended. We shared a view that this was not the right option for her.

'You are a creative spirit. Theatre is structured. You do your own gigs and you can ad-lib solo's, change your running order, drop songs, add songs, play it according to your audience. In a musical, you do the exact same thing at every part of the show, eight times a week, for as long as you can sell the tickets. It's a job for machines, not artists.'

She was back doing a few gigs a week, but this was more than I was achieving. It didn't matter. Royalties continued to flow from my previous work, and there were additional supplements to my workload that ensured a sufficiently steady income. More importantly, the two of us had time to focus on what mattered most to us, which at this stage was each other.

You can choose your friends, but you cannot choose your family. Except your spouse. Your spouse is your choice, and that person transitions from a special friend to the closest of family. It was starting to feel like the time was right to make that decision with Inge.

I had no family. Well, I had a family half a world away, but the relationships were so splintered that I couldn't say for certain if I would ever see any of them again. I hadn't come to Paris to escape them, but they certainly hadn't given me any lure to return to Australia.

My father Howard had a very strained relationship with his father, Leonard, and that in time led to a similar dynamic with his sons. Growing up, my sister Emma was his princess, while my brother Lewis and I were peripheral figures in his life. My relationship with his father became strong in my teens. Most people saw a lot more of Grandpa in me than any other member of the family. This led to Dad having an even greater resentment of me, and our relationship became more fractured each year.

I was always much closer with Mum, but the bitterness between Dad and I inevitably impacted all the relationships in the family. When I first moved out of home, I was speaking to Mum daily, but this slowly reduced when the awkwardness of Dad answering the phone to me gave me less intent to call the number. Emma's unwillingness to ever deviate from the path of following her father, ensured that my relationship with her became non-existent. Lewis and I weren't close, but he had his own issues with Dad, and that at least gave us enough common ground to ensure understanding and acceptance.

When I first travelled to Europe, I wrote letters home to Mum regularly. I called, making sure to do so on Saturday afternoons Australian time, knowing that Dad would be at the races, and I could speak to Mum without going through him. The responses I got from her diminished progressively. Last year I got a card acknowledging my birthday and another at Christmas. This year I'll be lucky to get that.

I did get a letter recently from Lewis. He has now moved to Sydney, his relationship with the rest of the family not much better than mine. There was a certain inevitability to that. Where Lewis and I would fit in each other's lives was hard to say, but at least we shared a certain affinity. I believe in family enough to want to start one. It would be an exercise in futility to go down that path without a fundamental belief that family ties matter. I don't consider them to be an unbreakable bond. When someone is so determined to sever those ties, then that is the result. Lewis and I don't want that same severance. We may never be close, but I like to think we share blood and experiences. Without doing anything to destroy it as the rest of the family have, we will always retain a bond.

The close bond I want isn't back in Australia. It is Inge. She is the heart of the family I want going forward. I don't see marriage as a significant change to what we have now. I guess that at this point in life we are each the most important person in the others world. The essence of marriage to me is the promise you make that your spouse will be the most important person in your world forever more. That may not end up being the case for everyone, for not every marriage ends up successful, but it is at least the intention.

I'm not going down this pathway to replace what I lack. I have an overwhelming love for her that has continued to surprise me. What I thought I had found with her was powerful, but it continues to grow bigger and stronger each day. When we were separated it stung me in a way I'd never known. Now I just want to be with her. Whatever we do, wherever we are, she makes my day.

Paris is the city of love and romance. There is an endless supply of places that celebrate this in the city, but surely there is nowhere more famous for romantic gestures than the most famous structure in the city. On our first night together she told me how it was such a part of the lure to the city for her, yet eighteen months on we have never gone there together. We've gone past, under, around and near, yet we've never actually set foot on the tower together. From the moment that I thought this may be our pathway in life, I was determined that we wouldn't do so until I was ready to take this step.

I did all I could to keep it a surprise, but it was hard to suggest dining at La Belle France on the Eiffel Tower after all this time, without there being something more to the evening. I told her the dinner was to celebrate a major breakthrough in my next planned novel.

'You know, I don't think we've ever been to the tower together,' I said to her, knowing with absolute certainty but pretending to downplay this as we got ready.

'I figured you were waiting until you were ready to propose to me, but just a simple plot idea is enough of a celebration, hey. I should have been more insistent on you working harder much earlier,' she said. Whether she was just playing with me or not, there was no doubt that she had thought ahead to the possibility of such a proposal coming in time.

I decided to change my plans slightly. We had the most amazing meal, and although my intention was to have a little extra surprise between the main course and dessert, I chose not to. I dragged dinner out for as long as I could. We had more wine, and then with the restaurant nearly empty, I paid the bill. We got in the elevator and taken down to the ground. There were still staff in the restaurant and a couple of customers yet to depart, but we were the only ones in the lift with the elevator attendant.

'*Bonsoir mademoiselle et monsieur*. Just make your way across there where you can see the exit,' the attendant said.

There were security guards at the gate, and the remaining staff and guests in the restaurant, but all of these were out of our sight. At this point, right under the Eiffel Tower, there was not a soul but the two of us. We got to the very centre, a place where at any time I've ever seen, there has been thousands of people. I never imagined there could be such a perfect moment. I dropped down on one knee and before I got a word out, the tears of joy were streaming down her face.

'Yes,' she said.

'You have to let me ask first.'

'*Oui,*'

'Inge, will you marry me.'

By now she was overcome and could only nod, her smile and tears merged into the most expressive display of emotion I was ever likely to see.

There are few moments more special in anyone's life than the proposal. It doesn't matter where or how, but there is not a chance in the world that there is a better city for it than Paris. There is not a better place in Paris for it than the Eiffel Tower. There is never a better moment at the Eiffel Tower than the freakish timing that enabled us to be there alone.

I can live until I'm a hundred. This day, this moment, will never lose its magical place in my memory.

15

11 March 2023

ELLIOT

I can live until I'm a hundred. This day, this moment, will never lose its place in my memory.

Sometimes in life, the view from the top is more symbolic than spectacular. Looking down on the city from the top of the Eiffel Tower was an amazing sight, but no more than being at the bottom the other night and looking up as the tower sparkled. It wasn't the view but the feeling that being here generated. Arriving in Paris and first seeing the tower felt like a dream had come true, but when I think back to those dreams, I'd always end up at the top. Now I am here, the dream is truly complete. I can think of nowhere else in the world that could deliver such a powerful feeling.

In my hometown, there is the Harbour Bridge and the Opera House that share centre stage. In New York it is the Statue of Liberty and the Empire State Building. Here, it is the Eiffel Tower. Everything else is secondary. The greatest drawcard in the city that attracts more visitors than any other. This is why the moment is so special.

John was not one for the commercial tourist spots, so I had decided to spend the day taking in the places that he'd be less keen to visit with me. I figured I'd decided to beat the crowds here by doing the tower at opening. Riding the elevator up had been amazing, the sight of the inner structure playing against the preconceptions formed through movies and other cultural references.

How many millions of people had taken these same steps in the century and a quarter since this structure was built? It was easy to feel insignificant when thinking of this, but at the same time it made the moment feel richer. The tower was a beacon that drew people from around the world. Surely the richest lives are those that share the most iconic experiences in life, along with their own unique moments. Paris may be a derivative destination, and the tower is the greatest example of this, but part of understanding humanity is experiencing the most obvious lures.

Part of me didn't want to leave, knowing that I was in the middle of a once in a lifetime experience. I was also aware that I had a tight agenda, and I couldn't do all that I wanted today while spending too much time in any one spot. I made my way back to the base and walked along the left bank of the Seine. It was an idyllic half hour walk that got me to my next stop, the Musee D'Orsay.

While the Louvre may be the world's most famous museum, the D'Orsay was commonly regarded as the greater attraction. Housed in a former train station, the building itself is a work of art. As someone who's always loved trains, I felt at home the moment I walked into the main area, looking so much like the layout you'd find at a classical old station. Art works up and down what would have been platforms, and a clock on the far wall for the trains timeliness to be measured against.

I'm not a great art lover, but the pinnacle of any aspect of life should not be walked past. You do not need to be a connoisseur to appreciate the very best in any facet of life. What defines the best is subjective, but in my limited knowledge of art there was nobody like Vincent Van Gogh. I had done a school project on him in Year 9, forced to select an artist and with no real interest in the topic, selected him at random. I became intrigued by the story of a man whose work is revered like few others, yet who couldn't sell a painting while he was alive. The D'Orsay has a room of his paintings, and all these years after doing that project, I was excited to see some of his works in the flesh.

I headed straight upstairs to find the Van Gogh display. Although the museum was not overly busy, as I walked the final steps to the room, it was clear that this was the biggest drawcard here. The crowds were far thicker here than anywhere else in the museum.

I walked into the gallery and was awestruck. There is a dedicated museum for Van Gogh in Amsterdam, and I assumed that most of his great work was there, but here in front of me were some of his greatest paintings.

Starry Night Over the Rhone, was to me the greatest of all his works. I was drawn immediately to it. If anyone should have crossed my path as I walked towards it, I feel sure I'd have knocked them over without even knowing, such was the magnetism I felt as it pulled me closer.

There is a difference between a beautiful picture and a picture of beauty. An artist can create a beautiful picture from a scene devoid of all beauty. Likewise, any artist can seek to capture the beauty of a scene, yet rarely can they deliver something that allows the viewer to feel the full extent of that beauty. This painting is the most beautiful picture of the greatest beauty. The lovers in the foreground representing the most powerful human emotion. The then very modern gas lighting from the town of Arles and its yellow reflection on the dark blue water of the harbour. The stars that have directed humanity throughout history provide a contrast to the artificial light below and blend perfectly with the aquamarine sky that house them. If a picture is generally said to tell a thousand words, then this painting tells billions.

I take a selfie with the painting behind me as though I will need a reminder that I actually stood in its presence. I take several more photos of the painting, hoping that a digital image on my phone could truly capture the feeling that seeing the work in the flesh has done. I know this is fallacious for I have seen it thousands of times online without ever feeling a semblance of what standing before the painting has given me.

Next to it, the Church at Auvers another of his greatest masterpieces, and as I slowly took in the detail of it, I wished I'd had enough time to take a trip out there. There was the Bedroom in Arles, the Portrait of Dr Gachet, and two of his better known self-portraits amongst the other masterpieces in the room. The commercial value of the paintings in this room would exceed the Gross Domestic Product of many nations. In reality, they are priceless. That one man could have created all of this is mind-numbing. That this is just a tiny part of his overall collection, and that his career was so short, defies belief.

I'd intended to spend no more than two hours in the Musee D'Orsay, but two hours had been taken up in just one room that formed a tiny part of the museum. I didn't have the time to explore all that it offered, but I felt compelled to seek out the famous outlook from the old station clock. On the top floor of the museum, the setting provides a vista across the river to the north of Paris, with a beautiful view of everything from the Louvre right out to the Sacre-Coeur. From the outside, the clock provides a reminder of the days the building served its original purpose as a station, commuters relying upon it to know how long they had before their train was departing.

Maybe next time I come to Europe I will visit the Van Gogh Museum in Amsterdam to take in more of his legacy. Maybe that is futile, for I should probably never visit another museum in my life. Once you experience perfection in any field, trying to relive or beat that is something that leads to frustration and disappointment far more frequently than the ecstasy of the first time.

John had reached perfection with his first book. That isn't to suggest that the book was perfect, but it may well have been the perfection of his working capacity. Maybe his life would have been better if that had remained his only published novel.

The perception I had of John as I grew up was of a hedonist, self-centred and self-absorbed. That stemmed entirely from the pictures painted by the rest of the family, whether or not that was their true opinion. Perhaps it was easier to cast aspersions on him rather than take any blame for the disintegrated relationship.

In my time with him, I have been struck by how far from my expectations he has been. Rather than someone who thought the world revolved around him, he was a man who seemed more absorbed by other people. In many cases these were people who in their own small way had made enough of an impact that he yearned to immortalise their stories through his work. More significantly was the obsession for those he loved.

16

8 July 1993

JOHN

It is our first wedding anniversary. To be honest, it feels like it has been ten years, such has been the way things have changed. My view, however foolish and naïve it may have been, was that marriage was a commitment to eternity. It wasn't meant as an invitation for change. Everything about us had been perfect until the day we walked down the aisle. There should not have been any reason for things to change between us, but as humans with all the associated flaws, I have started to understand where the problems stem from.

I didn't care about our wedding. That is poorly phrased, for I cared incredibly about it. What I mean is that I didn't have any particular cares about the details. I wanted Inge as my wife, and I wanted her to have the wedding that she wanted. With that, she chose it to be in her hometown of Rotterdam. The relationship with her family was strained, though at least it was far from the non-existent one I had with mine. To her, marrying a prominent author was a sign of success, and she wanted to show that off to her family and all those from her past. The word prominent is of course a subjective one, but there was enough knowledge of my name from my one great success, that I was hardly the kind of unknown artist with a dream, like many men she had dated in her young years.

Getting married in the Netherlands is a different process to what I envisaged. We had two ceremonies. The first of these was an official private ceremony held in the local registry office. This was conducted in Dutch and was just the two of us with two witnesses and thankfully for me, a translator. This was followed on the weekend by what I considered to be the traditional wedding. This one was conducted predominantly in English, and for this we had roughly fifty people in attendance.

Naturally none of my family were there. I didn't invite them, though that wasn't my original intention. I had contacted my parents after the engagement, but the reaction was typical of all interactions between us at this time. They weren't interested, and from that point I realised that my family going forward was Inge and any offspring we may have. I no longer was a part of the family that I had been born into.

I did have a few people come up from Paris for the event. Danny, another ex-pat Australian who'd moved to Paris, was my best man. My London based agent, Nicole, came over, conscious that she'd been one of the banes of my recent existence and needed to repair some damage. We'd lost touch with Jacques, the man who had introduced us, but I eventually tracked him down and invited him. He declined the invitation, offering his best wishes, but saying that he believed life was too short to spend a day out of Paris, whatever the occasion. That was fine with me. I didn't care too much who else was attending, as for me it was Inge's day.

Our honeymoon wasn't so much a destination, as a random road trip that took us a couple of hundred kilometres each day without any pre-planning. Across three weeks we saw an array of destinations through the Netherlands, Germany, Belgium, Luxembourg and France. When we surfaced each day, we had no idea where we would go. It turned into an idyllic way of seeing places that we'd never have been likely to choose. It was almost disappointing to arrive home to our apartment on the Rue de Rivoli.

'So where will we move to from here,' Inge said soon after we arrived home.

I had interpreted this as a comment about the constant movement of our honeymoon, but before long it became apparent that she didn't want to live here.

'Where do you want to go? Not back to fucking Rotterdam?' She had never given any indication of wanting to move prior to this point in time, but now that she'd gone from fiancé to wife, it appeared she was keen to set a new agenda.

'No, I want to stay in Paris, but this place is so small. I want a kitchen, a living area, a decent size bedroom a separate laundry and storage space.'

'You want to be in Paris,' I said, 'but you don't want to live in Paris?'

'What do you mean?'

'Paris isn't just a land mass, it is a lifestyle. That lifestyle is about 19th century apartment living. It is about life being based beyond the home, not confined to it. People speak about a person's home being their castle, but that is not a Parisian phrase. To have what you want means moving out of Paris.'

'There are decent sized places here.'

'With more than decent prices. Living here based on what we currently earn is challenging enough.'

It became a source of ongoing contention between us. While it never bothered her before the marriage, from this time on she always referred to home as my apartment, rather than ours. She accepted there wasn't an alternative at this point, but it was something that we should move beyond in the long term. I didn't necessarily have an unbreakable attachment to the apartment, but I did like the lifestyle we had where we were. I had my grocer, my tobacconist, my boulangerie, my cafes, my bars and bistros. I had no desire to move.

Attitudes to everything seemed to start changing. The places we went, the things we did. There seemed to be a progressively growing divide between what each of us wanted in any given situation. These were rarely major issues, but when you continually find yourself unable to agree on how you'd spend your free time together, it didn't help the harmony of the relationship.

Every morning I sit at my desk and write for two hours before doing anything else. The next few hours I spend out of the apartment, frequenting any number of my preferred locations for eating, coffee and most importantly, getting inspired to create new characters from the people watching I do. On returning home it is the consolidation of any notetaking I have done while out. All of this is exactly how I worked before the wedding, and never had it mattered to Inge. Now, she serves as a constant distraction, giving me little time to focus on work. It wouldn't necessarily bother me if she wasn't so determined to have us move up in the world. Her so-called needs are above and beyond our financial position and will be until such time as I release something else of significance.

We both take each other for granted now. Not completely, but enough that the extra effort we made for each other has changed from a pleasure to a chore. I want to make her happy and no doubt she feels the same for me. It seems now that it is all too much of an effort. When you devote enough of your energy into any task, you do so with an expectation of making a difference. The reward needn't be significant, for a good deed is its own reward, but when you see that the deed is either unnoticed or unappreciated, eventually you can't help but stop trying.

People evolve. Relationships also evolve, but not always in the same way that the individuals within the relationships do. I had always thought that each step forward in the relationship made it stronger, but marriage hasn't achieved that for us. I'm not falling out of love, but there are times when I feel like our love is falling apart.

There is a similarity between our temperaments and whether that is an asset or a liability depends on the day of the week. Our good times couldn't be more perfect, yet when we fight, we bring out the worst in each other. We are both idealistic, and in most cases those ideals point us in the same direction. When we see different pathways as the right ones, neither of us seems capable of yielding at all.

When Inge performed, it was always as a vocalist only, a trio of musicians backing her. At home she spent hours practising on keyboards. She wanted the ability to broaden her range sufficiently that she could do gigs in piano bars working on her own.

'What I can earn through a show on my own may be slightly less, but without having to pay musicians, I'd end up much better off,' she said.

'You need to be better than the other people currently doing that, or you need to have better material. If you're going to play the same songs that everyone else does, how do you start getting the spots that someone else currently has.'

She took my comments as criticism when it was meant as advice. She was a performing artist, and she had talent, but I wanted to help her find her creative voice. While she had previously played her own material when performing solo, she was now singing standards. I wanted her to add a few original songs to these gigs. While song writing was something that I'd never considered, I managed to translate her Dutch lyrics into French, making her far more accessible for audiences here. Most of her songs didn't fit with the rest of her repertoire, and her backing musicians talked her out of adding this to the set list. It did lead one of them to consider a different direction.

Xavier, was a Belgian ex-pat who had similar dreams. He was a guitarist, taking any gig he could in Paris to make ends meet, but had aspirations for a career in rock music. He convinced Inge that they should start a band. He'd recruited a drummer and bassist and wanted Inge to play keyboards and sing. He did most of the writing but worked with Inge on developing some of the material that her and I had previously worked on. While Xavier and I had previously gotten on fine, the greater presence he was starting to have in her life was more than I welcomed.

'He's an arsehole. He's doing this to get in your pants, not to develop your career.'

'You don't want to write for a tiny loyal audience. You want a novel to surpass *Of Virtue and Vice*. Why should I be satisfied performing in small clubs when I could be making music that takes me international? I can't do that on my own,' she said.

'What are you willing to do to get that?'

'Work. Nothing more.'

Nebefrux had their first public performance at a club in the Latin Quarter. They'd taken their name from the origins of their four members, with local drummer Jean and Luxembourg-born bassist Nic joining Inge and Xavier. The audience wasn't large, and the reception wasn't overwhelming, but gigs continued to get booked keeping the band keen enough to continue.

The rehearsing increased and my jealousy of Xavier grew similarly. When I met Isabella, his new girlfriend, my mind should have been put at ease, but instead it just led to a greater paranoia. Perhaps she was just a distraction he'd found to throw me off the scent. I wasn't going to be fooled by any display of forged affection, and I was convinced that the more it appeared he was all over her, he was playing a game.

Life at home became more difficult as Inge's tolerance of my jealousy became progressively more challenged.

'I can't do this. You trust me or you leave me,' was her ultimatum.

Our volatility had always made our relationship a minefield, but one we'd previously managed to navigate well. I had to face the reality that I couldn't change her, so had to change myself if I was to salvage what I wanted. I'd clung to a steadfast belief that she'd been the problem, but I had to accept that at this point, it was me. It wasn't even a fundamental fear of her sleeping with someone else, but the feeling that such an act would mean I wasn't enough. If that was true, what was I?

I gave her space. No more unannounced appearances. No more questions. Trust and faith, however hard it came to me. Before too long, the change in my actions were met by changes in results. Life at home improved. Inge spent more time rehearsing on her own at home and working on her own material. We spent more time together, both in and out of the apartment. The relationship was far more like it had been in our best times.

'Xavier quit the band,' she told me soon after. He'd joined a more successful band and couldn't continue with Nebefrux, who without their main creative force, chose not to continue. 'I know you'll be happy,' she said in an accusing manner.

'I'd got past that point. What will make me happy is you being happy. I think that will be when you're doing what your most inspired by. I don't think that's trying to appeal to the masses, it's by having the greatest possible impact on your specific audience. Inge Martin, front and centre performing her works, her way.'

She smiled. 'I wanted superstardom to take us out of here and into a mansion at Saint-Cloud. Guess we'll be stuck here.'

'This is us. A corner apartment opposite the Louvre is hardly a sign of failure. We've got a life that I'd say most people would envy. I have you, and that in itself is all that I could ask for. Do you really think you need more?'

'No. *La vie est belle.*'

17

11 March 2023

ELLIOT

'It is an eyesore. Your standing surrounded by the most beautiful structure, in the most beautiful city in the world. Then there is this monstrosity that conflicts with everything else around it. How can that be seen as adding to the picture?'

'Not conflicts. Contrasts. The modernity against the classical architecture brings out the best in each other.'

The broad American accents of the middle-aged couple in front of me were locked in a debate that had no doubt been waged thousands of times. We were waiting in line to enter the Louvre and the tourists were discussing the glass pyramid before us that had stood for over thirty years surrounded by the palace built more than seven centuries earlier.

'When something is perfect, don't change it,' the woman said.

'Nothing is ever perfect. Change is evolution. It isn't always for the better, but without it, we confine ourselves to the failings of today. What is the point of a museum if it doesn't use the past to point towards the future?'

They spoke loudly enough that it wasn't a choice on my part whether to listen in or not. I was tempted to join the debate given their seeming willingness to open it up to all and sundry based on their volume. The reality is there was nothing I could say that mattered. It was a reflection of personal opinion, with no right or wrong. Like any work of art inside, it is a question of taste.

Whether the pyramid was a good business decision could be argued definitively. The Louvre had become the predominant museum in the world, its status lifted enormously through the fame the pyramid had brought. Tourism was critical to the city, and the pyramid had played a role in maximising this.

Paris was a city dominated by older architecture. The previous great controversy of an addition to the cityscape came when the Eiffel Tower was built. With time, that perceived blight on the landscape became the ultimate symbol of the city. Similar feelings existed when the glass pyramid was built. For many, the modern glass structure was out of place against the style of the Louvre. Many others objected to the use of a pyramid, given its most famous place in human culture arose from its place in Ancient Egypt.

As we entered the museum, I was quick to ensure I turned in the opposite direction to the Americans I'd been waiting behind. My annoyance at their volume had grown progressively through the wait. In fairness, my frustration was out of proportion to their behaviour, but it is an inescapable fact that once your attention is drawn to something negative, the impact of each additional example grows exponentially. By the time we'd got inside, I had a great desire to strangle each of them. No action could be further from the type of person I am, but certain triggers will test anyone's patience.

As had been the case at the Musee D'Orsay, I'd arrived at the Louvre with one primary thing I wished to see. With half a million items on display, if you were to spend one minute looking at each item, it would take a year to see everything, even if it was possible to spend every minute of every day perusing the works. I'd hoped to see some of the highlights, but my one great determination was to see the world's most famous painting.

'You should go. If nothing else, make sure you see the *Mona Lisa*. The greatest painting of all time.' John had said this to me yesterday which surprised me. I didn't expect that he'd have such appreciation of a painting that seemed to be famous for being famous, rather than critically revered by aficionados.

'The value of any art, be it a painting, music or literature comes only with time,' he said. 'Trends allow trash to pass as treasure for a time. As time passes, the trash disappears and the treasure glistens more prominently. Van Gogh couldn't sell a painting when alive yet is more popular now than any other artist in history. Bach is regarded by some as the greatest composer of all time, yet the appreciation of his work took a century.

'All the different award ceremonies; Oscars, Grammys and the like, they should all be presented on a delay of decades. This year evaluate the work of fifty years ago and I guarantee the winners will be a better reflection of artistic merit than the winners at the time were.'

'Isn't the *Mona Lisa's* continued acclaim more about fame and hype than artistic merit?'

John agreed but emphasised that such fame arose four centuries after its creation, and only did so because it had remained such a revered work through that time. 'The brilliance drove the fame, the fame then had it more discussed which meant more people learned to appreciate its brilliance, making it more famous again. The circle never ends, which it would if it was a less remarkable piece.'

He'd mentioned, as many people do, how small the painting is. As I walk into the room where she sits at the near end, I know that I am looking at a painting roughly 75 by 50 centimetres, yet on a wall so large, and in a museum surrounded by works five, ten and twenty times larger, she looks tiny.

I spent the best part of twenty minutes paying homage to the work, or more accurately fighting my way through the crowd around the painting. Eventually, I made it to the front of the roped off and heavily guarded area around the piece. From the distance the public is kept, the ability to properly appreciate the *Mona Lisa* is diminished, but the crowds prove why this is necessary. Those crowds may not prove that this is the greatest painting in history, but they do indicate that this is the painting that has had the greatest impact on people. What is the aim of art? Is it not to have an impact on people? If that is the case, then everything John had said was right.

There's a claustrophobic feeling I get whenever I'm in areas that are too tightly crowded. It may seem strange that I've flocked to so many of the busiest and most crowded sites in one of the busiest and most crowded cities in the world if that is how I feel, but it is a fine line that separates atmosphere from discomfort. The buzz that surrounds events and locations that attract large numbers excites me, but there is a certain point when it goes one step too far. The crowds in the Louvre add something special. The scrum near the Mona Lisa is asphyxiating, and the feeling as I leave the room has an impact as great as the one when I walked in. Oxygen. Freedom. Of course, moments later, it is reflection on the experience that preceded it.

I check my watch and see that there's little time for further exploration, but this is the Louvre and as potentially a once in a lifetime experience, I was going to utilise every moment I could. I didn't have a particular section I wanted to focus on, so it was mere good fortune that took me to the exhibit of Ancient Egyptian antiquities.

Nothing says Egypt like the pyramids, and it seemed to make sense that a venue famed for the installation of a pyramid should feature Egyptian history so strongly. Whether this formed any of the inspiration behind the glass structure was uncertain, but after seeing the Luxor obelisk on the Place de la Concorde the other day, it seemed the connection between Paris and Ancient Egypt was no accident.

The Great Sphinx of Tanis stood at the entrance of this section, like a guard protecting the relics behind it. Statues of goddesses, works reflecting kings and queens, coffins, mummies, hieroglyphics and displays of life as it was thousands of years ago. I slowly worked my way through this section that had fascinated people throughout history. Ancient Egypt was a fascination globally, yet here in Paris it seemed on another level. I wondered if even Cairo could offer more.

I exited via the Louvre du Carrousel, an arcade that runs underneath the Place du Carrousel. I was brought face to face with the inverted pyramid, which served partially as a giant skylight, but more importantly as part of the greater creation of the Louvre's modern development. To some, the Louvre pyramid served as the male symbol, while the inverted pyramid symbolised female. The inverted pyramid hung to a metre below the ground, and under it was a small stone pyramid. If all of the theories of symbols are correct, then perhaps this smaller pyramid was the baby, born to those symbolised by the two main glass pyramids. I wasn't one for interpretation. To me, it was all aesthetics, and the design worked perfectly.

If I lived across the road from here, as my uncle does, I'm sure I'd make it my mission to work my way through the quiet sections of the Louvre that don't cram in the visitors. Everyone is drawn to the same things, for there will always be headline acts in every show. These don't necessarily tell the greatest stories, they merely shout the loudest to attract the most eyes. It is only when you're willing to look beyond the masses that you uncover the things that impact most greatly.

Maybe *Of Virtue and Vice* was John's *Mona Lisa*. He'd been stuck trying to find something to put next to it, when really his legacy was set with it standing alone. Any further growth he could have as an artist may have been better served creating work to sit in the quieter sections. Less people may look, but more of them may be spellbound if they had to dig a little deeper to find what was most inspiring.

18

21 November 1995

JOHN

Nicole had been my staunchest ally, but even she had reached the point where she was no longer wanting to represent me.

'You can't just fluke the level of success that *Of Virtue and Vice* brought. You have the ability within you, but I don't believe you have the desire to create anything that will have an impact.'

It had taken five years for my follow-up, *The Price of Success*, to be released. It hadn't reached that point with genuine enthusiasm from either Nicole or me. There wasn't scope for a sequel to the first book, but Nicole had sought a follow-up so similar, that it would be nothing more than the repetition of a concept that I'd already exhausted. I wanted to write a book that bore no relationship at all to its predecessor, stepping away as much as possible in both genre and style. *The Price of Success* was the compromise, one that neither of us completely believed in, but both of us understood was essential to satisfy the contracts that were in place.

It came as little surprise to anybody involved that *The Price of Success* was a failure, both commercially and critically.

'You've got one more chance,' Nicole told me, after the poor reviews and sales figures mounted up in the months following its release. The contract that had been negotiated was for two books, and while the publisher would have liked to have ripped it up at that point, they stood to lose more from doing that than by continuing. 'They're not going to help, you know. Marketing drives success, and they're not likely to spend a cent more than they need. You won't be doing any overseas jaunts with this one.'

'Good,' I said, despite having mixed feelings on that topic. Life was difficult enough at home that the opportunity to escape for a while would have been appreciated, but I hated the marketing trips. Saying the same things over and again to different audiences just to sell a few more books was not what being an author was about to me. Publishers view our job very differently, and as they pay the bills, they call the shots. For an author they see potential in, that means something very different to what it was likely to be for me.

The third book was again a fight, with my desire to follow my own path conflicting with everyone else focussed on cracking the market.

'You put another *The Price of Success* out there, and what do you think follows? Losing your contract mightn't seem like such an issue right now, but who do you think is going to sign you on the back of two failed books. One hit, a decade old. You think anyone else will pick you up? Don't kid yourself.'

The truth is, I didn't care. The royalties I'd earned from *Of Virtue and Vice* combined with the ensuing contract had provided me with financial security. I mightn't quite be set for life, but an absence of earning for a few years, if that was what it took, would not destroy me. I also had overwhelming belief that once I had complete creative freedom, I'd be able to produce work that would find its place. I had the basis of several books ready, from what I'd pitched to Nicole only for her to reject them.

Golgotha, the story of an innocent man on death row, ended up as my third release. It involved less compromise than we'd previously needed, with Nicole and I both on the same page regarding the idea's potential. After completing the first draft I wasn't sure what to be more concerned about. Part of me was worried that the finished product would fail to live up to the quality of the idea, while the other part of me was worried that the book would be great and deliver success that I didn't really want. Being resigned to escaping from the current contract and the requirements associated with it, a successful book now may put me back into uncomfortable territory.

Three months on from its release, those fears were unfounded. The book has failed to gain traction in any of the key markets. Even though a French language version hasn't launched, the English version has done better here than in Britain or the USA. The book hasn't even had any success in Australia, though I guess enough time has passed now that I'm a non-entity there.

Nicole had arrived mid-morning to meet with me. As usual, she chose the venue, a café out near the Gare du Nord. She believed that holding command in a meeting came not just from the relative roles of each party, but from the venue. In London we'd meet at her office. Here we no longer met on my choice of territory, for that would diminish her control.

'It wouldn't matter if it was the greatest book of all time, if nobody knows about it, nobody reads it,' Nicole said.

'My job is writing the book, not selling it.'

'So long as you believe that, success will be reliant on luck. The reader doesn't just buy a book, they buy you. They are invested in you. They like what they read, they want more. Once nothing of note followed *Virtue*, that investment ended. *Golgotha* may be just as good, and if it was out a year after *Virtue* it would have outperformed it. Nine years and one ordinary book later, nobody remembers you.'

'Nobody knew me when *Virtue* came out, but that didn't matter.'

'Yes. Back then they said John Martin, he could be anything, so they pushed the book into all the right hands. Now they say John Martin, we know what he is, and go straight past it.'

'You're telling me there is no way back?'

'Anywhere in life, there is always a way back, but I don't believe you have the desire or the discipline.' She paused, trying to find the right way to explain things. I knew she wanted to sever the relationship, but like everything, she wanted to do so on her own terms.

'You're with a publisher that works on selling 500,000 copies of a book. You can have a brilliant career working with a publisher whose business model is based on selling 5,000 copies. No loss of creative control. No world tours, no mass media, just a few in-store appearances. No million Euro pay checks, but a living. It is far more you. I can put you in touch with an array of people based here that can help you.'

'You're *my* agent. If this was all about the publisher, you'd be getting me a deal with someone more suitable now. The publisher isn't through with me any more than you are.' I felt betrayed by her. Over the years she had been a friend and confidante, not just a professional acquaintance. It felt now like I had been a cash-cow for her, and once the direction was fixed without the same potential for profit, I was set for her scrapheap.

'I'm an employee. I don't make the decisions. Ralph insists that I focus on authors associated with the major publishing houses. You'll go to a niche publisher and are best served with a niche agent.'

'How much time would I take? Handle me independently in your own time.'

'You need someone here.'

It would have looked like we were a couple, and Nicole was giving me the 'it's not you, it's me,' speech. Millions of people have used the line, but the reality is always the same. It's always you. However Nicole wanted to justify it, she was dumping me. I hadn't wanted to keep her for any great faith in her work, but I wanted to feel like the trust I'd shown in her personally had been justified. Maybe I should appreciate the fact she came from London to tell me face-to-face, but for now I was unable to see silver linings. My greatest professional supporter no longer supported me.

One huge success, one complete failure and one good, yet largely unnoticed novel. Would there ever be a fourth release?

19

11 March 2023

ELLIOT

John was waiting for me downstairs as I arrived at his apartment. He looked upset, and despite the fact I was no more than two minutes late, I feared it was my doing.

'You alright?' I asked.

'Yeah. I got an email this afternoon that my former agent passed away.'

'I'm sorry. Do you want to cancel tonight?'

'Nah. Nicole the mole. She was the first person to show belief in me, but when I needed her most, she showed her true colours and threw me to the curb. There's a whole lot of people who come into your life and shape you, but given time, you can count on one hand the people that genuinely give a shit about you.'

The cynicism of John's words sat in conflict with his demeanour. I couldn't know whether it was the impact on his own feelings of mortality, or a reflection of a genuine sympathy for the loss of someone who had played a role in his life. Either way, I felt that tonight wasn't the ideal occasion to be out celebrating, but the tickets were bought and if he insisted we continue, I'd be creating a greater conflict by talking him out of it.

We crossed the road and got a bus to the Boulevard de Clichy, the famous windmill of the Moulin Rouge right across the road.

'We've only got show tickets, so we're having dinner just down there,' John said, pointing to a bistro called Rouge Bis up ahead of us. 'This is nightlife central in Paris. It's not just the Moulin Rouge around here, there's a bit of everything. We'll take a wander after the show.'

'I thought the Latin Quarter was the place,' I said.

'A city the size of Paris, there is nightlife everywhere. Bastille, Grands Boulevards, Austerlitz.'

'I wouldn't have thought you'd be so up with all of this.'

'I might be too old to be a part of it, but I'm a writer. It's my job to know what happens and where,' he said.

After ordering, John got back on to the topic of Nicole, telling me that she'd been back in touch with him years later.

'She never felt comfortable about the way our working relationship ended. She screwed me over and she knew it, so she wanted to make amends. I've never be much of a forgive and forget person, but we caught up whenever she was in Paris. I mightn't have had the highest opinion of her, but I trusted her judgement on professional matters.'

'I thought the issues all started as she saw everything differently to you.'

'She always knew her stuff. I never doubted that, but she was a salesperson, and the art was secondary. I was an artist, and the sales were secondary to me. I knew what would sell, but I couldn't do it. She knew the art but her commitment to her job took precedence.'

'What happened to her?'

'A major stroke. She had a healthy enough lifestyle, but that's never any sort of guarantee. I last saw her about six months ago. She seemed well, so I never would have picked it.'

Reflecting on the more positive side of his involvement with her seemed to be bringing out more of his sadness, so when he changed topics I was more than happy to keep him away.

'So why are you still staying at that hotel? Why don't you come and stay in the spare room at my place?'

'It was already booked before I knew you had room for me.'

'Cancel it tomorrow. Come and stay.'

I realised the offer was probably more driven by his desire for company than as a favour for me, but it would work for me too. Getting to know John was much of the reason for being here, so it made sense. I said I'd see if I could get a refund on the rest of my stay, and if so, I'd join him.

We talked about other things I wanted to see and do while I was in Paris, and I said that I'd already visited most of the places that were priorities for me.

'So I'm free to fit in with anything.'

'The Paris of an old local is very different to the Paris a young tourist wants to see.'

'I thought you were taking me clubbing after the Moulin Rouge?' I said with a laugh.

'That is not quite what I had in mind'

Our meals were fantastic, or at least mine was. John was so conditioned to the French bistro scene that he was harder to impress.

'I eat out in places like this every day. I guess familiarity breeds contempt, so it takes more to have an impact on me. Don't get me wrong, I've eaten here pre-show before, and if I hadn't liked it, I would never have returned.'

We made our way across the road with plenty of time before the show. John pointed out that it was essential, as however great the show was, the event was typical of any commercial enterprise in modern times.

'They pack you in like sardines and maximise every cent,' he said.

'Doesn't everyone?'

'To an extent, but when you've got enough of a name behind you, the ability to do that is far greater.'

'I take it you wouldn't come here normally.'

'Some may say that love can't be quantified, but today proves otherwise. Your uncle loves you enough to endure the crowds and the lines of the Moulin Rouge, but not quite enough to endure the crowds and the lines of the Eiffel Tower or the Louvre.'

I laughed. 'I'll take that,' I said. The activities of the day were all more than suitable to be done on my own, but I knew full well that I'd never have come here alone.

Our seats were good, but he was right, space was at a premium, and anywhere else, such closeness of seating and tables would have turned me off.

The performance ended up being one of the most entertaining shows I had ever seen. So much for cabaret being too old-school. This was a performance that would work for young or old alike. It was a visual and aural feast, perfectly pieced together. The main show, Feerie, was filled with song, dance and incredible costumes, many of which were much higher on glamour than material which helped me appreciate them far more than such things normally would.

For me, the greater highlight was the variety of acrobatic performances that interspersed the main show. Four different acts performed feats of unbelievable precision and strength that took my breath away. I could have watched an entire night of just these artists and couldn't have enjoyed it more.

When we left, there was an array of vibrant pubs and clubs nearby that I wouldn't have minded checking out, but I knew John would be far more comfortable in somewhere quieter. We didn't have to search for long before finding an ideal median point between his ideal and mine. More than anything, the ease of getting a drink suited us both.

'Don't worry. You can bring a girl back to my place. You'll make a better impression than the dive you're staying in now,' he said.

'I don't think that will be happening.'

'Why the hell not. You're young and you're in the city of love. Make the most of it.' He paused for a moment before continuing. 'Or are you more worried about walking in on me and someone I bring home?'

'You do that often?'

'Not as often as when I was your age. Maybe more often than you do at your age though.'

Maybe staying with him would be more eye-opening than I had imagined.

20

3 February 1997

JOHN

There are billions of people on this planet. Every one of them has a story, and if you can mine their lives for the great highs and lows, there is a story that will move people. Even the most ordinary life has its share of extraordinary moments. Most people don't appreciate the unique magic that forms the lives of the people around them.

Eric Beeh was born in Bavaria in 1897 and despite one of the more amazing life stories I'd ever heard, it was unlikely that too many people today would know he'd ever existed. In his day, he was an enormously successful and famous entertainer. People who worked mainly on stage were often left without a legacy at the end of their careers. In those days, if you didn't see them live, you didn't see them. Movies could always be seen by new generations. Musicians work was constantly finding new fans. The live cabaret performer could have a greater impact in the moment than any of these, but they faded from memories with time. Without further exposure through another medium, their star would fade as quickly as it had risen.

In 1931, my grandfather, Leonard Martin, had written a book called *Rubber Man* that was a fictionalised version of Beeh's life story. Unfortunately the book didn't capture most of the magic of Beeh's life, for the greatest elements of his story came after the book was released.

When I was a teen, I read *Rubber Man* but was far more entertained by the stories that grandpa told me that weren't in the book. When I decided to become a writer, Beeh's story was always at the forefront of my mind.

After the success of my first book, I had pitched the idea to Nicole and to my publishers, but both were completely disinterested.

'People will jump at an uninteresting story about someone they know, far more than an inspiring story about someone unfamiliar,' the publishers representative said.

'It's a fictional character. They're always unknown until they're written.'

'They tend to look for more than the life and times of the main character. There needs to be something more.'

'There is more,' I said, but to no avail. It saddened me. I wanted to write this book as a tribute to my grandfather, but also because I had enormous faith in the story I was pitching.

I had moved on through necessity. I was contracted, and subservient to the whims of those who decided what would sell. Whatever merit existed in the idea, was irrelevant. Without the right people behind it, there was no point me going further.

My contract was completed with *Golgotha*, and I was on my own. Creative freedom was mine, but after padding out a range of ideas that I'd thought about over the previous couple of years, nothing was inspiring me.

I found some of my old notes about Beeh just after New Year's, and seeing it was the centenary of his birth, it seemed the perfect time to go back to the project that I'd yearned to write years ago. I wish Grandad was still alive to be able to read it once finished. Actually, I wish even more strongly he was alive to be able to help me with some of the stories.

Since late last summer, a brasserie on the Rue de Roule had become something of a second home for me. A couple of local authors were regulars here, and after recognising me, invited me to join them. We talked about my work, but equally about theirs. It was the dynamic I liked. I had the opportunity to learn from them as they did from me. Discussing every imaginable topic, we were all helping each other. With time, our numbers expanded, and now there is about eight in our loosely affiliated group. In amongst the group are people at all career stages. Claude and Didier who I first started drinking here with, were more experienced, and in Didier's case, more successful than me. At the other end, Gerard and Sandrine were not yet published. I was happy enough with their presence; every member of a group brings something different and every group benefits equally from the exuberance of youth and the wisdom of experience.

Without the backing of a major publisher, I was now more reliant on the opinions of others around me. I used the brasserie crowd as a sounding board for things and while the idea of a rehashed version of a book from the 1930's didn't win much favour, once I began talking about Beeh, the group was very interested. I had come up with the working title of *Contorted* for the book. His life had been twisted out of normal shape much like his body was during his performances, so I felt it captured him perfectly.

Claude, who was many years older than me, remembered Beeh, more by reputation than anything else. He was too young to have seen Beeh perform live, but he had seen some very grainy video footage of him performing.

'He was based in Paris in the late 1920's when my grandfather met him. At that stage he was working as a vaudevillian, and the club scene here was strong enough to have him constantly in work.

'Grandpa had spent a couple of years in America just after World War II and he again spent time with Eric, the two having never lost contact from the days in Paris. Eric had left Paris in 1934 to take advantage of the additional career opportunities in America. He used grandpa's nickname, Rubber Man as a stage name, from the time he arrived in America.

'He was an acrobat and a contortionist. He could bend his body in half and fit in a suitcase. He often played a drunk, the stagger accentuating a lack of balance before his routine became all about balance. His act was a combination of comedy and drama, but nothing he did on stage came close to the comedy and drama of his life.

'The best story was from after a show in Mexico City,' I said. 'It had been exceptionally hot, and Eric's routine was energy sapping enough that by the time he made it back to the dressing room he was at boiling point. Fortunately, the dressing room was equipped with a very high-powered fan to help cool things. Eric stripped off when he got in the room, but that wasn't enough. He had to get closer, to get the most possible benefit of the cool air on his hot skin.

'Have you ever seen what happens when you put a finger in a high-powered fan. Say goodbye to the finger, right.'

'He lost a finger in the fan?' Gerard asked.

'No. He stretched right out,' I explained while standing up to demonstrate. 'His arms above his head. His fingers were way above the fan and his toes were way below. He left something a lot worse than a finger in Mexico City.'

'*Non! Quelle horreur*,' Claude said amongst the gasps of most of the group and a chuckle from a couple of others.

'Yep, his cock-a-doodle do. Or as it then became his cock-a-doodle don't.'

There's a fine line between comedy and tragedy, and a story like this one straddles it. At the time nothing could have made me feel more traumatised, but when I first heard the story, it was decades the after the event. By that time, it was hysterical.

'I don't believe this story,' Claude said. 'Surely something like this would have been a bigger deal. He would have been known as Dickless rather than the Rubber Man.'

'That is a true story. I don't think it was one he wanted to share with the world, but if you can find his career history you'll see a big gap in his resume after June 1950 and you will now know why.'

'At one stage he was on the most wanted list. He was staying in New York City and the hotel he was booked into had a major fire. It appeared to be deliberately lit. He woke up in the middle of the fire and jumped from his window on the third floor. He escaped with only very minor injuries as he was such a skilled acrobat, that he did a safety roll as he landed. When investigations made it appear that arson was behind the fire, theories abounded that he may have been involved, doing the jump as a publicity stunt. Someone outside was filming, and to this day you can just see a body leap out of the building in the side of the shot.'

'Was he charged?'

'Nobody ever was. Eventually the investigation showed that the fire started in a room further down the hall. Supposedly he had been in deep sleep at the time.'

'Supposedly,' Sandrine said. 'You think he did it?'

'No. He was an artist. Artists would never do something wrong.'

Everyone laughed but I then added that the investigation had been thorough enough that if they'd had reason to believe he did it, they would have found a way of proving it.

Gerard asked when the fire had occurred.

'I think in the late 1930s'

'Maybe he did it. Mexico City was his punishment.'

Again, we were all laughing. There are few things like a comical severed penis story to continually get people laughing, at least once their initial discomfort is conquered.

I continued giving various stories from Beeh's life and career, which kept the group entertained. Rather than using them as beta readers, I was getting in before that stage. As writers, they were a suitable audience for getting an idea of what would work. I never went into great details about how I envisaged the finished product would be, but I was determined to get a clear idea of what stood out amongst the array of dramas and comic moments from this man's life.

Over time, the member of the group who was most intent on helping me along with her opinions was Sandrine. How much of this was driven by her enthusiasm for the story, and how much of it was a more personal type of interest was a little difficult to be certain about. It wasn't unusual for someone of that age to attach themselves to an older person in the career they aspire to. When I was first making my mark in the business there seemed to be an endless flow of young women like this. As a comparatively forgotten relic of the past, I'd forgotten what it was like to be held in such awe.

I had declined invitations to her home several times knowing it would lead somewhere I didn't want to go. As a happily married man I would walk away from the scenarios that I used to sprint towards. Sandrine eventually changed tack, aiming not to seek my expertise, but to offer hers, by showing me the potential time savings and efficiencies I could gain through working electronically.

I made my first visit there with a strictly business mindset. Despite my best intentions, I knew myself enough to feel unconvinced that it would stay that way. It took almost no time for me to be proven right. This quickly turned into a regular routine. Three months on, and dozens of visits later, she still hadn't shown me the bloody computer.

21

12 March 2023

ELLIOT

I made the excuse that I had to leave Paris today due to a family emergency. A refund would be provided to me for all but one of the remaining nights of my stay. A great bonus, but even without this, I still would have made the move. If staying at John's was the better option, it was worth doing irrespective of any financial benefit. That said, I was happy to ask the question, figuring the money was better in my hands than theirs.

Although it was after peak hour, dealing with luggage on the metro was an unnecessary hassle. Cashed-up to an extent from the hotel refund, it was easy to justify ten euros on a taxi, saving me so much more than just the three quarters of an hour that direct transit offered me.

John was on the balcony as the cab pulled up, racing downstairs, as best as he can, when he saw me get out of the taxi.

'You're early,' he said.

'I sent you a message. Didn't you get it?'

'You've seen how often I check my phone.'

I should have rung him. If there is a more significant change of plans at any time, I will remember to make sure I speak to him.

He took my smaller backpack as I dealt with my suitcase. The building, like most in Paris, had been built long before elevators were commonplace. One had been added in more recent times, but it was in a tiny shaft by the staircase and barely fit the two of us and my luggage. It also moved sufficiently slowly that I decided it would be the only time I'd use it.

'You're lucky that Inge and I had troubles all those years ago. She insisted on us getting a bed for the spare room and despite the fact it's never used, it has been there ever since.

The second bedroom wouldn't have been large enough for more than a single bed, but that was all I needed. There would be families living in smaller spaces than these, but from my perspective this was an apartment ideally sized for one. Why John kept the spare bed rather than clear the space in the room to utilise it as an office seemed strange to me.

'This was my office before Inge insisted on it being put to a different use. I got familiar with working in the living room, so I've never bothered changing it back.'

Whether either John or I were as happy with the arrangement after a few days was another story. He may feel lonely, but we all tend to romanticise what we lack, bemoaning what we have. The idea of someone sharing your space for a few days is often more appealing when looking ahead than when dealing with it.

'Do you want me to go downstairs and get a coffee?'

'I've got a machine here. How do you have it?'

He made us both a coffee and we went outside to sit on the narrow balcony overlooking the streets below. While the area was dominated by large square apartment buildings, this one was an unusual shape, sitting on a tiny block. John's apartment was right on the corner, with a view from different points of both the Rue de Rivoli and the Rue de Louvre. Only two of the five floors had a balcony, so John had managed to secure the most ideal spot in the building.

'This is perfect,' I said after taking a sip. I'd meant the view rather than the coffee, but he proceeded to tell me that it was easier making his own here rather than disappearing downstairs anytime he wanted a cup. There were two cafes immediately below us, though he told me he didn't tend to go to either of them.

'Each of them ripped me off at one stage or another, so I haven't gone back to either of them. I've got enough places I do like not far away, so anyone who crosses me once, that's it. I don't do second chances,' he said.

'Grandma used to always say that an eye for an eye leaves the whole world blind. I'm sure you would have heard that constantly growing up.'

'I did. And I don't say it's wrong as a theory, but if some bastard is going to blind me, I'm sure as hell going to make him pay some sort of price.'

This was the John that my parents talked about. It highlighted why his relationship with the rest of the family crumbled. Every relationship faces issues. If you're not willing to yield ground in any situation, walking away becomes the only option. I don't know if that was what brought John to Paris, but relationships can survive geographical distance. They can't survive emotional separation, and that is what that generation of the Martin family faced.

I wanted to know more about what had happened to make the divide so great, but I was sufficiently determined to nurture my relationship with him that I didn't want to threaten it by leading towards uncomfortable topics. If I could get him directing it that way, maybe I would get what I seek.

'Your grandma was a hell of a woman. I wish our relationship had been better after I left.'

'We can never have everything', I said.

'That's exactly it. My relationship with dad had decayed. Mum was stuck in the middle. She didn't want to lose me from her life, nor I her. But dad didn't want to be in my life, and he made it awkward and uncomfortable for anyone else to be. He begrudged mum talking to me, and so the contact deteriorated until I was basically no longer part of the family at all.'

'Where did it all stem from?'

'Where does a circle begin?'

He explained how his father Adrian always had such a poor relationship with his own father Leonard, and how that led to a similar dynamic a generation further on. John had looked to his grandfather as a hero and a source of inspiration. This had always sat badly with Adrian, who wanted his son to avoid the same type of life that Leonard had. He felt that is what had made him the depressed and distant man he became.

'It's human nature. We want the best for those we love. We look at the best of our experience of life and seek to influence those we love in those directions. We look at the worst and guide our loved ones away. Dad's intentions, in theory, were good. What he failed to understand is that each of us is different. I couldn't live the life he wanted. I was just like his father, and he hated that. The more he saw it, the more he resented me.'

I needed a segue to change the topic as he was getting upset dwelling on the past. We walked back inside, and I surveyed the living area again. It hadn't struck me until I looked for it, but there was complete absence of his life on display. Most homes I've ever been in have photos in frames showing the good times from the past, but there was nothing like this. Any sign of individuality was missing, leaving the place far from homely, but I figured that said as much about John as the personalisation's of most homes say about their owners.

John saw me looking around the room and sensed my thinking.

'You can tell it's the home of a single male, right?'

'I suppose so. There's normally a bit more of the person on display in a home. Isn't that what makes a house a home?'

'Home is what you make it. I don't live in the past, so I don't need reminders of it looking back at me. Simple, with everything I need, and as little as possible that I don't need. That is home to me.'

'There's got to be plenty from the past that is worth remembering.'

'Absolutely. But if it is worth remembering, I don't need a visual reminder. It's all within me. Not just the good, but the bad as well.'

'Most people don't celebrate the bad.'

'Maybe celebrate isn't the word, but you need those experiences. You can't appreciate the light without the dark. We want to avoid all the bad times in life, but if you ever did so, you'd never be able to enjoy the good times. Everything balances out.'

'Not completely,' I said, thinking of those who'd lived the most unfortunate of lives.

'More than you think, though. The smallest triumph takes on far more significance in amongst a sea of tragedy.'

I wasn't completely sold on his opinion but accepted the general gist.

John's work desk sat in a corner next to a relatively small bookcase. One corner of a shelf was filled with his catalogue, while a variety of genres found space across the shelves. It seemed a limited collection for an author, most of whom tended to be exceptionally widely read.

'I read surprisingly little. Reading helps writers to improve their craft, but at times it comes at the cost of blurring their originality. I do pick up books as I wander, but I read them and pass them on. I only keep those that really impact me.'

As I looked over his desk, I asked about his working patterns now.

'I may be half-retired, but that doesn't mean I've stopped. There is no contract anymore. I'm under no obligation to produce anything, but as long as I'm breathing, I can't envisage not having ideas, not expanding them, and when I end up with something good enough, who knows.'

'So *Paradoxical* may never come out?'

'True. Marchand will publish anything I finish, but there's no advances, so there's no requirements. If I'm not satisfied with it, it's never released and there are no consequences. That said, we all need a reason to wake up and face each new day. For me it is writing, and there is no point writing if nobody will read it.'

'You choose to work, but on your own terms?'

'I don't make it too easy on myself. I've learnt that anything in life that comes too easily is never completely satisfying. Anything you'll truly appreciate comes through working for it.'

22

4 April 1998

JOHN

Love is never perfect. True love lasts forever, while perfection can only exist in a moment. Inge and I had more than enough tell-tale signs that highlighted the imperfection between us yet there was still an unmistakeable feeling that our destinies were shared.

Every relationship is unique, but there are certain elements to their life cycle that are common amongst most. The consolidation of relationships with time sees excitement diminish, while security grows. Competing with this is the natural yearning of the human being to want what we lack.

Every child wants to be grown-up. As we age, we wish we were younger. The very prospect that makes something impossible adds to the appeal. Within relationships, as sure as time impacts the thrill that existed in the beginning, our desire to rekindle it grows. The ability for a couple to achieve this can never be understated. Without creating freshness over time, relationships go stale, unless the excitement comes from somewhere else.

'How many women have you slept with since marrying me?' she asked when I got home one evening. 'Don't make up a story. I saw you leaving Bernadette's apartment.' My instinct was to quickly create a story as to why I'd been there, but if she had seen me leave, the truth would have been obvious. We were past the point where well-crafted lies could suffice. She knew, and it would be an insult to her intelligence to pretend otherwise.

The more pressing question was how much of the past I should own up to. Whatever the consequences were for my indiscretions, would they be reduced or increased based on their volume? Whatever level of contempt she held for my actions, there was little for me to gain by hiding anything now. I'd never been a big believer in the phrase that honesty was the best policy, but with little left to lose, it seemed like the only approach worth attempting.

'I don't keep a running tally. A handful. Five, maybe.' In any element of life, the step from zero to one is much greater than any other step. I hadn't contemplated anyone else for the first five years of marriage. Once I stopped resisting Sandrine's attempts to seduce me, it seemed like no great extension of my error to continue down that path with anyone else. I wasn't actively pursuing other women, but I wasn't turning them down either.

Even after accepting the proof that the relationship between Inge and her former guitarist had remained completely professional, I remained suspicious that she had subsequently strayed elsewhere. I'd reached a degree of peace with that. Wherever we went, the attention that came her way was obvious, for she was an incredibly attractive woman. She enjoyed the attention and she loved to flirt, none of which meant that she did anything inappropriate, but it certainly enabled opportunity if ever she wanted it.

As our relationship deteriorated, I felt certain that there was something going on with a songwriter she'd been working with. Whether the primary motivation was any attraction she felt toward him, or merely a way of getting at me, I took for granted that the increased time they were spending together was creating more than music.

'What about you?'

'What do you mean what about me?'

'Other people.'

'Probably five.'

My eyes widened, a sense of rage starting to take hold before she continued, having seen what she expected from me.

'Actually, it's none. I guess my interpretation of marriage was a little different to yours. I wanted to see how you'd react if I had done the same thing as you. I was right, you set different rules between us.'

'It never meant anything.'

'Of course it did,' she said. 'It meant that you weren't satisfied with what we have.'

She didn't want to look at me the whole way through the conversation. She told me she needed to get away from me to think about things, and that we'd talk tomorrow.

'You're staying somewhere overnight?'

'I won't be sleeping with anyone. You should try it.'

It was mid-afternoon the next day before she came home. I didn't know what to expect, but she was calm and composed. She said it was important to get everything out in the open.

'I can forgive you anything from before this moment. I won't forget it, but I also won't use it against you,' she said. 'I married you because I wanted us to be a partnership. I wanted us to be a team. Us against the world.'

'Me too.'

'Somewhere that changed.'

'Relationships can't stay the same because people don't stay the same. We move forward together, or we move further apart.'

'What do you want now?'

'I want what I always wanted.'

'If all you wanted was us, where did all these other women come into the equation.'

'It was an accident.'

'A woman slipped, and while falling, managed to rip your clothes off, simultaneously losing hers, and fell on your dick? Many people wouldn't believe that, but even if I choose to, I think the same thing happening with five different women becomes a little far-fetched.'

'That's not what I mean.'

'Well I need the truth.'

I explained Sandrine. Every element of my resistance, the pretence that followed and then the weakness I showed once she had me in her apartment. I acknowledged everything that followed and how failing the first time had removed the taboo. From there, it led to me no longer resisting temptations as they arose.

'Accident isn't the right word. You chose those options. You can't undo them, but you can choose the path forward,' she said.

'What do you want?' I asked.

'Complete truth. Complete togetherness. I want to be the person who you come to with ideas. I mightn't be a writer, but I know you and your work better than anyone. I want you to write songs with me. I want you to be there when I perform. I want us to be a team in every possible way. I want to know what you're thinking, what you're feeling. I want all of you. The good and the bad.'

'All of this happened when I felt we were drifting apart. I chose the wrong way of dealing with the problem, but I didn't make the problem.'

'Don't turn this on me. We both took things for granted and I accept that is as much me as you, but I didn't turn away.'

She told me that she needed to tell me the truth as well. She said it was uncomfortable, but imperative if we were to move forward. My jaw sank as I contemplated what she had done that she felt wrong about. She'd just said she'd never been with anyone else during our marriage, so in the spirit of complete honesty, if she was to now change that, it would cast a pall on this entire interaction.

'When I felt you were pushing me away I did start developing feelings for Xavier. One night after a show we'd all drunk plenty, and he kissed me. You turned up, and we quickly covered our tracks. A few nights later when we were sober, I threw myself at him. He pushed me away. I felt rejected and hurt, and that was the beginning and the end of the band.

'Nothing happened, but I'd wanted it to. All the time you were jealous, thinking something was going on and I denied it. Your assumptions about him were wrong, but your assumptions of me weren't completely.'

What could I say to that? We'd both found an outlet for what we'd lacked within the confines of our marriage. We'd stopped giving each other all of our selves. What we sought was different, but they stemmed from the same issue.

'We can't force things to be perfect, but we can make a conscious effort to commit ourselves to give all we have,' I said.

'I believe in us.'

It would be unrealistic to think that everything was suddenly ideal, but every day we seemed to get closer. Often, any moment of silence would be broken by Inge saying, 'what are you thinking, what are you feeling?' I'd always answer honestly, even if the thoughts and feelings of the moment were nothing. There were times the questions frustrated me, but they were integral to what was essential in us moving forward. We needed the certainty that we were genuinely united. Everything you see and hear can present that image, yet it is what lies within that is most essential. We were getting this out to each other more than ever before, and with it came the certainty that we were on the same page.

We consciously tried to make each day special. I've always looked back on my arrival in Paris, and the days travelling through Europe before arriving here. Every day brought new special memories. Every day was unique. It is the nature of travel to provide that, but eventually we settle into life forgetting that those memories didn't just happen. We make them happen, and Inge and I were intent on doing this. It may be as simple as dining at a new restaurant, walking through a different neighbourhood, travelling to a different destination. Life is short, and we were determined to make each day stand out with something unique, but always sharing the experience.

Truth had set us free. It had brought us closer than the original honeymoon period. We were both determined to hang on to this. There were easier options, but the greatest rewards never come through ease. When our marriage was based on ease it crumbled. It had taken a lot of work to repair it, and ongoing work to maintain it, but this had provided the ultimate reward. Our marriage had finally become perfect.

Inge was playing two shows a week at a piano bar on the Left Bank. I was usually there, not because she still needed it, but because I loved watching her perform. There were enough regulars who formed part of the furniture that I developed many acquaintances there. It wasn't just watching Inge, but a night I could rely on having plenty of good company and conversation. Watching the most beautiful woman sing was an added bonus. Knowing everyone in the audience wanted to take her home, but knowing she was coming home with me, always made it perfect.

When *Contorted* was released, Marchand had used the sales from my previous book with them as a guide. They set only limited in-store appearances around Paris. The early success had them raising the stakes, and I was sent to several other towns in France to help promote the book. Inge always travelled with me, barring one overnight stay that clashed with a gig at the piano bar.

Sales were also up across the Channel, and Marchand sent me on a five-day tour of the United Kingdom. It was to be the longest time away from Inge that I'd had since we put our marriage back on track. I wasn't keen to go. I'd chosen Marchand specifically to avoid this extra marketing element, but the relationship between any author and their publisher was important, so I accepted it had to be done.

Inge and I spoke for a couple of hours across the course of each day. She still asked me what I was thinking and feeling in each conversation. We were out of each other's sight, but never out of each other's minds.

I was woken by the phone early on the Thursday morning in my Edinburgh hotel room. It wasn't the number I expected to see. I answered and it was my neighbour, Bernadette.

'You must come back immediately. I don't know how to tell you this. I am so sorry.'

23

12 March 2023

ELLIOT

'It destroyed me.'

Inge had suffered a major heart attack on the staircase of the apartment building. She didn't have a phone on her, and nobody saw her until it was too late. She'd had no health complaints, and no indication of any such vulnerability. Doctors suggested that it was probably the result of an irregularity she'd had since birth, but one that wouldn't have been discovered without specific testing. Such testing would only happen after symptoms showed, but in Inge's case they never did until the final tragic attack.

A tear ran down John's face. It was nearly a quarter of a century ago, but the severity of wounds like these never completely healed. There is never a circumstance which makes losing the person you love any easier, but the circumstances surrounding Inge's fate added an extra layer of pain for John.

'If only I had been there. I don't mean that she could have been saved, for it all happened too fast, but just imagine the pain she endured, the knowledge that she was about to die and being completely alone in those moments. It's gut-wrenching.

The tears were more plentiful. I took some tissues from a box I spotted across the room and gave them to him, resting a hand on his shoulder.

'Having your primary love beside you at that moment. It isn't for anything they can do, it is to have that visual reminder that everything was worth it. That comes from the certainty of that person's love. With all we'd endured in the previous couple of years, she didn't have that certainty. That was my fault.'

'She knew.'

'Is that so?'

'The greatest loves don't come from a lack of imperfections, but from the ability to grow through these imperfections. You'd done that. By that time, your marriage was as perfect as could be. She had everything she'd dreamed of. In her final moments she'd have wished you were in her sight, but she'd have known with absolute certainty that you were always with her.'

He nodded, raised his watering eyes towards mine, and the subtle hint of a smile began to show on his face.

'You really have read all my work,' he said.

'Naturally.' I'd quoted from *Verdriet*, a book he'd written several years after Inge's death. The title derived from a Dutch word for grief, it was the story of an old couple and the impact on the husband after the death of his wife. While the age and circumstances of the couple in the book varied greatly from John and Inge, it was quite clearly a story built from his personal grief.

'You're one of the few that did.'

John's general persona was tough and unemotional, so seeing this side of him helped change my perspective of him. I'd read *Verdriet* along with all of his other works a few years back, so I knew the depth of emotions that existed within him, but it was as though John the author was a different entity to John the man. An artist creates in part what he sees in the world around him, but his vision is always impacted by what lies within. The author and the man can never be completely separated.

Seeing this vulnerability, I knew I was right to be spending this time with him. While I was set to gain from developing a closeness to my uncle, I knew the more essential element to the relationship at this point was what he was gaining from my presence. He may be a famed and successful author, but beyond that, he was a lonely man in need of unconditional love.

We returned to the balcony with fresh coffee and conversation turned to the afternoon ahead.

'You want to come to Longchamp with me?'

My plan had been to spend the day with him, wherever that took me, so while I wasn't sure where he was talking about, the answer was obviously yes. He explained that Longchamp was the main racecourse of Paris. I lived a few blocks from Canterbury Racecourse in Sydney yet hadn't attended the races more than a couple of times in my life. It wasn't what I expected to be doing in Paris, but in my attempts to get to know my uncle, if it was part of his life, I was happy for it to be part of my day.

'You're a bit of a gambler?'

'Gambling is spending months writing a manuscript that my agent is likely to think is a piece of shit. Going to the racecourse is a far less risky way of earning an income,' he said.

John explained that he bet big, but rarely, and was very selective about the horses he put money on.

'It's a combination of my analysis and inside information. I've probably had ten bets this year, five of them winning. The two I've got today were pencilled in weeks ago.

'We grew up just near Cheltenham Racecourse in Adelaide. As kids, Dad used to take your brother and me to the races regularly. One day when I was 17, I told him to back a horse called Miss Parnassus. He put a small bet on for me, but after I raved for so long about her, Dad ended up having a big go himself. She was near last, but started making ground very quickly near the inside, until she was badly baulked. The jockey nearly fell, and this happened right in front of me. I swear, she would have won with a clear run. Dad had a different viewpoint, past the post, and he never saw what happened. In those days you didn't have video replays on your mobile phone covering every different angle. I knew she was a certainty beaten, but Dad and few others realised it. He was cursing me for days.'

'That wasn't where the bad blood stemmed from?'

'That's part one. Part two was a fortnight later when Miss Parnassus was running at Morphettville. I spent the previous 48 hours convincing Dad to follow her, but he very strongly told me where to go. I went somewhere else though. I went to three betting shops before I didn't get asked for ID and I backed her. I then went to Morphettville and found an old guy I knew well, Pete, and gave him the rest of my money to bet on her. Sure enough, 25/1 and she won comfortably. I won more than $10,000 that day, which would be worth about $50,000 today. It funded my trip to Europe and bankrolled everything that followed. Without that money, I never would have made it here.'

'How could you have risked so much money?'

'I was in a rut. I wasn't happy with life. I hated my job. I wanted to move out of home. I never thought gambling would be a solution, but I figured with where I was at the time, I had everything to gain and little to lose. Well, not little, but in the scheme of life, it was then or never to take one chance at blasting out of the trap I was in.'

'What did grandpa say?'

'He was pissed to say the least. I took the family out for dinner and splashing the cash probably made him more resentful than appreciative of the gesture. Tell you the truth, I probably did it more to piss him off than anything.'

'I guess winning that sort of sum it made sense that you keep betting.'

'I didn't have another bet for over a decade after that race. I realised that day that there are times when the odds are so overwhelmingly in your favour that it's foolish not to. A gamblers psychology means they think those real opportunities exist constantly, but the truth is they are incredibly rare. For every time those opportunities arise there are a million bets being placed by mugs who think they know more than they do. There was a good reason why the bookies used to drive home in Mercs waving at the mug punters walking across to the train station. I had the magic result that day, but steered clear of falling into the waiting traps. It was only once the odds tipped back my way that I returned.'

'How did that happen?'

'When I was a kid, I learnt from an astute judge back home about horses who never got space to release their sprint. Blocked behind other horses, they'd finish as though they hadn't raced, and they'd carry that energy into their next run. That was exactly what had happened with Miss Parnassus. On its own, it's a good method for finding winners, but like every method, it only works so well. When it's combined with a more significant resource, you then have a genuine edge.'

He was waiting for me to ask the question as I waited for him to give the answer. Eventually he won the battle of wills.

'What is that resource?'

'Information. They say knowledge is power, right. I know enough people in the racing industry here, and when I ask, they tell me what I need to know. I don't overuse them, so they keep doing the right thing by me.'

'They know when their horses will win?'

'No. I work out when their horses should win. They just let me know whether the horse is ready to perform at their best. I might pick several horses a week, but maybe only one in ten results in me betting. There are half a dozen horses today that I'd marked out, but it is only these two that have been backed up with the additional information I need.'

Dad had always retained his interest in racing that stemmed from the days at Cheltenham with John and Grandpa, but it had never rubbed off on me. Most of what John was telling me now, was as foreign as hearing the locals speak French to me. For all of that, I decided that the afternoon at the races would be another novel experience. Whatever interest the races would hold for me, watching John go about his business would fascinate me sufficiently.

From the moment we walked through the gates, he was interacting with people who appeared to come from all walks of life. A jockey yelled out 'G'day John,' in a thick French accent, while men in suits and men in torn jeans all took their turns to chat with him.

'You find every type of person here. Thieves, vagabonds, princes, sportsmen and business leaders.'

'And writers,' I added.

'Yeah. There's a hell of a lot of stories you can find on racecourses. Most of them stem from the level of diversity you find in the people here. And the fact you find triumph and tragedy right next to each other. Desperation and elation. The highs and lows of life.'

'Sounds like betting is secondary,' I said.

'That's right. I first came to Longchamp to people watch. I knew nothing of the French racing scene, but reminiscing about my young years at the races back home made me realise that the racetrack was a goldmine for stories. I never wrote about racing, but I wrote extensively about characters who had come to me from my times here.'

'The betting is just incidental?'

'Not these days. There's a lot of hours of planning into every bet. Putting the plan into action and seeing it come to fruition gets me over the frustrations I have with my writing. That said, I wouldn't be here if not for the interactions. People brought me here. It led to more people and more stories and the circle continually expanded. I often come to the track and don't have a bet, just to keep the connections tight and the circle growing.' His manner changed quickly as he added that today he was all business.

Before the first race I'd heard him mention to a couple of people that he fancied a horse called Zalacain.

'People always ask me what I fancy because they know I win. If I told them all the horses I'm backing, I'd lose the value. I don't hide, but I tell them what I've picked out, not what I'm backing. Zalacain was one that I had worked out, but I don't know anyone associated with the horse so it isn't one I'm putting my money on.'

Zalacain won, and several people congratulated John and thanked him for the tip. Little did they know, he didn't profit from it at all.

'I did though. I helped a few people out, and that keeps them in my corner. You never know who you'll need on your side at some point. Life isn't all about the instant reward. Sometimes your good deeds have a payoff way down the track.'

He put a 1000 euro bet on a horse called Cerisy in the second race. I couldn't imagine somebody putting such a large bet on a random event. It may not have been anywhere near as random as I would have thought, but he had already talked about luck in racing. There had to be a reasonable chance of the horse losing.

My unease proved more accurate than John's confidence. The horse was clearly beaten, running fourth in a field of eleven. It wasn't a case of bad luck, the horse just failed to deliver on expectations. I expected a deterioration in John's mood, but he seemed completely unperturbed by the result.

'You're taking that well,' I said.

'Half of my bets win, half of them lose. I never get over-excited either way. I don't see it as losing 1000 euros, I see my profit for the year has dropped from 20,000 to 19,000. Maybe if I have another 19 straight losers, I'll start looking a little angrier, but that hasn't happened in the 25 years I've been coming out here.'

His point stood the test of time. The next bet was in the fifth race, and his horse Le Petit Gegine won convincingly. He collected 5,500 euros, to give him a profit on the day of 3,500. Once again, there was no sign of excitement as his horse bounded clear, while standing alongside him, I was jumping up and down as the horse crossed the line.

After collecting his money and having several more quick conversations with other racegoers, he suggested we leave to see more of the surrounding area. Longchamp was situated on the western side of the Bois de Boulogne, a massive park in the west of the city that was nearly three times larger than New York's Central Park. We walked through it, and as we got towards the eastern edge he pointed out another racecourse, Auteil, where steeplechase racing was held. At its southern end, we arrived at Roland-Garros, the home of the French Open tennis championship.

'You still play tennis?' he asked.

'Yes. I've always dreamed of coming here, yet with all else there is to see, I hadn't thought of putting it on my sightseeing list.'

We went inside and our timing was perfect, as a walking tour of the stadium was just about to begin. It took us through the players locker rooms and out on the two main stadium's playing arenas.

'My first year here, I came and watched McEnroe play. He played like an artist, unique in the way he crafted his game.'

'I didn't pick you as a big sports fan.'

'We all change with time. As a kid I used to spend my winter Saturdays at Woodville Oval cheering on the Peckers. In summer I'd be playing tennis. When I moved here, I'd come to this part of town regularly. A few blocks from here you've got the Parc des Princes where Paris St Germain play football and the Stade Jean-Bouin where Stade Francais play rugby. I followed both a little back in those days, but I guess with time I lost interest.'

'So what excites you now?'

'Waking up each morning is its own thrill. The longer you live, the less impact some things carry. Things you took for granted start to become more critical. Things that used to excite you mean less.'

I remembered Dad taking me to the football back home as a kid. His mood was marginally better when we won than when we lost, but no-where near to the same extent as was the case for me. My weekend was measured by the football results, yet now I was half a world away and wasn't even checking the results back home. I guess it helped me relate to what he was saying.

It saddened me to think that the idealism of youth was hard to hold on to. For John, it had been replaced by a cynical view of the world. Was that the path for everyone?

24

1 January 2000

JOHN

Time heals all wounds. What a load of shit. Time heals physical wounds, but the mental scars of life's greatest tragedies doesn't heal. Perhaps they descend deeper within us, impacting less moments, but that isn't true healing.

Who each of us are is a small part tied to our DNA, but a far larger proportion of us comes from the totality of our experiences. Once we reach the summit of our lives, that triumph is forever part of who we are. Similarly, the worst tragedies of our lives shape us. The emotional connection to Inge, through all of the time that the relationship built and through all of the turmoil of our latter years makes me the man I am now. All of that is secondary to the tragedy of the end. If any one moment defines me as a person, that is the one.

Everything lost significance to me. All that I used to enjoy seemed meaningless, and nearly two years later, little has changed. I wake up each day with little desire to do anything. I try to write, but I seem to be incapable of producing anything that reflects what is inside of me. My work feels like dry retching, the heaving of the stomach trying to remove its contents with nothing of substance coming out. It is painful and seems to have no end.

Last night the world celebrated like never before as they saw in the new millennium. As midnight struck, I was outside on the balcony, seeing the fireworks ascend above the Louvre from the main celebrations on the Champs-Elysees and the Champ de Mars. The scene replicated what I saw on the television as the world's celebrations were beamed everywhere. From Sydney Harbour in our late afternoon through to Red Square a few hours later, everyone wanted to believe that a new millennium was a new beginning.

'May 2000 be a better year,' was the line fed to me by all who saw me yesterday. The forces that control our lives don't acknowledge the calendar. When a new year ticks over, another new day dawns in the same way it did on the proceeding days. The pains of yesterday would linger and a change of years wouldn't remedy this, only a change in my life.

I didn't search for the routine that my life currently follows, but it found me. Now, every day is so close to the same that the day and date are meaningless.

I wake before dawn to a pounding head and a ritualistic walk to the kitchen for a glass of water and the downing of painkillers before going back to bed and sleeping a few more hours. When I next wake, I feel better, though not great, and I drift in and out of sleep for another couple of hours before feeling ready to face the day.

A coffee accompanies several cigarettes while I sit on the balcony and watch the city come to life. I look at the people below, occasionally honing in on an individual who stands out in some way, trying to contemplate what life may be for them.

By late morning I make my way to one of a half-dozen different brasseries. A long lunch that served as my one main meal for the day with a couple of glasses of wine and the necessary human interaction with the familiar staff and in some cases customers, that ensured I retained some measure of socialisation and the sanity it helped provide.

I come home ready to work for a few hours, fuelled with a belief that this would be the day that I had something ready to come out. How much time is spent at my desk, and how much was spent back on the balcony varied, but the balance that should have been leading to greater productivity seemed to be heading in the opposite direction.

I head back out late afternoon for my second set of human interaction. Every day I visited four neighbouring shops, a boulangerie, a grocery store, a tobacconist and a liquor store. The four shopkeepers, Alain, Cedric, Raphael and Marc knew me and my movements well. One day's absence would be noticed. Anything longer would sound alarm bells. How sad that life had reached a point where only those I help keep in business would know or care about my wellbeing.

The evening starts with a review of what I'd written in the afternoon. How long this took depended on how much I'd achieved in the afternoon. More often than not it involved little more than putting a line through the lot. It had been a long time since I'd produced anything worthy of consolidating. The sooner I finished, the quicker I moved on from wine to spirits, and the faster my descent began. Most nights I'd stagger to bed on my own accord. Sometimes I woke on the floor with no recollection of when and how I'd ended up there. Drinking doesn't ease the pain, it enhances it. It had never been my intent to ease the pain. I sought it because I deserved it.

Pain is known to drive artists. It has never had that impact on me, though I like to believe that in time it may serve me well. I want my next novel to be about the tragedy of Inge's death, but more from the perspective of the suffering that its left me with. It may sound self-indulgent for a story to be about my pain when it stems from her demise, but I think that misses the point. It wouldn't be glorifying me or my love, it would be shaming me.

Every person has a story, unique, special and worthy of celebration. In time I will tell her story in a way that fully celebrates everything she was. At this point, I find it impossible to tell anything that would do her life justice. It is far easier to write a contemptuous story about a man who failed to give her everything she deserved. A man who wasn't there for her when and how she most needed him. A man who wasn't worthy of her love, yet who received it endlessly.

As contemptuous as I am towards the principle of new year's resolutions, I know that there are changes I need to make. The new year itself is irrelevant, but I need to escape the funk that I'm in, and to think it can just happen is futile. Change doesn't find us, we find it. We make it happen.

I live in one of the world's great cities. I shouldn't be caught in the same routine day after day. Paris has stories in every corner, every street and every building. I am determined to start seeing and experiencing more of these. I'd lived in this part of the city for twelve years, and for eleven of them I'd barely left the confines of a four-block radius of my apartment. It was time, not based on the calendar, but on the state of my life, to start extending this.

People and place are the cornerstones of our lives. I had taken the person I loved most for granted and now I had lost her. I had also taken the city I love for granted but I still had the time to re-establish my appreciation for that relationship.

25

12 March 2023

ELLIOT

'If you want the best Paris experience, you walk. Don't set a destination, just get outside and appreciate the journey.'

We'd got a train from Auteil to the Latin Quarter and I followed John's lead as we walked down streets barely wide enough for a car to make it through. The area seemed like a maze. My sense of direction is usually reliable, but I quickly lost track of where we were until making it to the Quai de Montebello. Before my eyes was the Notre Dame, one of the worlds grandest and most famous buildings.

The Notre Dame had been in the news a couple of days ago, as the third anniversary of the fire that threatened to destroy the great cathedral passed. The French president had toured the site to inspect the progress of the reconstruction. It is likely to be at least two more years before the cathedral can reopen, highlighting the enormity of the job that is faced. It is a shame not to be able to see one of the greatest sights of Paris from the inside, but even from across the river, the exterior was a sight to behold. Buildings nearly a millennium old aren't standard sights for an Australian.

'Don't worry about that,' John said. 'The world may have had sight of Parisians grieving at the prospect of losing it, but they never cared so much until that point.'

'We all take things for granted until we fear losing them,' I said, thinking more of people than places.

'Don't get me wrong. It's a part of the city's soul, but 99% of the people who step inside are tourists. As locals, we always appreciated its place on the cityscape, even without visiting.'

John didn't want to cross to the Ile de Cite where the cathedral stands, and we continued along the Quai, coming soon after to 'Shakespeare and Company'.

'Your great-grandfather first came here ninety years ago. This is where he wrote the first draft of his most successful book. This place has been an institution for all of those years. The owners let writers stay here in exchange for helping with the shop.'

'He stayed here? What about you?'

'He did, but I didn't. It wasn't this spot in his day, but a few blocks away. Sylvia Beach ran it, but it was closed down during the Nazi occupation of Paris. New owners revived it and used the same principles that had underpinned it, albeit in a new location. It's probably not quite the same as it was in the days of Hemmingway, Fitzgerald and your great-grandfather.'

'I knew he was a writer, but I didn't think he was usually referred to in that company.'

John laughed. 'I was grouping him based on familiarity to you, not on status.'

We wandered through the store, perusing the shelves with my focus on finding John's books rather than anything new. Sure enough, there was *Of Virtue and Vice,* along with several other of his works, yet he walked through the shop like just another anonymous customer.

'I've done signings here, but that's far enough back that I'm a non-entity now,' he explained.

'I haven't read this,' I said, picking up a copy of a book called *Spes Nova.*

'And you said you were a real fan,' he said with a hint of jest in his voice.

'I read from Dad's collection, If he didn't have it, I didn't read it.'

'I've got it at home. Don't waste your money buying it here.'

'You don't want the royalties?'

'Two Euros? I can live without it.'

In truth, I wanted to buy something from such a landmark shop. The purchase also got me a Shakespeare and Company bookmark, which although valued at next to nothing, was a memento that was worth something to me.

We crossed the road, stopping to look at the wares of some of the street vendors set up by the river. They mainly sold art and second-hand books, and John told me he regularly picked up books here over the years. He wasn't in the mood to look for long, and we turned at the Pont Saint-Michel.

'You get a better view of the Notre Dame from here than up-close,' John said. The natural inclination is to get as close as possible to any great sight, but the perspective often makes for a better look when set back further.

Once onto the Ile de Cite, we walked along a beautiful tree lined street. He pointed out a brasserie on the corner that was amongst his favourites.

'Should we eat here?' My hunger had built sufficiently that I wasn't so concerned about where we ate as when.

'No, I've got somewhere more appropriate in mind.' He said this with a smile that spiked my curiosity. I had little idea what 'appropriate' meant but was happy to trust him.

We passed Saint Chapelle on the left, and John recommended it as one of the more worthwhile tourist sights to see.

'The stained-glass windows are amazing. I haven't been in there for twenty years, such is my general aversion to the tourist spots of the city. It is better than most of those sorts of places.'

We were onto the next bridge making our way back off the island. A couple of blocks later, we were back at the Rue de Rivoli, but several blocks from home, and going further away as we turned right and approached a strange looking tower.

'This is the Tour Saint-Jacques. It was part of a church built in the 16th century that was destroyed during the French Revolution. Only the tower remained and was subsequently restored. I've never been up there. It's three hundred steps to the top, so there is no chance I will now.'

The tower, just a few metres in length and width was one hundred and fifty metres tall, which in a city like Paris stood high above most of the buildings. I imagined the view would be amazing from the top, but it had closed for the day so it couldn't be done now. I thought if time allowed it might be a place I came back to.

A few blocks along, the architectural marvel of City Hall took my eye, but rather than crossing for a closer look, John had me turning left. A block later we were stopping at a brasserie called *Un Nouvel Espoir*.

'This is the place?'

'Sure is. Understand the name?'

'A new um, something'

'A new hope.' He grabbed the book out of my hand and raised it. 'Or in Latin, *Spes Nova*.'

26

28 August 2002

JOHN

The transition from darkness to light each morning is gradual. As dawn breaks, the first bit of natural light descends on the city. With sunrise, the light gets brighter and continues to progress until the sun gets high above the horizon.

For a couple of years, I had failed to understand how the natural world shapes us and leaves us with the same gentle transition. The tragedy of Inge's passing had seen the light in my life extinguished as suddenly as the switch of an electric light being flicked. I felt that the same switch would be turned, and I'd be ready for light, albeit different, to return at some point. It doesn't. Light slowly begins to find its way back but for many of us, we keep our eyes closed while it is happening, failing to see the change.

You can set your clock to the dawn of a new day, but you never know when light will begin to shine on your personal darkness. When you've been out of the light too long, you begin to accept it as the new normal, but you always retain some capacity to invite the light in. I'd waited impatiently for far too long. It was an inner fight that I seemed incapable of winning, but I persisted, and eventually managed to take the first steps.

I loved Paris when I arrived. It was like the start of a relationship, with every move designed to make a positive impression. I saw the high-lights, not necessarily the most touristy ones, but elements of the city's greatness. By the time I'd committed to staying permanently, it was like a marriage. I saw the city without its make-up, hair unkept and dressed in its daggiest tracksuit pants. Such things weren't a detraction from true love, they were the natural point of evolution in a relationship. It was an exact replication of the relationship I'd had with Inge.

When I'd strayed in my marriage, it wasn't a lack of love for Inge, but a desire for the freshness and excitement that could only come with new experiences. Hindsight had taught me that such things didn't require someone new, they just required a commitment to find those things together. After long consideration of leaving Paris, perhaps by return-ing to Australia, or in moving on to somewhere completely different, I believed that the best approach was to rekindle what I could of my love for the city. This couldn't be achieved through routine. This needed a new approach.

For months, I got a train to a different part of Paris each day. I alighted in relatively unfamiliar territory and walked up and down new streets, taking in the sounds, sights and smells of different suburbs with their own unique elements and experienced somewhere and something new each day. It was twilight in my life, for there was no great feeling of positivity, but the complete despair of the previous couple of years had lifted. I was alone, though ready and willing to interact with people when the opportunity arose. There had been a turn on the road of depression, and though I wasn't at the point of life that I sought, I had reached a point of new hope.

On a day that had led me to discover quiet Charonne in the cities east, I'd felt sufficient energy to walk the whole way home. In Le Marais, I saw Un Nouvel Espoir. A new hope. The name was a reflection of where I felt my life was, so I stopped for a drink and a meal. There was nothing about this brasserie that indicated 'new hope,' yet the mindset I walked in with presented it as such.

It was busier than ideal for me inside, and rather than having empty tables around me, I picked out a table with only single customers either side. On my left was an attractive woman of about thirty, though she wasn't giving the best impression, seemingly frustrated at the poor service she'd received.

'*Encore combien de temps?*' she said as the waiter passed by.

She'd clearly ordered quite some time ago but was still yet to receive her meal. She made incidental eye contact with me, and the roll of her eyes further emphasised her impatience at the service. Perhaps it was only hope they were offering the customers that a meal may be forthcoming.

I'd already ordered a meal and a beer, and the drink had been served quickly. I decided to engage the woman, less interested in her opinion of the place, and more intent on a rare interaction with someone new.

'*Avez-vous un habitue ici?*' I asked. I rarely began a conversation in French, knowing my language skills were too poor to carry it far, but far too embarrassed by that fact after so many years in the city to expect people to indulge my failings.

'*Non. Plus jamais,*' she said indicating she would never be back. 'English?' she asked, my accent having given me away. Phrased like that, I never knew whether the question was about language or nationality, so I started to nod my head before saying that I was Australian.

'You join me,' she said, more as a direction than an invitation, but one that I was happy to accept. For so long I'd sought to avoid people. Perhaps the new hope I needed was nothing to do with the brasserie but with its customer.

'*Merci. Je m'appelle John.*'

'Zoe' she replied and outstretched her hand. 'How long in Paris?'

'I came for two weeks. It's now been eighteen years.'

'*Mon dieu.* You must have fallen in love.'

'I did. Love doesn't always last forever though.'

'True, but you are still here.'

Her meal finally arrived, and I felt awkward as her earlier impatience had suggested she was desperate to eat, yet manner suggested she should wait for me. I encouraged her to start her meal, and while she did I told her more of my story, intertwining commentary between French and English depending on my confidence in finding the right words outside of my native tongue.

My meal arrived just before she finished, and it was then her turn to do more of the talking. She'd been in Le Marias for a job interview and lived across town near Montparnasse. She was divorced and subsequently had struggled to make ends meet. She cursed her ex-husband, and the impetuousness of youth that had led her to marry him despite what she now knew as an array of warning signs against such a decision.

'When young we are fools. We see ideal and think it is real.'

It wasn't the mindset that I wanted to hear as much as experience had taught me the merits of her words. I'd suffered through reality and was seeking a return to the ideals that I'd had in my younger years. For now, her philosophies on life were irrelevant. Meeting and dining with someone, anyone, was an experience I appreciated. I continued to eat rather than suggest anything that would contradict a word she said.

'You still write?' she asked, as the waiter took my now empty plate.

'I haven't written anything of value for a long time, but it is my skill and my passion, so I never stop. I just need my mind to get back to the place it was so that I can produce work like I previously did.'

'How you make money if no more books?'

'Royalties from previous work. I am not rich, but even if I never produce another piece of work, I have enough to live well. I don't need the money, but I do feel a need to tell stories.'

I asked if she would like another drink, keen to extend the evening a little longer but before deciding, she asked me what I wanted to do when we left the brasserie. The way she referred to 'us leaving,' implied together, and I felt that suggested she was keen to extend the evening far beyond drinks.

'Well before I met you, I planned to do as I do every other night and go home alone, have a drink on the balcony as I look over the city, then go to bed. Any and all of those components would be far more enjoyable if I had someone to share them with.'

She smiled. When love has been lost, however it has ended, there are elements that are inevitably missed. There is a time it can take to be ready to move on, but sometimes circumstances collide to set you in that direction. A new hope may have been on Zoe's horizon as well as mine.

***

Every writer has their own process. For me, it often involves extended periods where little is achieved, but once a concept is clear enough in my head, it can move from an idea to a finished product very quickly. I'd spent more than two years trying to make sense of a story based around the guilt I felt after Inge's passing. Soon after meeting Zoe I had begun a story based on hope and new beginnings. Three months on, I'd reshaped the story, setting it in London rather than Paris and reworking the two main characters to be less like Zoe and I, but filled with the same message of hope. I chose a Latin translation for the place where the two characters met and decided on that as the title for the book to keep the message from being too direct.

I hadn't spoken to Nicole in over six years. She had tried to get in touch after hearing about Inge's death, but while I appreciated her condolences, a time of tragedy wasn't a time I was ready to forgive and forget anyone who'd wronged me. Now, with a product I believed in, it was going to be her professional advice I sought. From this, any chance of a change in personal feelings may stem.

'What do you want John?' she asked after reading the manuscript. 'Are you seeking a new deal?'

'I just want your opinion. I no longer have any confidence in my ability to measure my work. I know what I think of different things

I produce, but it's never reflected in sales or critical acclaim. After the first two books, the worst work I produced did best. The one book I believed in was canned. I'm not asking you about the marketability or anything else, but before I proceed, I want someone credible to tell me what they think.'

Her assessment was mixed. She felt my style had improved, but the plot was lacking. The characters were relatable, but they got what they wanted too easily.

'I felt like I knew what was coming at all times. I could see the final twist coming. All of the obstacles were set in their backstory. They'd overcome them before the book began and then they meandered towards the obvious conclusion only for you to throw the twist that was apparent beneath the surface. I think you have the basis of something very good, but it needs extra elements.'

This was exactly what I wanted. Like most people, I hated criticism, but I needed it. I'd been so busy trying to avoid obstacles in the new stage of my life that I'd transferred that into the world I'd created in the book. The book wasn't meant to be an examination of this stage of my life, it was merely inspired by that. I'd felt that the change of setting, change of names and change of particular characteristics had been enough to make the story of Samuel and Millie far removed from the story of Zoe and me. All I had succeeded in doing was changing the surface, not the soul. I knew how to fix this.

***

Spes Nova gained little attention on its release, and the sales figures were slow but steady. It had outsold the last two books I released through Marchand, the small publishers who I now worked with. Ratings were generally positive, but far from overwhelming. I did more than twenty book signings, both here and across the channel courtesy of a commitment I made to Marchand in exchange for them outlaying an increased marketing budget. It was still insignificant to the days of working with a major publishing house but was right at the extreme end of what I was willing to give.

I'd been philosophical about my place as an author for a long time now. If few people bought the book, and nobody liked it, I wouldn't be crushed. I knew the roads I'd walked for the past five years and all of them had led me to this point. I was comfortable with who I was as a man and as a writer, and how this work reflected that. I didn't see this as a masterpiece, but I believed it was a story worth telling. I knew that it was a story I had to get out. The benefits I had gained from writing this book were enormous. I was proud of it, and no critic nor sales figures could change that.

As far as I know, the book never hit the shelves in the United States or Australia. So be it. A new hope had given me new hope. Whatever may follow, I was back. It may have gone unnoticed by the rest of the world, but I knew what I believed, and at this point nothing else mattered.

27

ELLIOT

'It's changed hands a couple of times since then. Not that it was that ever that bad, despite the issues Zoe had with service.'

'So this became your regular haunt?'

John laughed. 'I've been here five times in twenty years. Four of those times have been bringing someone here following discussion of the book. Just the coincidence of the name and meeting Zoe, prompted what was to follow. I didn't mean for it to seem like a tribute to the brasserie.'

I was more than happy with the meal, particularly the exquisite chocolate tart I had for dessert. If not for the fact that great food was so commonplace throughout the city, I'd have been surprised that John had come back here so rarely.

'What do you want to do for the rest of the evening?

'It's been a long enough day so I'm happy with a pretty laid-back evening.'

'I was hoping you'd say that. But we'll take the scenic route.'

'Isn't everywhere in Paris scenic?'

'Far from it. Anyway, this isn't a more scenic way really, it just means seeing something different.'

A few blocks up we reached the Pompidou Centre. I wasn't sure whether this was the most impressive or the ugliest building I had ever seen.

'It's an inside out building. The structure, the mechanics and the circulation systems are all on the outside. Those green pipes are plumbing, the blue ducts are heating and cooling, the yellow pipes are for electrical wires and the red ones are for fire control.'

We did a full loop of the building which is home to one of the world's largest museums of modern art. Not really my thing, I wasn't sure about whether I'd come back to see things from the inside, but I was glad to have seen the structure. Perhaps in a different city it wouldn't have the same impact, but amongst the classic architecture of Paris, it stood out as unique. Whether this was good or bad was a matter of opinion. I thought back to the Americans I had stood behind in the line to enter the Louvre and imagined them having the same debate here.

A couple of blocks later we found Café Oz, a little reminder of home in the heart of Paris. Though the crocodile on the sign told me I could expect something far from the Australia I knew, but I couldn't help but pull John through the door. We had a quick drink, an Australian beer that I'd normally take for granted, and the entertainment of perusing a cocktail menu filled with such choices as a Ned Kelly Sour, a Bondi Iceberg and a Darwin Sunset. The appeal only lasted so long, and we were back on the road home.

'John,' a voice called out as we got to the Rue St Honore and passed another bar. It was a young woman, someone who I couldn't imagine being part of his social circle. 'Will you stop for a drink?'

He introduced me to Aimee and explained that she lived on the same floor in his building. She was now working with him, translating one of his earlier books in order to release a French language version. She was gorgeous, and I was happy to be stopping here and getting to know her better. I also wanted to know more about the dynamic between John and her. Surely there was nothing more to it.

'How long are you in Paris for?'

'I leave Wednesday.'

'Maybe I can show you around a bit.'

'You're not happy with your current tour guide?' John said.

'Two expert guides are better than one.'

'Well I think Aimee is better equipped than me to show you the side of the city that's of more interest to someone your age.'

'Sure,' she said. 'Not that your uncle is out of touch, but particularly the nightlife might not be his thing.'

'Well I'd love to see that,' I said. I wasn't really that interested in the city's nightlife, but I was certainly interested in her.

The three of us walked the few blocks back to their apartment building. We invited Aimee in for a nightcap, but she said with work in the morning she needed an early night. I wasn't too concerned either way, as I was keen to find out a little more about her from John.

'You'd be keen, right,' he said.

'You wouldn't be talking me out of it would you?'

'Hell, no. She's a great girl. Stunning, but funny and smart too. Mind you, if you hook up with her you mightn't ever want to leave Paris.'

'Sounds like you're in love with her,' I said.

'Geez, if I was thirty years younger, I would be.' He paused, trying to decide whether or not to divulge much more. 'I had a bit of a thing with her mother – that was a little more suitable. As a result I'm more of a father figure to her.

I asked for more details but he was a little evasive, so I'm not sure that it was so much of a relationship as a typically French *'cinq au sept'* arrangement.

'It couldn't have ended too badly if you get along so well with Aimee.'

'I never said it ended, did I?'

I raised my eyebrows. I couldn't be sure that he wasn't toying with me, but after pouring us both a drink and joining me out on the balcony, he gave me a little more detail about Aimee's mother Bernadette.

'Not everything has a convenient label. Age breeds cynicism. Bernie and I are both at the stage of life where we see more hassle than potential gain. It doesn't mean we don't still have some form of need. We pass on the stairs with little more than a greeting, but every now and again she'll come here, or I'll go over there. Neither of us want anything more'

'That's enough?'

'We get what we need without the complications that would come from anything more.'

'How complicated would dinner together be?'

John laughed. 'Where does the line get drawn? We're in the right spot for us. Take one step in a different direction and we'd no longer be in that spot.'

'You might be in a better spot?'

John looked at me with a degree of contempt. What could his young nephew teach him about relationships?

'I don't pretend it's perfect, but life never is. Let's say you hook up with Aimee. You'll have the best night of your life, but then what? You'll go home and have nothing more than a memory. It can't lead to anything more, but does that mean you turn her down? Hell no.'

For some reason that seemed very different. A one-night stand at my age was a normal enough encounter. An ongoing sexual relationship between people John's age with nothing more to it, seemed very different. How could I judge? My views stemmed from my life experience as much as John's did from his. Maybe in my sixties it would make sense.

The high-powered searchlight atop the Eiffel Tower shone bright, and from our spot on the balcony, watching it light up different sections of the sky was capturing my attention as much as the conversation. Down below, there was little movement along the Rue de Rivoli unlike the constant bustle of daytime.

'I expected similar at night in the City of Lights,' I said.

'Is it the City of Lights or the City of Light? There's a lot of disagreement about the origin of that term, but most people maintain that it originates from the Age of Enlightenment, when Paris was the global centre of progressive thought. On that basis, it should be a city you come to become enriched in the mind, not dazzled by lights.'

'I thought it came from being first to have widespread street lighting,' I said.

'There are many opinions. There is no indisputable fact. The reality is that someone once used the term La Ville Luniere which translates to City of Light. Over decades and centuries, the name became more commonly used and everyone picked the interpretation that suited them.'

In many parts of the city, the vibrancy only got greater as night took over, yet right here the city seemed to be ready to sleep. I was starting to feel that way myself, though John was getting deeper into the stories of his life.

'When Inge died, I swore that I'd never love again. When I met Zoe, I hadn't thought she could ever replace what I'd lost, as much as I wished she could.'

28

3 February 2004

JOHN

When you meet someone, you never know what you're in for. My initial impression of Zoe hadn't suggested any great promise, but I was at a point in life where I felt there was nothing to lose. I doubted there was much to win, but as the first woman I'd been with since the loss of Inge, the experience would no doubt help me, albeit for someone more suitable that I'd find in time.

Supposedly opposites attract, but whether they have the most successful relationships is another story. Couples usually evolve, and as they do, the opposites tend to meld far closer together. Zoe and I are both different people to who we were two years ago when this began. I don't think either of us has consciously changed who we are in order to suit the other, but to some extent it is an inevitable result that follows spending enough time together.

Zoe has an accounting background. While individuals rarely conform to stereotypes, it would be rare to find an accountant and an artist who had similar approaches to life. In keeping with expectations, Zoe was practical, detail-oriented, and managed time brilliantly. Qualities that were the antithesis of how I could be defined.

Soon after our relationship began, we developed a friendship with a couple who lived on the floor above me. Pascal and Vivienne were both chefs, and in personality as well as career, were exceedingly similar and claimed it as the reason their relationship was so strong.

'You know why we gel with them – they are the practical artists of Paris,' I said.

'They cook the same meals over and again. It isn't really creative art. It's far closer to the routine processing that I do,' Zoe said.

'They create daily specials, utilising additional stock in the most interesting ways. The dishes that form the main menu are still created from their inspiration.'

'No, they are based on what will sell.'

'Most of my contemporaries write what will sell. They are still creating. When Pascal and Viv plate-up, they are ensuring their own unique dish bares their individual touch, making it something slightly different to what you'll find anywhere else.'

Zoe and I had both developed a part of what I considered the chef's place between the practical and the creative. She had developed a small degree of spontaneity that had never been part of her life. There was no longer a mental cost-benefit analysis performed on every action before a decision was made. She started to read, and began paying more attention to the artistic world in general. It was far from a complete transformation, but she'd clearly developed a more multi-dimensional way of looking at the world.

I had a new lease on my working-life, building far more practicality and efficiency into my routine, becoming accountable for the hours that previously led nowhere.

We ate at Pascal's restaurant on the evening I'd planned proposing. As she commented on the creatively presented meal, I focussed on the ultimate practical consideration of any restaurant meal. Taste. I also reflected on our first meals together. Back then it was I who would have admired the artistry of the plate, while Zoe would have been halfway through eating. Time changes everything.

***

Before I was old enough to understand the advice, my grandfather gave me a warning about relationships. 'Never change to please a woman. When your blinded by the feelings at the beginning it all seems worth it, but that eventually fades. You no longer know who you are anymore.' I'd always remained conscious of that view, but by the time I'd grown up, his opinions on relationships of any sort didn't carry so much weight with me.

Leonard had lived more in his twenties than most people live in a lifetime. Spending most of that decade in Paris, he had enormous success with his first three books. He'd worked hard, but he was better known for how hard he partied. He was a classic example of excessive living that was commonplace in Paris in the roaring twenties.

He spent time in New York in the 1930's, but this coincided with a period when his work suffered. There were many factors behind this, but when his publishing contract was completed with his fifth novel, he was left without options. He moved back to Australia and worked as a freelance writer. Life was completely different to what he'd experienced in his years overseas, but at the time he found the slower pace appropriate for him.

He met Moira soon after his return and they were married just twelve months later. They'd been madly in love, or so I was always told, but by the time they had their first child, my father Adrian, the cracks began to appear.

Relationships often see people change. It is often unnoticeable to the person who is changing. Exposed to a different person in a close enough way, they start to become more like the person they are falling in love with. Leonard had done this, and it was these changes that had made him happier with the quiet life after all of the excitement of his time overseas. As time passed, the memories of his former life grew stronger and more positive while the staid life in a slower town was losing all appeal. Fatherhood only accelerated this. He became grumpier, angrier, more removed from those around him, with all pleasure and enjoyment disappearing from his life.

Dad always retained a strong relationship with his mother, but by the time I was born, he had little to do with his father. Leonard had been abusive, not physically, but verbally and emotionally to everyone in the family. Moira remained, through thick and thin, her commitment and loyalty never giving rise to any consideration of leaving him. Once Dad and his younger sister had both left home, her relationships with the children were compromised by the divide that existed between them and Leonard.

Most parents worry about their children falling into the wrong influences amongst their school friends. My parents primary concern was the bad influence of my grandfather. Dad hated the kinship I'd developed with him, but it was natural. I felt like we were kindred spirits. Grandpa was the odd one out in our family, but as I grew up, he was no longer alone in that. I was just like him, filled with an adventurous spirit that I hoped would see me follow in his footsteps.

'For God's sake, why the hell don't you bloody listen, you stupid woman.'

This was the one problem with my visits. Every time I saw him, I found the joy of his stories and experiences was negated by the way he'd speak to Grandma. Dad says she is a shadow of the woman she was. Decades of this treatment had normalised the behaviour and led to it becoming progressively worse. The scars it had left her with could never be healed. I could see each tirade still hurt, but felt too entwined in the relationship I had with Grandpa to ever question him.

At this time, Grandpa wasn't the only person inspiring me. Debbie and I had been together for several months, and it was getting more serious. Such was the role that Grandpa played in my life, she inevitably was getting to know him too. While he was generally on his best behaviour in front of her, she got to see enough to build an opinion about him.

'I don't care what you say, he is an arsehole.'

'That's harsh.'

'No, it's fair and accurate. The way he treats his wife is disgusting. Absolutely no excuse.'

'They're a different generation. You can't think of them in the same way you would do with people our age.'

'Bullshit. There is no love without respect, and he shows her absolutely zero. If that's who you look up to, I am scared for our future.'

'I want to live the life he had. It doesn't mean I want to be like him. Influence can work two ways. Emulate the qualities you admire, be more vehemently against the things you abhor.'

'And what about your grandmother? Your happy to keep turning up and worshiping the man who has been treating her like shit for forty years.'

It hurt hearing her say this. The main reason for the hurt, was that I knew it was all true. I'd seen it so much that it had lost all impact. It was just the dynamic of their marriage. I wasn't going to lose the admiration for the man he had been, but I wasn't going to ignore the other side of the coin anymore.

'Oh shut up and leave us alone,' Grandpa said after Grandma had come in to offer us something to drink. Doing something for us. An act of kindness. That is what generated such a response. Now was the time.

'No. Don't ever speak to my grandmother like that.'

'Who the hell do you think you are, to tell *me* what to do?'

'Someone who knows that the people I love deserve more respect than those words.'

I walked out on him, partly to show that I wouldn't tolerate his disrespectful treatment of his wife, but more from the fear that he'd unload on me more severely than I'd cope with. I said goodbye to Grandma, who was upset at me more than him.

'You know he'll be worse now.'

'I'm sorry, but I couldn't cope with anyone talking to you like that anymore.'

'I'm used to it. It doesn't upset me so much anymore.'

'I don't believe that. Take care Grandma.'

I kissed her and went home. It was a few weeks before I visited again. Grandpa was far less forthcoming in conversation than he'd ever been. The bond had been broken, and I was just another visitor who he largely ignored. It achieved something though, for he never said a bad word to Grandma in front of me again. I could never know what impact it had in every other moment of their lives, but at least there had been some change.

Soon after I found out that Debbie was pregnant, and it was Grandpa that I turned to for advice.

'You want *my* opinion?' he said.

'You're the person I most trust and most admire. Always have been.'

'You find some strange ways of showing it.'

'I'm free thinking enough that I will never blindly follow and accept everything that any person says and does. I didn't like something you said. That doesn't change the fact that I think most of what you say is based on more wisdom than I can find from anyone else.'

I explained how I didn't want to be a father but while I didn't want her to have the baby, she was determined to do so. I saw the life that I wanted to experience slipping away from me, to be replaced by something that may be wrong for me, or at least something that I was nowhere near ready for.

'I changed for your grandmother. She didn't try and change me, but subconsciously I was changing to fit into her world. This angry old bastard you see before you, was born from those changes. Never lose who you are for who you think they want you to be. You can't make choices for her, but you can make choices for you. You can be responsible for your actions, but if you follow that path, you'll be as bitter and twisted as me before too long, and if you think that is best for the child, you're stupider than I was.'

***

Last time I did this, every component came together at the last minute. As I prepared to propose to Zoe, the pieces had been planned to every last detail. The impulsive young man had grown into a man with a carefully structured lifestyle.

I had chosen dinner at Pascal's because it was a good enough restaurant to help make a night special, yet routine enough for us that it would keep her off the scent. After dinner, we walked to the Seine and along its left bank heading east.

As we got to the Pont des Arts, I was happy to see the bridge reasonably quiet. I had chosen this place for a number of reasons. The bridge linked two of the most beautiful buildings in Paris, the Institut de France and the Louvre Museum – the practical and the artistic. The bridge itself was also a tribute to love, millions of couples placing a lock on the bridge to symbolise their love for each other. I suspected that she would understand the symbolism of the two buildings and saw that as an example of the change within her. When we first met, she never would have noticed such a thing.

There had never been a doubt about her saying yes. I knew she was more resolute in her desire for us to marry than I was. After Inge passed, the loneliness was something I abhorred, but I didn't need marriage as the alternative. Zoe did, and unconcerned either way, I felt it was right step to give her what she wanted.

I thought back to Grandpa's advice about not changing for a woman. I had changed enormously in my time with Zoe. She hadn't forced this, and I hadn't tried to be different. The difference within me was age and experience. Everyone changes with time. For me, this meant becoming more responsible, more mature and more dependable. These are standard examples of growth, and most people whose younger years had been like mine, followed this same path. It wasn't change, but evolution. Surely Grandpa couldn't have believed that the lifestyle of the young adult could have been maintained forever.

29

13 March 2023

ELLIOT

There are certain moments that I find awkward when staying at someone else's home. When a knock on the door came before John was out of bed, I faced one of these. I felt obligated to answer it, but whoever was there was bound to be confused when a stranger opened the door. With my inability to speak the language, how I'd rectify the confusion deepened my issue, but it was something I accepted I had to deal with. Worst of all, I'd be opening the door in my pyjamas. In a city of style like Paris, this was hardly the impression I'd want to make on anyone.

'*Bonjour,*' Aimee said with a smile as I opened the door. She looked as glamorous as I looked daggy, making me feel more self-conscious.

'*Bonjour.* I thought you were meant to be at work.'

'I'm on my way, but I wanted to see you first and make plans for tonight.'

'Sure. I'm in your hands. Whatever suits you.'

'I will come by at 7. We'll go and have dinner with John – I know the perfect place. Then we'll do a bit of a city by night tour, which I think John will be happy to skip.'

'Sounds perfect.'

'I shall see you then. By the way, you might want to be dressed slightly fancier than that,' she said with a chuckle.

John surfaced just as I closed the door. 'Was that Aimee?'

'Yes. We're going out to dinner tonight.'

'Where are you going?'

'You're coming too.'

'Three's a crowd

'Sometimes three reduces the tension and makes things a lot smoother for the two. We'll be going out afterwards. You come to dinner, and then afterwards when we hit the nightspots, you can choose to go home.'

John nodded. 'You think you're a chance with her, do you?'

'You tell me.'

'What? Does she bang every nephew I have come and stay with me? There isn't a precedent I can call upon.'

'Yeah, but you know her.'

'True. Realistically I know her better than I know her mother. For starters, she speaks fluent English, is an avid reader and loves my work, so we have more in common which leads to us having a decent friendship. She looks at me like an uncle, so she might well be thinking of you like a cousin. To that end, I wouldn't go getting too hopeful.'

Sometimes fantasy gets the better of all of us. A beautiful young French woman showing an immediate interest in me, had not surprisingly done this. I needed to take a step back in my thoughts and appreciate it for what it was. Twenty-four hours ago, I wasn't contemplating any prospect of someone like this falling in my lap. The fact that someone had entered the scene didn't mean that her role was quite as I hoped. She'd show me a different side of Paris, one that will round out my experience of the city really well. That was something to appreciate and savour without it turning into anything more.

'What do you want to do today?' John asked.

'You're the tour guide trying to outperform Aimee. What do you suggest?'

'You're the tourist who has to decide what they most want to see.'

'I've seen everything I'd picked out, so I'm in your hands.'

We'd already planned a trip to Versailles on Tuesday, so that left today as my last full day in the city centre. The main attractions already done and dusted, I had little concern about the agenda other than getting home in time to rest up for a big night ahead with Aimee. In truth, I wanted my time in Paris to be building my relationship with my uncle more than anything else, so I was happier spending this time with him wherever it took us and whatever it involved.

John wanted me to take the lead. 'Well what's the best thing about Paris?'

'That's a matter of opinion, I guess.'

'Opinions are like arseholes, everyone's got one. Most conflict in the world, whether it is international affairs, politics or the issues inside of relationships don't stem from facts, but from beliefs. The facts of how the world keeps turning are largely irrelevant to the lives we lead, but it is the opinions that shape everything.'

'Aren't most opinions shaped by facts. I mean, you have to justify your opinion with facts in many cases.'

'Interpretations of facts. When the economy is shit, one side of politics wants to up taxes so they can raise funds to pay off debt and stabilise things. The other side wants to cut taxes so they stimulate the economy. People spend more and more taxes get collected that way. Both are based on economic facts, but it is how those facts get interpreted that dictates the opinion of what will work.'

'How does that affect our plans for today?' I was confused by the tangent John had taken.

'I'm just saying that only you can decide the best way for you to spend your last day in the city. If you follow my lead, you get my version of Paris.'

'I'm happy with that.'

John said that his version of Paris was about the diversity across the neighbourhoods. Each of the twenty arrondisements were unique and the best way to appreciate all that Paris offered was to get a taste of each of these. He said that we'd seen bits of most of these, but some of the outer areas to the east and the south of the city offered some of the most authentic parts of the city that were so often missed by tourists.

From Louvre-Rivoli we got the train to the end of the line at Chateau de Vincennes.

'Although not a strictly Paris thing, you can't visit France without seeing a chateau, right,' John said as we made our way out of the station. Before we entered the chateau, my stomach was demanding we make a pit stop, and the sign of a creperie seemed a more relevant piece of authentic France than any old castle.

'Not here,' John said. 'Around the corner is a fantastic creperie.'

'You obviously know the area well.'

'No, but right next to anywhere that draws tourists you get the places that cater accordingly. Higher on price, lower on quality. The best spots are where the locals go, and they're always slightly off the beaten track. I have eaten up there a long time ago, so I can vouch for how it was rather than how it is now, but that standard philosophy generally serves you best.'

He was proven right. I had lemon and sugar crepes that were divine. I'll never know how much better this was than the first place I saw, but they were flawless and took us through a bit more of Vincennes than I otherwise would have seen.

It is fair to say that the Chateau de Vincennes would be classified as a second-string attraction amongst the myriad of options for tourists in this city. Built in the 1370s, it predates the era of true opulence that led to the next home of French monarchs, Versailles, which I would see for myself tomorrow.

One of the positives about the experience here was the lack of crowds. People visited tourist sites in their masses when they were conveniently enough located, or spectacular enough to justify travelling. Vincennes was neither, so the crowds kept away. Perhaps in most cities this would be an attraction that would pull in a constant flow of people, but with all else that Paris offers, it stays off the main tourist radar.

After spending some time wandering the lower level of the chateau, he encouraged me to take the stairs to the top on my own.

'Been there, done that. I'm no longer capable of doing it again,' he said.

From the upper section I looked down at him seated on a bench below with a hand on his head looking tired and older than his sixty years. My presence may have been emotionally uplifting for him, but trying to give me the best Parisian experience was stretching him physically. He may not have said much about it, but I'd already seen enough of his lifestyle to know that he hadn't cowered into middle aged. He drank like a fish, he smoked like a chimney, and it would be unrealistic to think that such a lifestyle wouldn't come without a toll on his health.

The view from the top hadn't stretched beyond the immediate area. Just beyond the mote was downtown Vincennes, a world away aesthetically, yet no more than a stone's throw in distance. The chapel across the courtyard was my main focus, and where we'd head to next. It looked much newer than the fortress it had served, though I found that it was actually completed prior to where I stood. Even in this domain of kings and queens, the fear of God had ensured that what was built for Him stood proudest and most spectacular of all.

Named Saint Chappelle, it was modelled on the famous chapel on the Ile de Cite and had similarly spectacular stained-glass windows. John and I were amongst just four people in the chapel and were able to take our time appreciating these in a way that wouldn't be so easy at its downtown namesake.

'Alright. Time to get a taste of the full universality of the city,' John said once I'd fully surveyed the majesty of the chapel.

'Where are we off to?'

'Olympiades.'

'The Greek sector of the city?'

'Surprisingly enough not. Definitions can change with time, so that the meaning doesn't always match the name. One way or another, names always carries some form of significance.'

30

20 June 2005

JOHN

'*Je ne suis pas Inge.*'

There are few more certain ways of creating trouble than by calling your lover by the name of your former wife. If that alone is not enough, then doing so in the height of passion can only magnify the impact.

Accidents happen, but rarely without a cause. I may have called her Inge in an instinctive moment, but there was no doubt an underlying reason. My error stemmed from a reality I couldn't escape. Whatever feelings I had for Zoe were secondary. I was using her, albeit subconsciously to relive the love I'd lost.

Knowing something and choosing to act upon it are two different things. I realised the imperfection of our relationship, but the comfort I gained from it was something I didn't want to lose. I did genuinely love her, but love comes in a range of forms. Family, friends and lovers have all had their own place in my heart. Inge's place had been unique. Zoe hadn't ever filled the same place. It didn't mean I didn't love her, it just wasn't the same all encompassing love I'd known before. It didn't render the relationship worthless, just not ideal. Marriage, when not based on perfection, probably isn't the right option. I'd come this far though and felt that it remained the best way to proceed.

My slip of the tongue hadn't led to any ongoing issues and like many conflict points in any relationship, the anger was forgotten before too long. A good day at work was all it took for Zoe to come home seemingly no longer affected, and for everything to be back to normal. While I hadn't previously thought about the next step, I felt that it was time to start making plans for our wedding.

'What do you want Zoe?'

'We've both been there before. There's no point making such a big thing of it the second time around,' she said.

'A second marriage doesn't matter so much?'

'You tell me.'

'Of course it does. You get married because you want to spend the rest of your life with that person. It can be the second time around and it doesn't change the intentions, right.'

'That's why I said yes. Not so sure that's why you proposed though.

'Why then?'

'To make me Madame Martin, just like she was. Marriage is about the future, but you're stuck in the past.'

'You married an arsehole and it didn't work out. I married someone ideal and tragedy took her from me. You can't expect us to look back in the same way.'

'I don't expect that. Thierry was perfect at a time, but I don't try to make you be like those parts of him. I fell in love with you for being so opposite to him. The more time passes, the more I see the tell-tale signs of similarity. I see your eyes pop out of your head every time a cute young woman passes.'

'It doesn't matter where you get your appetite as long as you come home to eat.'

'Says the man who eats out every day.'

I realised the poor choice of expression didn't help my cause. The main cause of Zoe's marriage to Thierry failing was his infidelity, something I'd been similarly guilty of with Inge. The fact that Inge had been more forgiving had led to a very different result. We'd overcome the difficulties that my failings had caused, the challenges leading to our relationship becoming stronger. For Zoe and Thierry, the opposite had occurred.

'So where do we go from here?'

'Nowhere,' she said. 'We live in the moment. Save thinking about tomorrow until you've moved beyond yesterday.'

***

The sound of the phone ringing early in the morning always disturbed me. It was before sunrise when I got the call in Edinburgh that brought me the most horrific news I ever experienced. There'd never been anything since to compare, but the anxiety remained.

'Hello John,'

'Mum.' I paused, still half-asleep. 'What's up?'

'Nothing needs to be up for a mother to ring her son.'

In some cases that may be true, but we hardly had the happy family relationship where phone calls were made at random. She asked me what time it was and apologised after I told her. She had miscalculated the time difference, with the clocks having just gone forward an hour in Australia and gone back an hour here. The   conversation then meandered through a range of insignificant elements, with her having nothing of note to say leaving me uncertain of what had prompted the call.

Mum had been calling me more regularly since Dad passed away. At the time, my failure to return home for the funeral had deepened the rift between the rest of the family and me, and it had taken a couple of years for anything to change.

More in keeping with marriages from earlier generations, Mum had always been subservient to Dad, and it would have been at his behest that she refrained from contacting me in years gone by. Now on her own, there was no reason for her not to try and rebuild bridges. I appreciated it. I doubted it would lead to any form of true family bond re-emerging, but after so many years of feeling like I didn't exist to them, some level of relationship was a decent first step.

I had contemplated going home for a visit, yet after all this time the thought was uncomfortable. I would overcome it, but now wasn't the time. There were so many issues between Zoe and I that needed sorting. While part of me thought spending a month apart may be the best thing that could happen to us, I thought it was more likely to be the division that was the beginning of the end. She had a tenuous relationship with her own family and would have considered any move I made to repair damage that I hadn't caused was inappropriate.

'Stop living in the past. You don't need those that proved they didn't need you,' Zoe said to justify her position. I wasn't sure at this stage of the relationship that she'd proven she needed me, but at the time I retained enough belief in us that we'd work all that out. Australia could be considered once we were married.

***

'John, this is Cherie.'

Fabrice was the manager of my publisher, Marchand, and had convinced me to attend a drinks function at the office. They ran these events a couple of times a year, but I was generally able to talk my way out of attending.

'We have met,' the woman said. She noticed the look of confusion on my face as I racked my brain trying to remember her. 'At a function here several years ago. I spent the evening trying to get your attention, but you were the star attraction and I got nothing more than a moment of your time. I decided to stay by the boss tonight to increase my chances.'

She needn't have bothered. Years ago, I was the stable star for Marchand. As a somewhat famed author when I arrived, I had a profile that set me apart from most authors working with such a small publisher. Now I garnered little attention, and in the eyes of most I was a *has-been*, though Cherie clearly found that more interesting than the *never-has-been's* that filled the rest of the room.

Cherie was another of Marchand's authors. She wrote non-fiction. Each of her published books was the story of one of Paris's Arrondisements. She'd explained that she released one each year, currently working on the thirteenth of these.

'What do you do after you've done all twenty?' I asked.

'That would have been twenty years work. I might be due for a break, though I might just push on and do the areas outside of the city limits. Saint Denis, Versailles, Nanterre, Creteil. There is just as much material in these areas if I choose to continue.'

She was attractive, but not the kind of head-turner that would have lingered in my memory when we first met. Behind glasses, tightly tied back brown hair and decidedly non-Parisian drab clothing, she looked like the stereotypical librarian. The longer we talked, the more I could appreciate the beauty she was hiding.

We chatted for the best part of two hours, only briefly interspersed with quick greetings from others in the room. She hung on every word I said about my work, and I was equally intrigued hearing about hers. I'm not sure if it was her words or the sound of her voice that was having the greater impact, but I didn't want to leave.

She gave me her number, and we made loose plans to catch-up the following week. I'd learned enough from my past that I wasn't going to make the same mistakes going forward. This first interaction hadn't been so much a lure towards her as a signpost of what was wrong with my current relationship.

***

'Let me guess, you were with her again?'

'Cherie? Yes. It is good to spend some time working with someone who appreciates me as a writer and doesn't try directing me away from that.'

'Working? Sure.'

'You know what, I haven't spent a single moment with her when there hasn't been other people around.'

'It's not just about what you do, it's about what you feel.'

I'd had exactly that issue all those years ago with Inge. My meaning-less romps with other women hadn't destroyed us, but the prospect of her developing an emotional attachment to someone else was a bigger threat. Now, however I tried to paint it, I was developing genuine feel-ings for another woman. There had been nothing inappropriate in my actions, but I couldn't pretend that it wasn't a constant thought.

'I proposed. I was the one trying to get on with the wedding, and it was you who pushed back.'

'So that justifies you looking elsewhere?'

'That may be relevant if I had.'

'You're in love with a woman from the past and in love with a woman you want in your future. I'm just the convenience of the present. *Va te faire foutre.*'

She rarely said a word to me in French unless she was swearing at me. Usually this was followed by the sound of a slamming door, and this time was no exception. The door reopened a couple of minutes later and she emerged with a small bag packed.

'Si c'est ce que tu veux, tu peux putain l'avoir.' She headed straight to the front door and another slamming followed. By telling me I could have what I wanted, I didn't know quite what she meant. I had no idea if she was walking out the door for a day or for good.

It took three days before she returned. She said little, but when I asked where she'd been, she had no hesitation telling me she had stayed with Michel, a work colleague who lived a couple of blocks from us. I had no doubt what the sleeping arrangements would have been. I wasn't convinced that this was the first time. At this stage I didn't care. Any-thing that would speed up this ending, would accelerate the beginning of the next stage of life.

'Feels good to be honest. You should try it,' she said.

'I've never said a word of a lie to you. You don't understand the difference between a fact and a belief. You can believe anything you choose, but it doesn't change the facts.'

She was unwilling to listen, though it was better that way. I knew it was over, and while I wanted her aware that I didn't own the blame for that, nothing she believed was going to change. There are two sides to every story and the truth usually sits somewhere between each of them. The inevitable end wasn't my fault, but I accept it wasn't hers either. Some relationships end not through the fault of either party, but the fact that things were never right in the beginning.

31

13 March 2023

ELLIOT

We got a taxi to Olympiades, right in the heart of the 13th Arrondissement. It was lunchtime, but having indulged sufficiently with our brunch, neither of us felt the need to eat again at this stage.

'When I first met Cherie, she was spending most of her time in this area, doing the research for her next book. I hadn't spent much time here, so it was like discovering a new city.

'This is the Quartier Asiatique, or the Asian Quarter. Paris might not appear to have as much of an Asian influence as many western cities when you stay right in its heart, but out here it is very prolific. There's a significant Chinese population. An even greater Vietnamese one. It escalated quickly at the end of the Vietnam War, and this became the centre of their community.'

There were many modern high-rise apartment buildings, far different to what dominated the more central parts of the city. Asian restaurants and supermarkets lined the streets that we started walking along. Seeing shops with signage in Asian characters made me appreciate how comparatively simple my own language barrier was here. It was one thing to have issues with vocabulary and grammar, but at least I could read anything and have some idea of what I was looking at. For those who had come here for a better life from many other places, it wasn't so much a variation on the world they'd known, as an entirely different world.

We made our way west and decided to stop at a brasserie for a drink and something light to tide us through to dinner. On a corner we had a choice of multiple options, some French and others Asian. Compared with the scene fifteen minutes earlier, the block felt more Parisian, but still with a strong Asian influence. John pointed to Le Mandarin de Choisy, a Chinese influenced Parisian style bistro, giving us the best of both worlds. We had a beer and shared some entrees, before continuing our walk westward.

'This is the Place d'Italie,' John told me. Offering no more hint of Italy than Olympiades had paid tribute to Greece, he explained the origin of the name stemmed from the road out of Paris heading to Italy.

'It's the centre of the 13th. Each of the nine roads that converge at the square leads to a different part of the Arrondissement, all of which have their own separate cultures.'

We headed out in the direction of the Seine towards the neighbourhood of Rive Gauche. This area was a comparatively new business district, dominated by modern architecture, sustainable and home to a more upmarket community. Along the Avenue de France, office and residential buildings alike looked as though they'd be more in keeping with a 21st century city than the traditional cityscape of old Europe. Trees flanked bicycle lanes in the middle of the road, the clear focus of the area's plan being on the environment. Paris was traffic gridlock in so many spots, incentivising other means of transport. It was clear that in a new area like this, they were thinking not just of today, but planning for the future.

'I thought the different Arrondissements were meant to have a distinct culture. This couldn't be any more unlike where we were.'

'Each neighbourhood does. An Arrondissement is just a political boundary. For convenience, people may describe the greater area based on one small part of it, but it isn't a full picture. I guess Cherie's books weren't just short stories because they explained that depth.

'She also made the connection of what linked those differences. So for the 13th, there was a link between that run down area and this modernity. Right here you have a new beginning for an area. Back at Olympiades, the population is heavily geared towards people who have come to Paris for a new beginning in their lives. There may be people who have been in the 13th for generations, but their lives were surrounded by, and influenced by the new beginnings around them.'

'I should take a flick through her books.'

'Your time here is limited. See it and live it for now. Read about it some other time.'

Food was central to living in this city. Although I didn't want much to eat, my stomach had started sending signals that I wasn't going to make it through to dinner without something beforehand. I mentioned this to John, and he agreed.

'Don't worry. We're heading to the 14th, and my favourite boulangerie in Paris.' He hailed a taxi, telling me that although it was nearly walking distance, there was enough still to see that he didn't want us killing ourselves at this stage of the day.

As we walked into the Boulangerie d'Alesia, any thought of something light was quickly overtaken by the array of rich delicacies catching my eye. Spoilt with unbelievable choice, I decided on a Religieuse. The name sounded spiritual and the appearance looked divine. Two choux pastry cases filled with a chocolate cream and coated with a chocolate ganache topping. As good as it looked, the taste was a piece of heaven. I'd always enjoyed chocolate eclairs, but this was the same principle taken to a whole new level.

How John had chosen to settle for a sandwich was beyond me, but he remarked on how good that was too. His opinion of the place had brought us here, so I'm sure he knew what he was choosing.

'Everything I've ever had here is great, but after crepes this morning I didn't want to stay on the sweet stuff all day,' he said.

'It's a long way to come for pastry. How do you find these sorts of places?'

'I've spent over 35 years in Paris. That's 12,000 days. If every third day I try somewhere new, that adds up to a lot of places. There's not a part of the city I haven't explored at some stage, and I've always had to eat. Mostly those experiences are good, and when they are good enough, they're places I go back to.'

'And this is the best, you reckon.'

'There are a hundred bests. Every boulangerie does something better than anywhere else. At least in my opinion.'

'And here it's a sandwich?'

'More the Recette Fraisier,' he said, referring to a decadent strawberry filled pastry that I nearly had chosen myself. 'Best nun is in the 11th,' he added.

'Nun?'

'Religieuse. It means nun. The pastries are shaped like a woman, the choc coating and cream are the black and white of the nuns clothing.'

I never would have seen it like this, but now that John had told me, it couldn't look more obvious. 'If you know where the best one is, you must have tried them all.'

'No. The prominence of each item on display shows you what the pâtissier considers their best products, usually reflected by what sells best and impresses the most customers. That dictates what I try in each place. If someone does a better Religieuse, it will be front and centre, and the few times I have found that, they haven't quite matched it.'

I took another look at the display cabinet as we were leaving, and if it wasn't for the fact of dinner tonight, I'd have taken something with me. Almost drooling, John made sure I followed him to the door. It had started to drizzle, and for the first time since I'd been in the city, I saw an imperfection in the weather.

'We're heading to the metro station. It's only a couple of doors down.'

The boulangerie was on the corner at an intersection of half a dozen roads, something very common throughout the city. On the opposite corner was a Hausmann-era church squeezed into its triangular block.

The belltower was striking, and I'd have taken a closer look if John wasn't so intent in getting out of the rain and into the station.

'So where to next?'

'If everything falls into place and the weather clears, you'll be getting the best view available in Paris.'

32

1 November 2010

JOHN

There are rare times in life when everything seems to fall into place. At my stage of life, there are really only two elements to consider: work and relationships. On both scores, I couldn't be happier.

Harbourside was released three months ago, and despite virtually no promotion on my part, it has done better business than anything I've previously released through Marchand. However much I try to convince myself that I don't care about sales, it is impossible not to take heart from success or to feel disappointed by failure.

My consideration of success and failure has always been built upon my own assessment of my work, but even I am not stubborn enough to completely disregard the opinions of others. Sales figures reflect more on the quality of marketing than the quality of the product, so it's hardly a reflection of my work. That said, no writer produces a novel without the hope that it will impact people. The more you sell, the greater the impact, and the greater justification for the labour you've endured.

My happiness with *Harbourside* is somewhat secondary. It is Cherie that has seen life transition to the place I wanted it to be. She had been much of the inspiration for *Harbourside*, a story that centred around a man who had shown a single-minded approach to achieving his goals, only to find an emptiness when he climbed the summit of his profession. Only then does he realise that his truest desire had been right before his eyes the whole time.

I'd named the main character Elliot after my nephew. When Mum passed away two years ago, I returned to Australia for her funeral. The week I spent in my old hometown was amongst the most difficult of my life. I'd been racked by guilt for having not made it back before she passed. She had cancer but had insisted that I never be told. She knew her time was nearing its end but remained steadfast that she didn't want to see me if it was based around pity or guilt. She would have loved me to have come back, but only if it was motivated by other reasons. Naturally if I knew the circumstances I would have returned earlier. I had already booked a trip back for later in the year, with no idea of the situation, but it had been in vain. It's a regret I'll carry forever more.

The one bright side of my time in Australia was meeting my nephews and nieces for the first time. Emma had three children under the age of six, while Lewis had two sons; Elliot who was eight, and four-year-old Michael. While all the adults in the family resented my presence and shut me out, the children were great. I don't interact with children, and I had found the idea of meeting them daunting, yet from the first moment they showed no judgement. I was the long-lost uncle, and it didn't matter why that was, once I was there, they showed nothing but innocence, acceptance and wide-eyed wonder.

As the oldest, Elliot seemed most comfortable with me. For the first time in forty years, I was kicking a football, and although getting shown up for my comparative lack of coordination, he loved having an uncle spend time with him.

Blood is thicker than water, but not thick enough to survive anything. My family had cut me out of their lives, though I'm sure they'd say the reverse was true. Either way, the blood ties alone hadn't protected us from this point in life where we were effectively strangers to each other. For all of that, the children and I felt a connection that couldn't be manufactured. That was the natural order of life. Until such point as those ties are severed, the natural order wins out, and through Elliot and the other children, I'd learned this powerful lesson.

A couple of months after the release of *Harbourside*, I got an email from Lewis, one of the few times any family member other than my mother had made contact with me in all of my years in Paris. He was angry and resentful that I had dragged up our family's dirty laundry just to sell books, and that I had used his son's name for the main character. His interpretation of the story made no sense. Apparently he saw himself in the character of Elliot. It was set in Sydney, where he had moved years earlier, and unbeknown to me, featured many other elements of his life. The motivation had stemmed from my life and experiences. Half a world away, there'd been enough similarities in his life for him to interpret my story as his.

I'd long come to accept that the relationship with my siblings was non-existent, so my response didn't need to be an attempt to build bridges, but the impact of Elliot and the other children had made me assess the situation differently.

Dear Lewis,

Thank you for reaching out to me. It was wonderful to hear from you. I am so happy to know that you have read 'Harbourside', though I'm quite surprised by your interpretation of it. The book was very much a tale of the last decade of my life. I don't see any connection to anyone else in the family within the plot, and I am very sorry if you have read it that way.

The character of Elliot was certainly named after your son. It is a tribute, not so much to him, but to the lessons I learned from him, Michael and Emma's children. In one of the hardest times of our lives, the innocence of the children took me back to my own childhood. They didn't judge. They took everything and everyone at face value. Age may bring us wisdom, but it also delivers cynicism to our lives.

The turmoil I endured when my wife passed away was beyond anything I can adequately express in this form. While I appreciated a couple of cards and a couple of phone calls from Mum, it wasn't quite the level of support one would normally hope for from their family after losing the love of their life. Yes, I have failed others at points of time, but it is hard to believe that anyone could perceive that I was alone in that.

I will always carry the guilt of not seeing Mum before she passed. Had I known the situation, of course I would have been there. I understand why she didn't tell me. I understand why both Emma and you failed to tell me. Whether you were right or wrong is a matter of opinion, but I accept your decision on that with no judgement.

My failure to leave my home to visit her was wrong. I had often asked her to come to Paris to visit me. Dad too. You and your family. Emma and hers. Those invitations are open and always will be. You will always be my brother, and there is always a place in my life for you when you want it.

I am getting married early in the New Year. Nothing would please Cherie and I more than having my family share that joyous occasion with us.

Your brother, John

It couldn't have been further from the response I would have given in years gone by. I didn't expect it would change anything. Given the way he'd interpreted *Harbourside*, who knew what spin he would put on my email.

I had no expectations about the reply I'd get. My motivation wasn't a happy reunion, but the prospect of Elliot one day reading *Harbourside* and asking about his uncle. I didn't want to be painted as the villain, even if I was destined to be talked of in a less than glowing light. I also envisaged the possibility that he, his brother or one of his cousins may well grow up with a desire to pursue a direction that wasn't welcomed by their parents. I hoped, that in some small way, by doing what I could to bury the hatchet, that it may provide a small insight to another side of the story. Maybe through that, I could have played a role in making the pathway easier for any of the kids that applied to. Maybe I was fooling myself, but sometimes we need to approach life without focusing on the end result. There are times when we can accept defeat, but only after we have done all we can to shape things towards victory. I felt with this response I had swallowed my pride and played my role towards family unity.

It took weeks before I got any response, and when I did, it was short and non-committal He congratulated me on the pending wedding but said that he wouldn't be able to make it. The fact that I hadn't said exactly when it would be, indicated that it wasn't any particular prior commitment that would keep him away. Truth be known, I wouldn't have wanted the extra complication at that point.

***

When Cherie agreed to marry me, my fourth long term relationship had led to my fourth engagement. I didn't want to wait too long to get married. One marriage from three engagements wasn't a great strike rate. One from four was really going to look bad.

The wedding was never going to be a large event. With no family in my life anymore, the invitation list was Cherie's domain. My life had been filled with people, but they'd always come and gone. There were few people, other than those who'd come into my life through Cherie, that I wanted at the event. Cherie was more than content to keep the event small. Having been through an extravagant wedding years earlier, the smaller occasion was ideal to me, but I'd expected my fiancé to have more grandiose wishes. Most women have grown up dreaming of their wedding day, but Cherie's wishes were few.

'It's a monumental event. Sharing it with more people doesn't make the event grander, it just dilutes the joy amongst a wider group. I'm happy with intimate, and a day that those special enough to be there will remember forever,' she said.

I loved being able to say we got married at the Notre Dame. The tiny detail that I tended not to mention was that it wasn't the famous cathedral, but the Eglisse Notre Dame des Champs near the Tour Montparnasse. Cherie had been baptised there, and though she'd never looked ahead with any great desire for marriage, once a wedding was happening, this was where she wanted it to be.

Fabrice was my best man, which considering our relationship was nothing more than professional, said plenty for the volume of people in my life. He had introduced the two of us, so that earned him the position.

All around the city there were people who knew me and enjoyed my company, but they were all more acquaintances than friends. I didn't let people get too close, for a lifetime of precedent told me that the closer people got, the more difficult it was when they let go. Everyone needs someone, and I had that in Cherie. What reason was there for anyone else?

33

13 March 2023

ELLIOT

'The greatest view in Paris comes from the top of the Tour Montparnasse. Not so much because it is the highest point in the city, but for the fact that it is the only place where you are spared the eyesore of the ugly black stump that this tower is.' John was right, it was hardly the ultimate in Parisian beauty. In many cities, such a building would blend into the skyline. Even in the newer business district of La Defense, this tower wouldn't stand out in such a way, but in Montparnasse a sixty-story tower surrounding buildings that were all no more than a tenth of the size, could never just blend in.'

We got in the lift and exited at the top, but had three more flights of stairs to encounter. John was ready to cope with this. He said he hadn't been here for several years, but knew it was worth the effort.

On the roof, the views of the city surpassed what I'd had on the Eiffel Tower. If there was no other advantage, the fact you could look straight out at the Iron Lady earned it that status.

We walked the perimeter of the rooftop and whenever I stopped to read the displays pointing out prominent sites to look out for, John would add a little extra information on less prominent parts of the city that had formed part of his life story. Many of these were neighbourhoods that that had been prominent in special moments with Inge, Zoe and Cherie.

'It's obscured by other buildings, but just down through there is the Notre Dame. The other Notre Dame that is, where I married Cherie. By the time we got married she was working on the book for the 15th, so we were spending a lot of our time in this area, rekindling her youth.'

I imagined the view up here at night would be even more spectacular, but there was too much more to see and do to stay and wait for that. It was late afternoon, and I knew that John was keen to move on and show me more.

'You're alright to cover a few more kilometres on foot? He must have known that if he could manage, I certainly would be able. I may have a longer night ahead of me, though adrenaline would get me through that with no problems.

From the bottom of the tower, we walked along the Boulevard de Montparnasse and within a couple of minutes we arrived at a church.

'This is it. The Notre Dame des Champs,' he said. 'Our Lady of the Fields.'

Although baring little resemblance to the famous cathedral, it still appeared far grander than the picture in my head that had formed from his description. For a wedding as small as he'd intimated, I had pictured a chapel designed for a very intimate crowd. Along a street filled with traditional Parisian apartment buildings, the church stood out markedly. It was set further back from the street than all other buildings and was surrounded by greenspace that seemed to be in short supply in this city.

'This is beautiful,' I said.

'It was far more than the event warranted, but if you ever get married, you'll see that the safest approach to a wedding is to say yes to whatever your bride wants. Cherie had gone to church here as a child. She wanted it, so she got it.'

We continued through narrow streets, now in the 6th Arrondisement. In the first few of these, the apartment buildings here had few businesses on the ground floor which was different to most of what I'd seen of the city. Turning on the Rue de Fleurs, this changed, and the familiar sight of brasseries, boulangeries and other small businesses made me feel like I was back in the Paris I'd come to know.

At the end of this street, we arrived at the gates of the Jardin de Luxembourg. While Paris doesn't have the volume of parks that are part of most suburbs back home, it compensates by having a few grandiose parks. These give locals an opportunity to appreciate life away from the crowded concrete maze that defines the city. The east and the west of the city were defined by the Bois de Boulogne and the Bois de Vincennes respectively, while the Jardin de Luxembourg was the green heart of the south side of the city.

'This is one of my favourite parts of Paris. Always has been. When I first settled down in Paris, I lived just over the other side from here. I'd come here several times a week. I'd find a different spot, and just sit with a bottle of wine, a baguette, a notebook and a pen. I spent so much time indoors that it seemed like exposure to the outdoors inspired a whole lot of ideas. At home I was able to write for hours, but it was always just the expansion of concepts. Almost all of my best ideas came here.

'When I moved across the river, I still made my way here whenever I felt short on ideas. Maybe superstition was part of it, but however stuck I felt, something always seemed to strike me when I was here.'

'Shouldn't that have led to more books getting finished?'

'Hell no. It led to more books getting started, but finishing isn't about the search for inspiration, it's about the clarity of those ideas. For me these were the *Jardins d'Inspiration*, not the *Jardins de Clarity*.'

We passed tennis courts, playgrounds, walking trails and children on pony rides. There were park benches with business people seeking escape from their stresses. Easels with canvasses capturing the beauty of the scene. Older men battling over chessboards. There was something for everyone, and the diversity of people around the gardens proved it. There were people everywhere, yet not in such numbers that it made the experience asphyxiating.

The gardens were originally the private estate of Marie de Medici, and were an accompaniment to her home the Luxembourg Palace. The estate now not only serves as a community hub, but the Palace itself is home to the French senate. In front of it, the Grand Bassin is the centrepiece of the gardens. There would have been more than a hundred people sitting on chairs around the perimeter, with many more people closer to the water's edge as they navigated colourful remote-controlled boats across the pool. While this was mainly children with a touch of parental assistance, I couldn't pretend I didn't want to be joining in myself.

'I'm not letting you wrestle the controls from a five-year-old,' John said. 'Come on, there's more to see.'

We continued on a track to the right of the palace, reaching the Medici Fountain. A long basin of water flanked by rows of plane trees and adorned by elaborate and spectacular sculptures depicting the lovers, Acis and Galatea. It would have been the perfect place to be wandering with a young lady rather than my uncle, for it was one of the most romantic scenes I could imagine. Most of the people gathered around here were young couples, and I couldn't help but think I'd rather be coming here with Aimee than hitting the nightspots of the city.

'If you ever spend more time here, this is the place to bring women.'

'That's from your experience?'

His face answered my question without the need for further explanation. I could understand why. What surprised me was the comparative quiet of the scene, with so few people gathered around.

We walked back along a track and John sat down on a park bench, seemingly worn out from covering so much ground across the day.

'Over the years I would have sat on hundreds of different benches and chairs throughout these gardens, but this one I remember more than most.'

'Who was the woman?'

'Millie.'

'Who was she?'

'A figment of my imagination. Well, not entirely. One of the most beautiful women I'd ever seen, but she walked right past me here. I saw her for just seconds, but as I thought about her, she shaped the character that was the missing ingredient from *Verdriet*.'

34

29 January 2013

JOHN

However prolific an artist has been through their career, they will be remembered mostly for one standout piece of work; their magnum opus. One work that shines above all others, and that will define them forever more. In some cases, the work that the artist considers their great masterpiece may contradict what the public considers their ultimate work. *Of Virtue and Vice* may always be what I'm remembered for, but finally I feel that I will break free of the hold it had on my career. It may never be revered in quite the same way, but I envisage my true legacy will lie with *Verdriet*. After fifteen years of trying, I finally feel like the last pieces of the book I've always wanted to write have fallen into place.

I'd been upfront with Cherie that the basis for the story was my grief after Inge's death. While Zoe had taken it as a personal rebuke that I'd write about the despair from that loss, Cherie's greater understanding of creative inspiration had seen her encouraging of my intent.

I never saw *Verdriet* as a retelling of my experiences in the aftermath of Inge's death, but an exploration of the guilt that plagued me. I had felt guilty when I first slept with Sandrine. I felt guilty when the full extent of my indiscretions came out. The truth, and more importantly Inge's forgiveness set me free of this guilt, but after the idyllic period that followed, the guilt came back harder than ever after her passing.

I had felt guilt for my absence, though the tragedy wouldn't have been avoided had I been here. She experienced no warning. Death would have come in moments and having anyone at her side could not have helped save her. Such reality didn't help. My absence hadn't been a choice, but this didn't impact the feeling. I felt further guilt that a woman who deserved the best of me, had been forced to endure the worst I offered for much of the time we were together. Marriage always means taking the best and worst of your spouse, but I couldn't escape the fact that over the course of our marriage, we got a different balance.

My protagonist in *Verdriet* was Oliver, a man who had escaped consequences throughout his early life. An act of selfishness sets of a chain of events that ends in tragedy. While he accepts no responsibility, an inner guilt begins to consume him until suicide appears his only option. While preparing to jump from an upper story balcony, he contemplates life as it would have been had he made a different initial choice. The appearance of Millie in the alternate reality makes him reassess the origin of his selfishness and re-evaluate the real reason for his guilt, prompting a final twist.

The various elements of the story had come to me at different times, but the twist that brought it into a story that flowed only came to me in recent weeks. From that time on, the book has become a constant obsession. While Cherie had always been a constant support in my creativity and my intent to write this book, she was far less welcoming of the overriding way the current stage of the writing process had impacted me.

'The great thing about being a writer is that work-life balance should be easy to attain. You've lost that balance.'

'That's easy for you to say. You go and walk down a street, take a couple of photos then write about what you saw. I explore the ultimate depths of human emotion. You can't just switch that on and off.'

'Thank you. Wonderful to know the respect you have for my work.'

'I respect it greatly, but there is something very different going into it.'

'You know why you can't complete anything to replicate your early success? You've lost touch of life from any perspective bar your own.

Every character carries your perspective because you've lost the ability to see things from anyone else's angle.'

All too often, fights start out as a different view of an issue but descend into something altogether different. Cherie felt that she wasn't getting the best of me as I invested more of myself into my work.

She wasn't completely wrong about my assessment of her work. I admired what she'd achieved, but I didn't consider the production of coffee table books to match the creation of literature. I never sought to belittle her professional legacy, for I considered her work to be every bit as good as mine, albeit in a far less creative pursuit. I'd never read any of them in full but had flicked through each of them multiple times. The coffee table style books she'd produced were conducive to that, and I believed that proved my point. I created worlds in my books. She explained elements of worlds that were there for all to see and experience. The emotional investment that we each had to undertake couldn't ever be compared. The fact that in the seven years since we met, she had completed seven books while I had finished one was testament to that fact.

It seemed like she believed I should produce work as she did. Each of her books ran to a timetable, and every step of that timetable was met religiously. A first draft was created, it went to the editor, it came back, and she worked on it until the final product was with the publisher right on the due date. Every year, another book, right on time. My work could never be conducted that way. It was ready when it was ready and that was the only timetable I could ever work to.

I'd originally believed that her profession was an asset to the relationship. I had thought that two people who both identified as authors should be able to understand the ups and downs we had in our career. Clearly that wasn't the case. As sure as a house painter bore no correlation to a portrait painter, sharing the title of author didn't really connect us.

Cherie was so easy-going that we'd never faced issues before this. I couldn't have envisaged that this was going to be an issue. I apologised and clarified what I had meant, hoping it would bring an end to the argument. I only seemed to make things worse.

'You're right. I want to put the book aside for a little while so that we can spend some quality time together.'

'It's convenient for you, so I should drop everything.'

'What do you want?'

'Respect would be an ideal start. Treatment as your equal.'

'You are my equal. I couldn't have more respect than I have for you.'

'You're always good with words. What about deeds?'

Credit where it was due. By invalidating any words I could use, there was no way of me progressing. At least not at this stage. Just the way she wanted it to be.

Change is easiest to see from a distance. The more we see someone, the less we notice any form of change in them. Change in ourselves is the most difficult to notice. I never noticed it happening. In my younger years, I would have stormed out of a situation like this. I had to win. It didn't matter whether it was an argument, a tennis match or a best-sellers list, when things didn't go my way, quitting the contest always seemed preferable to losing it. Getting a D at school never bothered me when I didn't try, but getting a B when I'd studied hard made me angry. Age and experience had taught me that while defeat may never warrant celebration, it was integral to life. I couldn't win this argument, so I was conceding defeat.

'Je suis désolé.' Saying sorry was a foreign concept to me, so it made sense to say it in French. I repeated it in English, to emphasise the sincerity.

She was grateful, for she knew me well enough to know how unforthcoming I was with apologies. The gratitude only extended so far, for there remained a degree of tension between us in the ensuing period. She believed that I was sorry for what I'd said, but she knew full well that the words had stemmed from something I believed. She didn't want an apology as much as she wanted a change in my belief.

I'd grown up with a domineering father and a submissive mother. They both grew up in environments where the dynamics were the same. My relationships with women had always followed the same pattern. It was only now at the age of fifty that I'd realised I had to take the lessons from the flawed marriages that had been my early examples.

The age difference between Cherie and I was fifteen years. She'd approached me as a young fan. The dynamic that ended up defining our relationship had carried a level of dominance and submission. It wasn't based around any belief that we weren't equal partners. Equal does not mean same, and while our roles in the relationship were different, there was no way I believed that my role mattered more.

Cherie launched 16th, her tribute to the arrondissement sandwiched between the Bois de Boulogne and the Seine. I introduced her at the launch, speaking in my improved French and speaking of my pride in her work and detailing how my love for her was irrelevant to the opinion I had of this particular book. It was the first time I had thoroughly read any of her books, doing all that I could to express my respect and my admiration.

'You were very convincing,' she said as we returned home for the evening.

'Because it's true. Difference doesn't need to be followed by a categorising of better and worse, higher and lower, more and less important.'

'It might not need to be categorised, but maybe it can be. You still don't value what I do as highly as your work.'

'I've watched Roger Federer play tennis and I've watched Tiger Woods play golf. They're both the best at what they do, but as I played tennis and have never played golf, I appreciate what Federer does more. It doesn't make him the greater sportsperson. It doesn't give him a greater legacy. Everyone sets out on their own pathway in life, and that is essential. Your book sales are proof that there is a demand for what you provide, and you do it better than I do in my segment. Maybe your Tiger and I'm some battling has-been on the tennis tour.'

She'd been to Roland-Garros with me the previous year, but was no great sporting fan, and didn't like my analogy.

'So you don't respect what I do, though you admire how I do it.'

'You could stock shelves in a supermarket, and it wouldn't change how much I love you.'

'That doesn't address the point.'

'I respect what you do and how you do it. All of this stems not from anything to do with that, but the fact that what I create is something different. Not better, not worse. It takes something different out of me. I don't have your ability to work eight hours then switch off, forgetting all that has come before it.'

We both made our living from words, yet words continually escalated the hassles between us. The ensuing period saw us use less of them as we talked less. She was in the promotional stage with the new book and spent more time away from home at bookstores and libraries around the city. When she was home, I started making myself scarce.

Life cycles don't follow a linear path. There are ebbs and flows, peaks and troughs. Throughout a relationship, there's an inescapable reality that tough times will occur. More often than not they create wounds, but as these heal, they don't need to ruin the future. Through the hardships of the present, we were making progress.

Absence makes the heart grow fonder. We had spent less time together, and that led to the time we did share becoming better. With more time to dwell on the relationship and less time experiencing it, we had both found the desire return. We began making time for each other. We both made efforts to put the other person first. We accepted the flaws, and we thrived on the things that had defined our love in the beginning.

On my birthday she'd organised dinner at one of my favourite restaurants followed by drinks and dessert at a cocktail bar a few blocks from home. It was the same way we had spent the evening of my birthday in the first year we together. Whether the night felt quite as perfect as it had when we were a fresh couple didn't matter. We'd matured and reached a stage where we knew what our marriage was. Imperfections were part of the reality, but we were ready to appreciate that.

'We aren't perfect Cherie. No relationship is perfect. However much we want it to be, and however much we fall for the fairy tales that make it seem perfection exists, we must accept that reality brings limits. I love you with all my heart. I am proud of you, and I am inspired by you. I hope that works both ways.'

'It does John.'

35

13 March 2023

ELLIOT

I was under no illusions. Tonight wasn't likely to end up quite where I hoped, but it didn't need to. A meal in a quality Parisian brasserie followed by a tour of some of the best nightspots in the city with a beautiful guide was destined to be memorable, however it played out.

She knocked on the door right on seven, but she wasn't alone. Bernadette was joining us, which suited me perfectly. Two couples, in my mind, could only play to my advantage.

'*Maman, voici le neveu de John, Elliot. C'est ma maman Bernadette.*'

'*Bonsoir Bernadette,*' I said, creating the illusion I might be able to speak French with her.

'Hello,' she said, playing the same game.

John didn't look overly excited about Bernadette's presence, the nature of their relationship having never previously extended to such an occasion, but for my sake he accepted that this was merely a group dinner that by chance involved both him and his occasional lover.

Aimee looked stunning. She was a beautiful woman, but dressed for a night on the town, she took it to a whole other level. The cleavage revealing top, and the short tight skirt were far from ideal for someone who was trying not to spend the evening ogling her. I guess the occasional test of our discipline does us good.

Dinner was at a restaurant opposite the Opera House. It had looked like a routine Parisian bistro from the outside, but the menu changed my perspective quickly. Not so much the menu, but the prices. I wasn't sure the etiquette of the evening and had no idea how we were splitting the bill, but there was going to be a lot to split.

With Bernadette not speaking English, and me not speaking French, the conversation ebbed and flowed in terms of what I could understand. The language barrier wasn't likely to be an issue once our meals came, not just while we ate, but discussing the meals which could be done as easily with facial expressions and simple vocabulary. Until that point, things remained awkward.

John and Aimee were discussing a man who had unsurprisingly been staring at Aimee as we walked in.

'When you advertise such an attractive product, you can't pick and choose who is going to look at the ad.'

'I'm not a product John, and I'm not for sale.'

'We live in a transactional society. You may not be a product, but it's impossible to stop some people thinking you are. Everyone gets it one way or another.'

'You get that sort of leering often John?'

'I've been treated like a product my whole career. Editors, publishers, consumers, they've all at different times fought each other to buy me, sell me or these days throw me out.'

'That's very different.'

'It should be, but what should be and what is, are not always the same.'

I didn't want to get involved. I'd had enough trouble keeping my eyes off Aimee myself to understand what the guy had been thinking, so I could see Henry's point, but I didn't want to get on her wrong side. I focussed instead on the most simplistic French I could use to converse with her mother.

'J'aime Paris.'

'Ah, bien. Qu'est-ce que tu préfères à Paris?'

Fortunately, Aimee was paying attention to us rather than John by now and helped me out by saying that her mother had asked what my favourite part of Paris had been.

'I don't know. There are too many wonders in this city to pick just one,' I said. After pausing for a moment, I looked at my uncle and then said that getting to know him had been the biggest highlight of my time in Paris.

'What an arse-kisser,' John said.

Aimee explained that to her mother, before saying she thought it was a very sweet sentiment. Good move or not, it didn't matter. It was true.

Our entrees arrived, which for me was a dozen snails.

'Surprising choice,' John said.

'Why? I'm adventurous.'

'You've obviously never heard that the reason the French like eating snails is that they hate fast food. Nothing slower than a snail.'

'Clearly you don't need to be a dad to tell dad jokes.'

How can you come to France and not have snails? I had been hoping to do so at some stage, but for all the preconceived notions of them being a staple on every menu, this had been my first opportunity. Served in their shell with a heavy garlic sauce and parsley butter, they were quite the delicacy. The texture seemed like a combination of oysters and mushrooms, but the flavours were strongly accentuated by the sauce and herbs.

I had lamb for my main course, while around the table I was even more impressed at the sight of the risotto, the beef and the sole that the rest of our group had ordered. The meal was good, but considering the price, it needed to be.

'Food. That has been the other great highlight of Paris,' I said.

'They don't have it in Australia?' Aimee said with a laugh.

'An inferior version perhaps. Well, not even so much that. There's great food in Australia, but by comparison it seems that you have to seek it out, whereas here it is everywhere.'

I offered to pay the bill, but John and Bernadette had already agreed that they'd split it between themselves. Aimee and I parted with them as they got a cab back to the apartments. Whether they chose the taxi option over walking to save their energy for anything else was something I didn't want to contemplate.

Aimee took me around the corner, along the Boulevard des Capucines. We came to what looked like a standard downtown building, with commercial enterprises downstairs and residences above, but we got into a lift to the top, then another flight of stairs before we stepped out to a rooftop bar.

'There's no better way to start a night out than with a drink at a rooftop bar. You might think that locals are immune to the beautiful views of our city because we're so used to it, but you don't have to stop and stare at something to appreciate it's beauty.'

I didn't think I'd been staring at her too much, as tempting as it may have been, but her words certainly could have applied to her body as much as her city.

The drinks weren't cheap, but the surrounds made it worth it. We found a table near the edge of the balcony and had a view out towards the Eiffel Tower. Aimee said we'd just have one drink here as there was enough other places to go to get the full experience of Parisian nightlife. We couldn't leave until I'd gone around the full perimeter and seen the view in each direction.

'C'mon Elliot. Let's make the journey more fun. After all, the journey is as important as the destination, don't you think? We'll ride scooters to the next place.'

I thought it was better that such an activity happened now rather than after several more drinks. A few glasses of wines with dinner had followed a beer at home while we were getting ready and now a cocktail. I hadn't ridden an e-scooter before, so I was apprehensive about making a fool of myself. That wouldn't be so unusual, but in front of Aimee it was the last thing I wanted to do.

I had no idea where we were going, so I rode along behind her. As we made a few turns I lost all sense of where we were, more focussed on the view immediately in front of me than anything we were passing. Eventually we made our way off from the main boulevard and into a side street and Aimee pulled up outside of a laundromat.

'Got any dirty laundry on you?' she asked.

'Um, no.'

'Doesn't matter,' she said as she opened the door. She fiddled around with the controls on one of the washing machines. Next thing, she pulled open the side of the machine which proved to be a door through to a bar.

'These speakeasy style bars are scattered around Paris. This is my favourite, *Lavomatic*.'

It was busy, but our timing was perfect as two seats became available just after getting our first drinks from the bar. Not seats in the traditional sense, but swings. There wasn't space to start rekindling childhood memories on playground swings, but sitting on a swing drinking cocktails inside a laundromat made for a major point of difference to any night out I'd ever experienced.

'You know, if you see someone you fancy, you don't have to worry about me. You can go for it,' she said.

'What if she was sitting on the swing right next to me?'

'I think that would be a bit strange. We are like brother and sister. Or maybe cousins.'

That wasn't the case at all, but I figured it was her way of having me cast aside hope for what may have been. I hadn't considered the hope to be realistic, but there was no chance of me spying anyone else who was going to win my interest while sitting with Aimee, irrespective of the relative prospects.

'I don't plan on going home with anyone. Tonight's about seeing Paris nightlife, not a stranger's bedroom,' I said.

'Well let's see the main part of that.'

We left *Lavomatic* and headed towards the Place de la Requblique, finding scooters for the next trek.

'You went to *Moulin Rouge* the other night didn't you?'

'Yes.'

'Well we're headed back near there. Pigalle is the centre of Paris nightlife.'

It was a bit under ten minutes before we left our scooters on the Boulevard de Clichy, a few blocks down from the famous windmill. There were people everywhere, and as we walked in the direction of the *Moulin Rouge*, Aimee was catching everyone's attention. She took me by the hand. I knew this wasn't a sign to me of any changed intentions, but a signal to the lustful eyes of everyone else that was cast upon her.

'This is one of the best clubs in Paris' she said as we arrived at the back of a short line to get into *Cuba*. We were just a few doors down from the *Moulin Rouge* and the restaurant where we'd eaten that night was diagonally across the road. We didn't have to wait more than a couple of minutes to get in. 'Try this on the weekend and it wouldn't be so easy,' Aimee said.

It was busy and loud inside. The dancefloor was full of what seemed to be predominantly tourists based on the amount of English I heard being spoken.

'It's a different crowd mid-week,' Aimee said, sounding slightly disappointed.

'It's cool.' Dancing wasn't really my thing, but irrespective of where it was headed, I wanted to play the right cards with Aimee. I must admit, however misinterpreted it may have been by anyone watching, it felt good to be the centre of attention as I danced close with Aimee. I knew they were all wondering why she'd settled for me, but of course she hadn't and wouldn't.

We stayed through a couple of rounds of drinks, most of our time spent on the dancefloor before I was relieved to have Aimee suggest moving on. I'd enjoyed it there, but I'd felt stifled inside for that long, and couldn't wait for the coolish night air to refresh me.

'We'll head back in the direction of home. There's a cool Irish club halfway there.'

O'Sullivan's wasn't too far from where we'd started the night. We walked straight in to a small but crowded club, and I headed to the bar. The walk down from Pigalle had rekindled my thirst, and the beer went down a treat, but it seemed like Aimee was feeling the effects as she settled for a water.

She heard a song she liked and dragged me onto the dancefloor again, but we only stayed out there briefly. We had one more drink each and then she asked if I was ready to call it a night, which suited me.

'It's a twenty-minute walk from here. You up for that?'

'Yeah, it's a good way to end the night.'

It was nearly 2am and Aimee was working tomorrow. I don't think I'd have spent a Tuesday night like this if I was working the next morning, but she said she usually went out one night during the week.

'But I wouldn't be backing it up night after night,' she said with a laugh.

It was cool, but comfortable as we made our way along the quiet Rue Montmartre towards the Rue de Louvre. After a few hours in loud, crowded clubs, it was good to be able to talk to her and get to know her better.

'I can't believe that you're single,' I said.

'I had a bad break-up. I had been very much in love with a man named Claude.'

'Really? I had a bad break-up with a woman named Claudia. Must be something in those names.'

'Love always ends.'

'You don't believe that it always does, do you?'

'Of course. When it is perfect, it ends at death, which proves to be the ultimate imperfection. More often it ends when you realise the other person isn't what you thought they were. You start out seeing the best of the other person because that is what they show. Sometimes it takes days, sometimes years, but with time you see more and more of what they were keeping hidden. It's often just small things, but with Claude it was much more. Perfection is fleeting.'

As the apartment building came into sight at the end of the road, I imagined the fleeting perfection that I could have over the rest of the night if she'd only wanted it.

'Don't I know it.'

36

13 November 2015

JOHN

'We never knew it happened until the end of the game.'

I had just got home from the football, nearly two hours later than expected. Didier, my one remaining friend from the writing group on the Rue da Roule had been given tickets to the match between France and Germany at the Stade de France. I think it was more the escape from home than the desire to go to the football that made me say yes. It seems like it was a fine line away from being the worst decision of my life.

Three terrorists launched an attack at the stadium. Their plan had been for one to detonate a suicide vest inside the ground, leading to mass panic and escape outside where two other bombs would be detonated. They didn't get inside, and all three bombs exploded out of the stadium without enough people close by for the carnage to be too great. Other than bombers, its yet to be confirmed how many were killed, but it would have been substantially greater if they'd got inside. President Hollande was at the game. Initially it seemed that he may have been the prime target, though in hindsight it seems they just wanted as many victims as possible.

I heard explosions, but when the game continued and nothing official was said, I thought there must have been another explanation. Because of the damage done at the gates, we had to exit via the pitch when the game was finished. Leaving became a long process, and it was midnight by the time we'd got on the train back to Chatelet- Les Halles. As we travelled, the anxiety was enormous as we began hearing what else had happened in the past couple of hours.

Terrorists had taken over the Bataclan theatre and had been shooting indiscriminately at concert goers. There have been shootings in the 10th Arrondissement, by the Canal Saint-Martin. A bomb had exploded at a café near the Place de la Nation. It seemed like the whole city was under attack, and public transport wasn't a comfortable place to be. France had won the match, but nobody was reflecting on that. Everyone was eying off everyone else on the full, but silent carriage. Who knew where the next threat would emanate from?

It is only ten months since the Charlie Hebdo attacks. As a city, we haven't recovered from that. This now seems substantially worse.

There was an eerie feeling on the streets. Sirens were a constant sound, as emergency service vehicles headed in every direction. The situation at the Bataclan was still unfolding. It was less than three kilometres from home, and while every available police vehicle and ambulance that would be needed was already there, an obvious need also existed for the police presence to be strong and visible across Paris. Such a combination of events couldn't be coincidence. There were clearly many other people involved that the authorities needed to chase down. More importantly, fear was omnipresent across the city. There was no easy cure for that, but the more that people saw police everywhere, the less vulnerable they would feel. Not that there were many people out on the streets at this point. It was Friday night, but those of us who were out of our homes were making our way back.

Cherie seemed remarkably calm when I got home. She was watching the events on television as they unfolded. The phone network had struggled to cope with the level of calls and messaging that had been going on due to the widespread panic across the city, but we had managed to maintain contact with each other through the evening. That said, I'd been in the vicinity of three bombs, and had been out on the streets of a city under attack. I still found it surprising to get little more than a nod and a grunt for a greeting.

'It's unbelievable,' she said, without looking away from the screen.

'Yeah. Your relief that I'm safe is overwhelming.'

'I knew you were safe. The city is in crisis. It isn't all about you.'

I didn't disagree with anything she said, but I still felt that normal behaviour in circumstances like these would mean a sense of relief would be visible in her greeting. When everyone is feeling a degree of panic, even that which would normally be taken for granted, warrants appreciation. I guess she took my existence for granted even more than I realised.

I went to bed soon after. I'd been too close to the dramas to want to dive further into them now. Cherie wouldn't join me, only sleeping much later for a few hours just as I was starting my Saturday.

The attacks had been the deadliest in France since World War II. One hundred and thirty dead, several hundred more injured. Unofficially, it also killed one marriage. Paris had been placed into a State of Emergency by the President, while Cherie had made a similar decree on our relationship. Of course, the marriage was in a state of decay prior to the attacks, but the contrasting attitudes that surfaced over the ensuing period turned the situation terminal.

***

'I'm leaving you. It's over.' One week on, she was launching her final attack on me.

It came as a bolt out of the blue. Five years of marriage had been far from bliss, but there had been nothing within our marriage to prompt this. We disagreed and did so more frequently with time. She considered my attitudes to the events of November 13th typified my selfishness. I felt there was absolutely no basis for that. She was at every public memorial, waving her flag and being part of the unified public standing-up against terror. I shared her disgust at what had happened but considered such symbolism to be a useless measure for change.

'If you cared about this city, you would be out there with us, standing up for Paris.'

'If you think your little symbolic gestures are going to stop terror, you are fooling yourself.'

'It shows that we won't live in fear. They are trying to attack our lifestyle, but our presence shows them that they have achieved nothing. We live as we did, and no attack will stop that.'

'Remember *Je Suis Charlie*? The January attacks had you saying the same thing. All the rallies for peace didn't stop a bigger and worse event before a year had passed. The issues go far beyond marching the streets saying you're not scared. I want the same results you do, but I'll invest my time in something with a little more chance of achieving something, thanks.'

There was no infidelity, no cause for jealousy. If there was, I didn't know about it. A mind as suspicious and cynical as mine is more likely to see something that isn't there, than to miss something that is.

None of our arguments went to the core of who we were. The political and social climate of the country had caused fights, but they weren't built around contempt, but love and the desire to influence each other.

'What are you talking about. We've had issues, we've worked through them. Things have been better. I can't for the life of me work out where the fuck this has come from?'

'We've been heading this way for a long time. You know that just as well as I do.'

'I know we started taking each other for granted, but marriage takes work. Once we started working at it together, things have been better.'

'Marriage shouldn't be work.'

'Everything in life takes work.'

'What is meant to be, just is.'

I tried talking her around but got nowhere. I unsuccessfully suggested going away together, then changed tacks towards recommending a little time apart. When we first had troubles, a little less time around each other had proved a boon. She wasn't ready for trial mode. Her mind had been made up.

'What has changed?' I asked. I was going to have to accept her intentions, but that would be far easier done with a level of understanding.

'You are like Paris' she said.

'You love Paris. Your life is about telling of your love for it.'

'No. I understand Paris. My life is about sharing my understanding of it. Paris saddens me, for it is a constant reminder of losses and change that make it less than it was when I look back. I fell in love with the city as I fell in love with you. The City of Enlightenment and the enlightened author. The city's only claim to that richness is where it hangs on to past glories, just like the author.'

'My recent work isn't good enough, so you fall out of love with me.'

'No, your work deteriorates because the love within you is lost.'

'What do you mean? I love you as I always have.'

'I imagine you believe that, but you don't know what love is.'

Does she want to lecture me on love? Realism is idealism plus experience. Perhaps all our problems lay therein. Rather than taking the lessons of experience, she was clinging to an unrealistic ideal. Did she want to run back to her parent's castle and hide away from the world until the next handsome prince rode into town?

I had seen from the misery of my grandparent's marriage, it was better to sever the tie than to continue in a miserable relationship. We hadn't reached that point, and from my perspective, we weren't headed in that direction, but I can't pretend the enthusiasm remained the same as in our early days. You fight for what you truly believe in. When I realised how disinterested I was about fighting to salvage the marriage, it said enough.

She moved out, initially returning to her parent's place near Falguiere in the 15th Arrondissement, but soon after, moving into a small apartment in the 6th. Interaction between the two of us remained regular at first as we dealt with the inevitable issues that follow a change of address and a change of status.

I did what I could to stay up to date with what was happening in her life. It appeared she was still on her own. I was too, at least emotionally. I took what else I could get, but it no longer seemed like a relationship could possibly have a payoff that matched its investment.

***

'That's your problem John. Everything has become an equation.'

I usually only saw Didier every couple of months, but since that fateful night at the Stade de France, we've been in more regular contact. Both of us had a reclusive streak, but he considered this dangerous for his wellbeing. After the events of that night, it was natural to retreat further, but he fought this through our more regular interactions. We both understood how much there was to gain from the wisdom and care of others, and at this point of life that had changed from desirable to essential.

'Verdriet didn't make sense at times, but it worked. You wrote from here,' he said, pointing to his heart. 'Most of what you've done before and after has come from here,' tapping his temple. 'What you think and what you feel rarely sit in alignment. When they don't, which one are you meant to follow? All of us can form our own opinion on that, but you have to live with the consequences of that opinion.

'As a young man, I lived as my heart directed me, yet I wrote from the head. I tried to ensure that all of the lessons melded my work into exactly what it should be. Success only came after breaking up with the great love of my youth, Pierre. I wrote from my heart, as broken as it was, and the result changed my life. Ever since, men have come and gone faster than I could keep count, but none ever had my heart. My head ruled every element of my life, bar my career.'

Didier was more than ten years older than me yet would have been universally accepted as my junior based on appearance. He had an incredibly healthy lifestyle, testament to that approach of living based on rational choices. He hadn't come to see me because he felt like it, but because his scheduler reminded him it was time for his fortnightly couple of hours with me. I couldn't take task with that, for without it, who would I see? Who would offer me the choices and not judge me for the foolish ones I made?

'You can't just change the fundamental approach you have to life like clicking your fingers,' I said.

'When you are broken enough, you can't avoid changing your approach to everything. You don't choose it. Where the choice comes in is at the point of time when you begin to recover. That is when you return to how things were, or you commit to the new way of life. I think there lies the difference in how you changed after Inge, and how I changed after Pierre.'

'And now?'

'All you've ever known of love is loss. Family. Debbie. Beth, Inge. Zoe. You'd do whatever you could to drive anyone away, because unless you lose them, it ruins your narrative.'

'What bullshit.'

'Perhaps. I don't have the answers, I just ask the questions. Only you have the answers.'

'Cherie has the answers, not me.'

'Not the ones that matter. Why she left is irrelevant, all that matters is she has. Where life takes you from here on in doesn't get decided based on that, but based on what is within you.' He stood up and asked me to come for a walk with him. I'd been couped up inside as much as I could get away with since Cherie left, but I only had the energy to fight his persistence for so long.

'*Bonjour* John.' My neighbours Bernadette and Aimee were returning home as Didier and I were walking out. I explained the strange dynamic that had emerged between us.

'No, it never happened until Cherie left. She just invited me in one day. I thought she was offering me a coffee, but I got far more than I bargained for. Three times since, same circumstances. I don't think I've had a word from her other than that.

'Her daughter barely stops talking to me. She's a very good English student, and loves coming over and having me help her. It's the only thing that cheers me up.'

'Does the kid know about you and her mother?'

'No, though I think she'd like it to be the case. At first, I was worried she was directing her teenage adulation towards me in an awkward way, but I think she looks at me as more of a father figure. There doesn't seem to be any male role-models in her life. I think she likes the idea of her mother finding someone, and I'd fit that role perfectly through Aimee's eyes.'

'But?'

'I don't need the complications again.'

'You can't avoid complications; your choice is merely which ones you let in.'

'Casual encounters don't involve complications,' I said, prompting Didier to laugh.

'Until they do. I remember you and that girl many years ago. Sandrine?

We'd walked as far as the Jardins des Tuileries, moving through to the octagonal basin where we took a seat. I pointed to the giant wheel, giving tourists an overpriced yet spectacular outlook across Paris. In the moment as the wheel takes them to the top, they feel that fleeting moment of perfection as all the iconic sites below them stand out.

The success of *Verdriet* had been the greatest feeling I'd had as an author, given the hardships it followed. *Of Virtue and Vice* may have sold fifty times more, but at that stage I knew nothing else of the business and had no appreciation for what had happened. This was a feeling I loved. It coincided with a period where all the unease within the marriage had lifted. For a short while, life seemed perfect.

Perfection is always fleeting. We all aspire to reach a point in life where our day-to-day life is exactly as we'd hoped. If ever we reach that point, our hopes tend to get modified to include something more. It is the human condition. What we have shapes what we want. Every time the first of these changes, a moment of appreciation is followed by a change to the other.

How quickly perfection had sunk to devastation.

37

13 March 2023

ELLIOT

'Do you want to come in?'

'I think it's best not to, alright.'

I'd been almost certain of the answer, but I still had to ask. In the one time I met John when I was a child, there were certain things he said that had stuck in my head. One of these was the saying that it was better to regret something that you did than something that you didn't do. If ever I was to find out that the chance had been there and I didn't take it, then I knew I'd look back with regrets. By asking the question, I'd know that hadn't been the case. There was nothing to regret by asking, for I'm sure the desire it revealed was nothing that Aimee couldn't have seen from the first moment I saw her.

She kissed me on the cheek and thanked me for a great night. She said she hoped that I'd come back to Paris before too long as she knew it had meant a lot to John who was special to her. She also said she'd love to get to know me better.

'With time on our side, who knows how much fun we could have had.'

I didn't know whether that was a gentle way of rejection, or a genuine sign of any mixed feelings she had. It didn't warrant further consideration at this hour of the night. The situation was what it was. The reason why did not matter.

I gave her my gratitude and best wishes and asked that she keep an eye on my uncle. 'Family hasn't been a big thing for him, but I've pushed through his thick skin and seen what's inside. Whatever he pretends, he needs people, and he really values you.'

She walked down the hallway and only after she left my view could I bring myself to close the door. Nearly 3am, I didn't expect the welcome from John that I got.

'The night didn't quite end the way you wanted?'

'It was a great night,' I said. 'But yeah, I could have seen a different ending that may have taken it from great to perfect. What are you doing up?'

'I'm always up a couple of times through the night. Getting old is shithouse.'

'I don't think the alternative is better.'

He nodded, conscious I was right, even if he didn't particularly feel that way at that moment.

'So, what's wrong?' I asked.

'At this point of life, the simpler question would be what's right.'

'C'mon, you're only sixty. You've got more than a quarter of your life ahead of you.'

'You're basing that on average lifespans. They are averages for a reason. Some people live longer, some much less. Thanks to the bad choices and excesses of my past, there is little chance of me getting any-where near that.'

'Is there something specific?'

'There's a lot of things. I have breathing issues, heart issues, hyper-tension, high cholesterol.'

'They're all common enough things to slow you down, but they don't give you a deadline.'

'They all keep reminding me that the clock is ticking. They don't just impact how much longer I've got, but they impact the quality of that time.'

'But you still smoke, drink and live for the moment.'

'I can't undo the damage I've already done. I'm better off making the most of what I've got.'

'And you're doing that?'

'I guess that is a matter of opinion.'

He seemed a different man to the one I'd seen through our time together. John generally presented an image of indestructibility, but now he seemed vulnerable and scared of what the future had in store for him.

'What do you want from the rest of your life?'

'That's the biggest problem. When you are young, you have dreams. Some of them are unattainable, but mostly they are things you know you can reach if you work hard enough towards them. When you're old, you know you have to make the most of what you've already got. When you've got nothing, what can you make of it?'

'What do you mean you have nothing? A career that has an eternal legacy. A home on one of the world's most impressive streets...'

'A career that peaked decades ago and has floundered ever since. A home that you yourself said was unhomely. The truth is that the people in our lives make life. Love is what gets us through. Without family and friends, there's an emptiness. It doesn't matter when you're younger, as you're capable of finding any number of other options of making the most of life. Eventually your body and mind don't allow the same array of choices.'

'You've got family. Sure, there are complications with distance and history, but those can be worked through if you want it. The past few days have proven that.'

'We didn't have history against us. Come Thursday, distance is against us once more.'

'We'll make the best of that though. And what about Bernadette and Aimee.'

'Bernadette will never be more than what she is to me now. She hasn't got the slightest inclination to become emotionally involved, and to be honest, nor do I. Aimee's wonderful, but the friendship a sixty-year-old man can have with a twenty-year-old woman isn't quite the relationship that carries us through.'

His mental health was as concerning as his physical health. There wasn't any quick fix I could offer after such a long day and night. I'd also worked him out enough to know that any genuine solutions would be something he wouldn't be willing to choose.

'It's all bullshit,' he said.

'What is?'

'Life. Each of us is insignificant in the scheme of it. We're born, we die, and in between we do what we can to make it through.'

'And until we're dead we've got to keep striving to make it through the best we can.'

'Yeah. Well, I'm going back to bed. Once the day dawns I'll be ready to see it that way too.'

'Ok. Good night.'

I'd felt like I was fighting to keep going when we'd got to the last club a couple of hours ago, but now I wasn't ready to sleep. The unfulfilled desires of earlier had been replaced by the concern and worry for a man who I didn't know a week ago, but loved now like I loved the rest of my family. I grabbed a beer from the fridge and made my way out on to the balcony.

When Aimee talked about Claude, she highlighted the familiar fact of how relationships often deteriorate as you get to see more of the person. The same rules shouldn't apply in non-sexual relationships. These were never built upon false impressions that were given to attract the other person, so from step one they were built on a more sincere view. It didn't mean those relationships didn't have their own separate life cycle. Friendships fade, and in some cases die completely, just as John's had with the rest of our family.

I was shattered when I lost Olivia. This trip had been part of the re-cuperation process, but before I stepped on the plane, I'd already reach a degree of acceptance of the situation. One of the key components to this was hope. Hope that someone better, something better, was wait-ing in my future. John had that hope when he came to Paris. He found that hope after he lost Inge. He found it again when Zoe left. He found it as he worked on *Verdriet*. His problem now was the fact that he no longer had any hope that something better existed.

How do you retain a lust for life when you have no capacity to believe that every great experience in life is behind you?

38

3 February 2019

JOHN

Some say you're only as good as your last book. If that's the case, then had I retired after *Verdriet*, I was a great writer. Instead, I allowed *Words and Deeds* to be released. To the poor bastards who wasted their money buying it, I'm a useless nothing.

Success, failure, irrelevance. That had been the trajectory of my career from the time I arrived in Paris. From a sales perspective, *Verdriet* had not been the phenomenon that *Of Virtue and Vice* was all those years earlier. If sales were measured against the dollars spent in marketing, then the returns were similar. The critical reception was as great. Burdened by the more realistic views that accompany middle-age, my view of success had changed so much by this point, that I considered *Verdriet* every bit the success that my first book had been.

Learning from mistakes means not repeating them. Success had previously been followed by failure, and back at the same point now, it was important to reflect on where I'd gone wrong after my first book. The longer the time it took before the next release, the more the expectations grew. One of the reasons it took so long, was the constant dither in what the follow-up should be. If I'd had the courage or the freedom to stick to my first idea, success may not have followed, but the failure would have been minimised. A quarter of a century on, I had ploughed through ideas, eventually relying on the consensus of others to direct me. I was headed down the same road for the second time. How could I be surprised when I arrived at the same destination?

People usually show humility when speaking publicly. They heap praise on those who have aided their success and accept responsibility for the elements of failure in their life. Few people reflect quite the same beliefs privately. I was no different. The success of my first book came from the raw elements of the story. The failure of the next book was the result of the corporate management that were so insistent on shaping the product which followed. Of course, the publishers would say my initial success was the result of their quality in painting over my cracks, while the follow-up was a turd that just could not be polished. Claim responsibility for the success, pass blame for failure. It happens everywhere.

I couldn't do that this time. I was responsible for this failure. It doesn't matter where things went wrong outside of my contribution. My decisions, and the shortcomings of my work allowed no opportunity for anything but failure. I had learnt nothing. I deserved what I got. Depression followed and has been with me ever since.

Nicole and I had ended our professional relationship decades ago, yet she still remained the most trusted voice I had on anything career related. She told me what I didn't want to hear sometimes, and my stubbornness usually meant that I chose not to listen, then similarly avoided her for a long time afterwards. Once down enough, I'd go back seeking her advice again, and the personal relationship reverted to the beginning and the circle continued. I went to London to spend some time with her, hoping she could help me make sense of the muddle in my mind.

'You don't need to work, so fine. Stop. Say you live until eighty, that leaves you twenty years. Seven thousand days. How the hell are you going to fill them?'

'Enjoying life,' I said.

'You wouldn't know how. How many of life's best moments have not been accompanied by feelings of fear?'

'Plenty.'

'Bullshit John. Almost every great memory that anyone has is from a time when they overcame fear, nerves, anxiety. The feeling that something could go wrong is what makes things going right seem so valued. You're not talking about stopping writing, you're talking about stopping living. You can't keep the pros without having the cons. Live life, or choose mere existence, but don't think existence will be pain-free as you age.'

'That's bloody cheery.'

'Why did you come here John?'

'To get the most reliable possible opinion.'

'Would it be a reliable opinion if I told you what you wanted to hear?'

In some respects, Nicole had been the most significant person in my life. My family had failed to be part of my life beyond the first twenty years. Inge had been in my life for a decade. Cherie less than half that time. Nicole was here discussing my future with me, just as she had done the first time I woke up in her bed, more than thirty-five years earlier. Nobody else had retained a role in my life for anywhere near that length of time.

'Do you have regrets?' I asked.

'About what? Us? No. You're a dreamer. I'm practical. We had our moment and that was all we were ever destined for. People come into our lives and play all sorts of different roles for all sorts of different reasons. We've played our roles exactly as they should have been.'

She convinced me that I needed to write, but I was less convinced about ever publishing again.

'If writing isn't read, it has no purpose,' she said.

'You know how they say that if you find a career you love, you never work a day in your life. I found that in writing, but every part of the publishing process is when it does become work. And I am retiring. I've had enough of humiliation.'

Forty years ago, I heard my grandfather say the same thing. His career had followed a similar trajectory to mine. Although the circumstances of his marriage were very different to any of my relationships, there is perhaps a degree of symmetry in how the momentum in our personal lives correlated with the direction in our careers.

Leonard released ten books over the course of his life, just as I have. His biggest success came with his first novel, just as mine had. His ninth book, *Conceding Scores* had been the equivalent of *Verdriet* for me; books that we considered our greatest works despite a lack of interest from the wider public. Leonard regretted publishing his final book, just as I had regretted publishing *Words and Deeds*.

Leonard had believed he was married to misery. I feel like I am divorced from life. Only one of those relationships had died, yet both had equally lost all sign of life. There is a point of existence where all quality of life has disappeared. From that stage, continuing is often more painful than the release that accompanies death.

I've never made the decision to break-up with anyone. I've been the dominant personality in every relationship, and while that usually means making the decisions, when I felt it time to end things, I couldn't. Perhaps I was taking the easy way out. I wronged the person. I lied. I cheated. I ran. I made it impossible for the woman not to cast me out. The engagement with Zoe and way back to Beth in Australia, were examples of the same thing. My actions were the same with Inge, yet foolish or otherwise, she decided to stay and rebuild what we had.

Cherie was the most submissive partner I'd ever had. I led and she followed and that was the basis for our relationship from the beginning. It was only after we got married that the balance begun to change, albeit marginally. Perhaps I deserved what I got for the accumulated sins of my past, but the divorce knocked me down hard and kept me down longer than I'd imagined possible.

Twenty years on and I miss Inge every day. Three years on and I rarely think of Cherie. Losing her hurt me less than having her squash my pride. When *Words and Deeds* failed so badly, whatever pride was left was crushed just as mercilessly, and it was all too much.

Even when it has been perfect, love always ends. If nothing else destroys it, eventually death becomes the dividing force to end the relationship.

39

14 March 2023

ELLIOT

John insisted that we start early.

'The Eiffel Tower aside, there is nowhere busier than the Palace of Versailles. It's not somewhere I've been in the best part of a decade. The palace doesn't change, but the number of visitors keeps growing.'

I was surprised that he'd be willing to go somewhere so touristy, but he'd said it was an essential place for me to visit. For him, the crowds of Versailles were destined to be an ordeal he'd normally choose to avoid, but he admitted that the surrounding town was a place he enjoyed, as was the journey out there by train. After our middle of the night inter-action, I wasn't sure that he should be doing any of this, but at least it seemed like it would be a less packed day than yesterday. While not saying anything about that now, he did say he was keen to save effort where possible, so we'd skip any additional walking.

We went downstairs and across the road to the station, going just one stop to Chatelet before transferring lines to go another two stops to Saint-Michel. All of this may have taken longer than just walking to this point, but it left us fresher. From Saint-Michel we transferred to the RER train for the leg we couldn't have done any other way, the forty-minute trip to Versailles.

We arrived at the terminus, which had the far from simple name, Gare du Chateau Versailles Rive Gauche.

'I thought Rive Gauche was where we were yesterday in the 13th?'

'It's a direction rather than a place. It means left bank. Paris is famed for its left bank, so you find Rive Gauche in many spots. Versailles originally had its own main station that is on the main line to France's west. This was added as a convenient spot for the tourists heading to the chateau.'

We walked out of the station and courtesy of the pedestrian crossing, made our way immediately across the road. Opposite the station I was confused. The world's most omnipresent take-away restaurant had an outlet, but without its golden arches and distinct colour scheme that usually made it stand out. Had it not been for my need for a bathroom, I probably wouldn't have noticed it at all. As it turned out, entry to the bathroom was dependant on a receipt that showed you had made a purchase. I bought something small, partly for the ticket to relief, and equally to expose John to the type of food he would never taste of his own volition.

'You think so little of French cuisine you drag me here?'

'I've had a taste of your world, it's only fair you have a taste of mine.'

'It was more than enough, thanks.'

John couldn't have been keener to leave the experience behind him, and we continued down the street. At this point it became more apparent that the buildings on this side of the road were relatively new and uniform in their external appearance. However big the brand, they'd been required to conform to the blue awnings and discreet white lettering. Across the road was a building that looked nearly as palatial as the destination we were heading to.

'City hall,' John said as we reached the next intersection. 'Don't worry about it too much. Look that way,' he said gesturing to our left.

The most magnificent boulevard I'd seen in France was leading a couple of hundred metres ahead to the palace. A statue of Louis XIV on horseback welcomed us as we arrived outside of the gates.

My knowledge of history is limited, but I have heard of the Treaty of Versailles, the document that was signed in this palace which ended World War I. What other role it had played over the years was unfamiliar to me.

We made our way through a seemingly endless range of rooms that had been home to Louis XIV, his successors and their queens, including the most famous of all, Marie-Antoinette. My favourite room, by name rather than style, was the Salon of Abundance. It captured everything about Versailles. Abundance and opulence. It captured the most incredible beauty, but at the same time the grossness of inequality which led to the downfall of the monarchy. Centuries later, it is still disturbing to think thar such wealth could exist in a society where so many had nothing. Has the world really learnt the lessons of history?

'If the wealth that was held here, in the Louvre and in the range of other museums was sold, the money raised would mean nobody would ever struggle again,' I said.

'You think? How long would that last? These displays generate billions of Euros each year. The people who visit spend everywhere else too. That is what funds the nation.'

I shrugged my shoulders, accepting that the complexities of economics couldn't have solutions as simple as my ideals would like. John told me to appreciate what I saw and focus on the lessons it offered later.

'This is the pinnacle,' John said, as we walked into the Hall of Mirrors. 'This is where they signed the treaty. It is also where the German Empire was first proclaimed, which was part of the reason this was chosen for the treaty to be signed here, effectively dismantling that empire. I've never seen a more stunning room. Then again, I haven't been to your house.'

'It's a bit like the family room back home,' I said in jest. Full length windows looked out on to the seemingly endless gardens of the palace. Full length mirrors stood opposite reflecting the light and highlighting the opulence of the room's other features. Golden figurines. Elaborate chandeliers. Incredible artwork on the ceilings. Marble sculptures of Roman emperors.

'Look at the ceiling. It is not just beautiful paintings, they tell the story of the early part of the reign of Louis XIV.'

'Just the early part?'

'He was king for over seventy years. This was built midway through that time.'

Looking out from the Hall of Mirrors, the magnitude of the grounds became apparent. The French monarchy was overthrown as the impoverished masses rebelled against its excesses. Nowhere were these excesses more evident than Versailles, yet rather than seeing it dismantled, it was now celebrated. To me this seemed counter-intuitive, but John had an explanation for that.

'We want what we don't have. Those with nothing fought against those with everything. Once they'd won the battle, there was nothing to rebel against, thus romanticising it became far more common. Mind you, you're talking about centuries of evolution between those times.'

We began our trek through the grounds, not just to take in the majesty of all that it presented, but to escape the confinement we felt amongst the masses inside. As incredible as the palace itself was, the greatest highlight of Versailles was outdoors. Covering more than 800 hectares, it didn't matter how many people were sharing the experience, there was room to move and appreciate all that was here while retaining breathing space.

We spent a couple of hours wandering, stopping on benches at times to sit and savour the sights before moving further on. At the grand canal, we watched people rowing boats along the enormous waterway while other groups sat near the edge enjoying picnic lunches. People on bikes passed us, using this method to see more than we could ever hope to see on foot. It would have taken days for us to cover the entirety of the grounds, time we didn't have.

We walked hedge lined pathways to perfectly manicured gardens, elaborate fountains and magnificent sculptures. Eventually, John's fatigue looked as great as my own felt, and we made our way back up towards the palace.

From the top, I took one last look back at the land behind me. It had taken my breath away when we first walked outside, but after covering so much of the grounds in the past few hours, I had another level of appreciation at the sight. Turning back to the view of the palace itself, I doubted that there could be a more complete estate anywhere in the world than Versailles. I wouldn't have come had it not been for John's insistence.

'Worth your while?'

'Absolutely.'

'Beauty should always be celebrated. In amongst the horrors of the world, it is all too rarely we get the chance, so when we do, we have to grab it.'

'And this is the most beautiful part of greater Paris?'

'Visually perhaps. Genuine beauty lies not in this sort of extravagance of the senses, but in people and our relationships with them. All the palaces in the world can only serve as a reminder of what limitless resources can offer. For most of us, the small attentions and displays of care from those around us is all we can hope for. It genuinely is all we need and ensures that there is the same potential happiness in life for a pauper as there is for a prince.'

40

21 February 2023

JOHN

'*Bonjour* John.'

'Aimee! *Comment ça va?*'

She asked me to join her. Despite being immediately below my apartment, I was rarely a customer of this café. I journeyed further when I ate out, and I made my own coffee, but my machine is on the blink, so I popped down to grab a take-away. As depressed as I have been in recent times, Aimee remains the one person who seems to be able to temporarily lift the fog from me, so I was happy to join her.

'You've been keeping a low profile.'

'Yeah, I haven't been my best for a while.'

'What is wrong?'

'That is a depressing topic. Why don't you tell me about what is right?'

She laughed as she said she was no more able to avoid depressing topics herself. She told me that her former partner Claude had just moved in with his new girlfriend.

'I can't even get a second date and he's already at that stage.'

'You can get any date with anyone, you're just yet to find anyone worthy. I tell you, you ought to start looking at sixty-year-old Australian ex-pats.'

'Don't let my mother hear you say that.'

'I don't think she'd care. It's good for each of us to have that level of contact and interaction, but that's as far as it will ever go. Your mother is a good woman, and she's had as much hurt as she's willing to accept through life. She won't put herself in the position for more.'

Bernadette had lived in the building since divorcing Aimee's father more than a decade ago. She became familiar by sight, but I barely spoke to her in the early years.

Aimee was studying both English and literature at school and was intent on getting to know her author neighbour at that time. After Cherie and I separated, she moved into the role of matchmaker, trying desperately to encourage her mother and me to get together. Neither of us were interested, but in time we found an arrangement that worked for both of us. No obligations, no commitments and barely a word of conversation. Years later, it continues. With a knock on the others door, one of us would arrive and the other would either open the door or shake their head. It varied from a couple of times a week to once every couple of months, but over the course of five years, there has only been a couple of head shakes. In recent years, Aimee became aware of this.

'What's wrong John?'

'My nephew is coming to Paris.'

'That's a good thing, surely?'

'In theory, yes, but I'm worried that in practice, it will be a disaster.'

'Why?'

'I met him when he was eight years old. I was the famous author, the long-lost uncle from the other side of the world who he'd never met. For all the issues within our family, he looked up to me with admiration. Ever since, despite no contact, I've always clung to that memory whereby one small part of my family had an appreciation of who I was. I feel like I will lose that, when he sees the decrepit old bastard I've become.'

'Family ties bind until there's a reason for them to be torn apart. I can't believe he will be needing or wanting something more than the real you. If he does, what have you lost?'

'The purity of that memory. At my stage of life, what do I have but memories?'

'I remember reading a line once. What was it? Life is a gamble. So long as the potential upside outweighs the potential losses, bet with confidence. *Spes Nova*, by John Martin. The memories of the past won't die whatever happens, but you might build something much stronger.'

'Perhaps. I think it's putting my focus back on the rut that I've been in anyways.'

'I've been there. Life doesn't change to make you feel better. *You* change to make *life* feel better.'

'Maybe you should be writing books that I should be reading rather than the other way around.'

'I wish.' She had talked about the dream of being a writer in her last year of high school but hadn't taken any serious steps in that direction since. She'd taken a retail job a couple of years ago wanting to earn while building a life with Claude. It was a waste. Whatever she was to become, she was a young woman of great intelligence, and I would have loved to see her achieving her potential, whatever field she wanted that to be in.

Despite the odd subtle flirtatious comment, she was like family to me. I had nephews and nieces in Australia who I'd met once, but Aimee was part of regular life here. I'd seen her grow from girl to woman and had played a small role in that development. Now she seemed to be more of an influence on me than vice-versa. As loneliness had grown in recent years, her place in my heart grew to be progressively more important. Like most people that age, she lived a busy life, so I didn't see so much of her these days, but it didn't reduce her impact on me.

'What are you going to do?'

'Today?'

'No, longer term. You have the potential to be anything. Why are you settling for something that doesn't utilise your capabilities.'

'I'm not. I've got a job as a translator. I'm starting Monday. It's only casual work, *but* it's an opening at least.'

'That's wonderful. Congratulations.'

'*Merci beaucoup.*'

I don't know why the combination of her keen eye for literature and her mastery of both English and French hadn't raised the thought in my head previously, but I had an idea that had the potential to be ideal for both of us.

'Are you interested in the idea of having your name on the cover of a book?'

'Writing is a dream, but it's for the distant future.'

'Not writing. Translating my books. Everything I've done with Marchand has only ever been released in English. Maybe some of them don't warrant it, but pick one to start with, and let's see what happens.'

I'd spoken to Fabrice many years earlier about the prospect of a French language translation of my books. He wasn't willing to fund it, but said if I found a translator, they'd be happy to run a limited release. I'd need to pay the translator, or sort a royalty share with them. It had all seemed more trouble than it would be worth at the time, and I never gave it any subsequent thought. Now, there seemed a good reason to proceed.

'Three hundred pages. Three hundred hours work. How about fifteen hundred euros and a fifty-fifty split of the royalties?'

'How much are the royalties?'

'They won't get you rich, but they'll ensure your hourly rate starts seeming a bit more reasonable. It will give you a taste of the author life though, and it will be a hell of an addition to your CV.'

She was excited by the offer. I clarified that there was no timeline and no obligation on her part, and she could work on it as quickly or slowly as she wanted.

'It won't be released without you, so work to your own pace.'

'How will you know if I've done a reasonable job?'

'It will go through an editor.'

'I'll start today. *Verdriet*?'

'It's the best work, so why not start there?'

My expectations were limited, but it gave me something to look forward to. Four years on from my last release, dismal failure that it was, there was no grand enthusiasm when the emails arrived with my monthly sales figures. All going well, by the end of the year there would be something else out there. If it ended up as a break-even, I'd be ecstatic. It wasn't about money. It was an opportunity for someone special to me, while also providing me with an answer to a question that I'd always been curious about. Could French language versions of my book sell?

Life is a gamble. So long as the potential upside outweighs the potential losses, bet with confidence. Maybe I needed to reread my catalogue and start living according to the lessons within it.

41

14 March 2023

ELLIOT

'One last night in Paris. What do you want to do tonight?' John asked.

I really didn't want to do anything more than sit with John and talk. I felt like we'd been catching up on a missed fourteen years of our lives, and there was little enough time left that I wanted to make the most of this. I'd seen the best show in town, visited the best clubs, bars and brasseries. If I was here forever, I would never get sick of all that the city has to offer, but with just one more night, there was no one spot that stood out enough to select. There was however, one uncle, and spending time with him was my choice.

He suggested we get off the train on the outskirts of the city, and we disembarked at Javel-Andre Citroen. We walked across the Seine, stopping half-way along the bridge as he pointed out the strange sight just along the river. It was the Statue of Liberty, or at least a small replica of the icon of New York.

'The French gave them the original, so the Americans gave France one back, albeit just a quarter of the size. It isn't such a special attraction, but when we get to the other side of the bridge, you can get the ideal photo with the Iron Lady towering over Lady Liberty.'

I took the photo as he'd suggested, which proved to be the only reason behind coming across to this point. John took me back from where we'd come, though once across the bridge we turned to walk alongside the river. He pointed out a restaurant that he considered to be close to his favourite in the city, but being too early to consider dinner yet, I wasn't going to find out for myself.

The next opportunity to get across the train tracks presented itself soon after and we were in the 15th Arrondisement. This particular section couldn't have been less like traditional Paris, with tall and modern high-rise structures on the blocks closest to the river. We weren't more than a ten-minute walk from the Eiffel Tower, but it wasn't an area that I'd noticed when looking out from there.

A couple of blocks on, and the feel of residential living returned, but much of the area was filled with a different style of housing. Apartment living remained the dominant theme, but these weren't from the vintage most commonly seen in the city, but developments from the postwar area. Boulangeries and brasseries were still prevalent, but not in the same constant pattern, one block after another. After a few random turns through side streets, we came across the first bar we'd seen in a while. We'd walked far enough to feel as though we'd earned a drink.

'This is the most populated area of the city, yet it's a spot that has nothing to bring people to it. You're seeing a part of the city that few other than the locals ever do.'

Cold beer on a warm day when you've covered enough territory on foot, is one of life's truest pleasures. I could be anywhere in the world, and the moment the first drop hit my tongue I'd be exactly where I wanted to be. Gulping down a significant proportion more, I stopped to focus on the part of Paris we were in.

'It's strange. The travel snobs always talk about getting away from the tourist sites and experiencing the real city, but I think there is more to it than that. Dodging the major sites I understand, but you can do that and still visit incredibly vibrant parts of town. Here, not so much.'

'This is authentic Paris.'

'Where you live isn't?'

'It is, but for probably about a tenth as many people as this is.'

Paris may be the world's greatest city, but it is a city nonetheless. It has its strengths and weaknesses and for all the appeal that tourists see, there is another side that is no more appealing than you'd find anywhere else.

John and Paris will always go hand in hand to me. In every travel brochure, Paris is the Eiffel Tower, the Arc de Triomphe and the Louvre. When you get to see the fullness of the city, you realise that it is so much more than landmarks. Most, but not all of it is wonderful. This doesn't diminish the magic of the city, it rounds it and completes it. It makes it more real, accessible and understandable.

John is like Paris. From all I'd read of his work I'd seen the equivalent of a brochure. The strength of his work, his creativity and originality. Spending time with him I'd seen the vulnerability and the human weakness. It didn't diminish my love of him, it built it. He was a combination of positives and negatives and as such it made him more real, accessible and understandable.

A city constantly changes. Old areas are reimagined. Empty spaces are filled to make the city what it needs to be as times change. People do the same thing. We fill the empty spaces in our life. We shed part of who we were, often subconsciously, as we grow into the person we need to be moving forward. Even after we pass, everything we've been, has the potential to live and thrive in new forms. John, through his books, through the influence of his work on numerous other authors and to an extent through me, my brother and our cousins, will live on. As unrecognisable as the city will end up being in time, the legacy of John will follow the same way.

'It mightn't be the most exciting spot, but I was thinking we could eat at Alexanders.' He was referring to a restaurant two doors down from his apartment building. I hadn't paid much attention to it, but I wasn't concerned either way. If it was satisfactory to John, it was satisfactory for me. The past few days had taken a physical toll on him, so I think he considered the closer to home the better.

We headed back on the metro, taking the train to Concorde where we had to transfer for the three stops back home. Running the gauntlet of peak hour madness ended up being as tough as the walk was destined to be, so John motioned me in the direction of the exit.

'May as well have one last look at one of the best parts of the city,' he said. 'I think I've got just enough energy to make it this far.'

One last look from the Place de la Concorde, to the National Assembly in front of us, with the gold dome of Invalides shining above it. The Roman columns of the Madeleine in the opposite direction. From there it was into the Jardins des Tuileries, and a walk through the natural beauty that is equally part of Paris as its grand architecture. At the end of this was the Arc de Triomphe du Carrousel, the smaller relation to the Arc at the end of the Champs Elysees.

'You know that this is the end of the Axe Historique, a line of monuments that runs for nine kilometres. A straight line takes you from here to the grand arch at La Defense.'

I admired the Louvre pyramid for one last time before walking out along the Place du Carrousel and making our way to the Rue du Louvre.

Dinner was good without being special, but that was all we needed. I can have a good meal anywhere, anytime. I was happy to be back at the apartment early enough to have some downtime with my uncle. We chatted for a couple of hours, talking about the time we'd shared, life back home, and the future for each of us.

'I'm not looking forward to you leaving,' John said, as we came back in from the balcony. 'I've enjoyed the past few days more than I have for a long time.'

'My presence is only part of that. It's also been getting out, seeing and doing different things. That's something you can do without me being here.'

He gave me a nod of his head. I interpreted this as an acknowledgement of the merit in what I said, but a refusal to commit to acting upon it. Whoever you are, it is easier to make effort for another than it is for yourself alone.

He looked spent, and as I refilled my glass, he told me he was going to bed.

'Alright, see you in the morning.' He gave me a hug, and thanked me, without any specification of what for. He wasn't one for overplaying the emotion of a moment, so I knew the experience of this week, and the closeness of this moment, had really meant a lot to him.

I decided to head back out on the balcony and take in the view of the Rue de Rivoli, bathed in the electric light that the city is famed for. One last time with a glass of wine, I sat and reflected on the time I'd spent away from home, particularly this past week in Paris. Travel, they say, is the one thing where the money you spend makes you richer. I have been enriched far more than I could ever have imagined.

ever have imagined. The glass now empty, I stepped back in wrestling with the decision of another glass. I wasn't ready for sleep, though didn't really feel like another wine. Hearing a knock on the door, I regretted not already having gone to bed, to save the quandary of whether or not to answer it. It seemed far too late for anyone to be dropping in, so it may be someone to avoid, but equally, it could be something urgent.

'Bonsoir Elliot,'

It was Aimee. She explained that she had seen me out on the balcony so she knew I was still up and thought she wouldn't mind if I dropped in. Of course I was pleased to see her again.

'You know, your uncle once told me that it is better to regret something you did than something you didn't do.'

She wrapped her arms around me, moved in close and kissed me, simultaneously closing the door with her foot.

42

15 March 2023

JOHN

They're trying to keep it quiet. I don't know whether they're trying to avoid waking me, or just trying to keep the tryst a secret. Given how badly I sleep, they're wasting their time. I heard Aimee come in and I've heard everything since. It doesn't bother me. Two young people who mean a lot to me; why wouldn't I be happy for them to have the best of each other.

Normally when I've laid here awake long enough, I get up and have a drink and a painkiller to try and help me sleep. I'm not going to embarrass them by being in the living area when they show their faces.

I hadn't known what to expect from Elliot, but now I'm dreading the fact he's going home. People cause frustration, heartache and pain, but without them, what is life? However much I've tried to isolate myself from the need for having others around me, the few days I've spent with flesh and blood has filled me with reason. I haven't just learnt about him, but I have learnt about myself. How long I can hold on to those lessons once he's gone remains to be seen. Learning is only so valuable. Remembering the lessons is the most important thing.

As the noise from the next room abates and my eyes start feeling heavier, it may be one of those rare nights when I can return to sleep unassisted. Maybe that's another product of feeling good about life. I feel more content than I have in a long time.

***

Elliot's flight left at 4pm, so I'd suggested a taxi at noon.

'It may be more time than you need, but you can never take Paris traffic for granted.'

He didn't surface until after ten, just as I was starting to worry that he was cutting things too fine. I couldn't help but bring up what I'd heard during the night, partly to embarrass him, but more to give him the opportunity to talk about anything without the need to hide it. I'd popped down the street earlier to grab a couple of pastries so he had something to eat with his coffee, and after finishing that off, he quickly showered and got all of things ready to leave. He may have only been staying with me for a few days, but his European trip had been six weeks, so he wasn't light travelling.

He asked what I'd plan to do with life returning to normal after his departure.

'Back to work.'

'The Paradox of Paris?'

'No. I've got a different idea floating in my head now?'

'What's that?'

'It's about an old man. No, a middle-aged man, who has been separated from his family for most of his adult life. He's now washed-up and alone in Paris. His nephew visits from Australia, and they explore Paris, both learning lessons from each other and from the wonders of the city.'

'I like it. But I hope it doesn't end with a sad farewell in Paris, for I think it would be so much better finishing with a happy homecoming in Australia. And while we're at it, if the uncle has a stunning young brunette living next door to him, I think the story would work best if he brought that neighbour to Australia with him.'

'Think your stretching the believability a tad.'

'It's fiction. You can pull the strings of all the characters. You can make anything happen. You could call it *Perfection Doesn't Have to be Fleeting*.'

'If I'm pulling every string, I think the stunning brunette would have a thing for much older men.'

'Now who is stretching the believability?'

We both laughed. He said he was serious about the idea, though he prefaced that for every idea that has ended up as a published novel, there were a dozen that never made it to the end of a first draft.

'If I use the basis of the past week for a story, there is every chance it takes a tangent and turns into a completely different story. Don't expect to be reading your own life in my words. Wherever it leads, it has me inspired for now, and at this stage there is nothing more I need.'

We still had a little time left, so I made him another coffee and we went out on to the balcony together one last time.

'You need to come back home for a visit,' I said.

'My days of long-haul travel are probably over.'

'They don't need to be. You've traipsed around Paris with me through the past few days with no difficulties. Twenty-four hours spent mainly sitting on a plane isn't that hard to manage if you want to.'

'You might be happy to have me, but I'm not sure if anyone else would be.'

'I'm not enough?'

He laughed, impressed that I kept finding ways to better his argument.

'I couldn't avoid everyone else.'

'You wouldn't need to. There is a way back for everyone and every relationship if you take the right steps. The only thing stopping you and Dad or you and Auntie Emma from turning things around is your willingness to make it happen. I'm sure all of you would move on if the others took the first step, but each of you has always waited for the other to take that step.'

'I've taken the step a couple of times,' he said.

'That's what they say too. There are two sides to every story, and the truth is always somewhere in between them. You told me that the other day.

'You know, when I first planned my trip here, I never knew if you'd see me at all, but I took the first step and made contact.'

'We never had problems, so there was nothing to repair.'

'No, but we haven't really had a relationship. You welcomed me with open arms, but only after I took the step of initiating things. I think it's your turn now.

'I'll think about it.'

'You know, a man I greatly admire once told me that it was better to regret something you did than something you didn't do.'

'Sounds familiar.'

'Apparently you gave Aimee that same advice one time, and I will be eternally grateful for that.'

43

15 March 2023

ELLIOT

'I wish we had more time together.'

She looked at me and shrugged her shoulders. 'Perfection is fleeting. We had our moment of perfection. It is natural to try and squeeze the most of every experience, and if we had more time we would, but do you think it could have stayed so perfect?'

'If that was how life was meant to be, then nobody would ever find long-lasting love.'

'That's not true, but that sort of love isn't perfect. It has good and bad moments. It is great in its own way, just as this has been. Remember it for what it was. Perfect, albeit fleeting.'

After walking her to the door, she gave me one last kiss. Like every moment before it, I will enshrine it in my memory where it will stay precious forever. I had hoped she'd stay and allow me the pleasure of waking up next to her, but she'd insisted on going home. All that she'd said about perfection was true and advancing her departure had actually made the time we shared feel more perfect.

I didn't sleep much, but as I lay in bed, I felt a strange combination of satisfaction and regret. It didn't matter that I accepted her words about perfection, I still knew that less never feels like more. I doubted, however long I'd live, that I would ever feel a higher peak than tonight.

I remembered John say that once you've experienced the best life can offer, it is difficult finding the motivation to look forward to what lies ahead. Of course, tonight was only one of life's peaks. I had a career to look forward to. Marriage. Children. Who knows what else? But for the ultimate fulfilment of instinctive desire, tonight would surely never be topped.

I didn't get out of bed until late morning. John had been concerned if I didn't rise soon that he'd have to rouse me in order for me to be ready in time for my flight.

'I thought I might choose not to, so you'd have to stay longer.'

'I'm flattered that you'd want me to.'

'It's meant a lot to me having you here. I hope it's not the last time.'

'Of course not. I want to come back so long as you'll have me.'

'Is that to see me or Aimee?'

'Aimee? Why would that be?'

'I might be falling apart, but I'm not deaf.'

'Oh. Um, sorry.'

'Don't be. Very happy for you.'

'But living half a world away, I'm well aware that it was a one-off.'

'Some people come into your life for a season, some for a reason and some for a lifetime. You had a season in Europe to learn lessons that will carry you through life. You had Aimee be the reason that all those experiences stay with you forever as you realise how perfect life can be in moments. And you've got an uncle who will be part of you for a lifetime.'

He gave me a hug, and I felt a closeness beyond anything I'd ever known with my own father.

I packed my case and backpack and was ready in advance of the taxis arrival. John took the case downstairs in the lift as I took the stairs, and after putting everything in the cab, he gave me another hug. He was tearing up as I said goodbye and thanked him for the most amazing week of my life.

Five days ago, he met me for the second time ever. How could he be so overcome when he was saying goodbye to someone who'd barely been part of his life? I guess to him, he wasn't saying goodbye to me, Elliot, but to the unresolved part of his life that lay half a world away. It was goodbye to the Martin's. When he lost Inge, the pain was disproportionate to the quality of the relationship at that time, for the grief gave cause to remember the best times that preceded it. I suspect he'd never done that with our family, but as we bonded over the past few days it has given him the opportunity to reflect on all of life. Like with most conflicts, I am sure the issues he had with our family were ones where blame lay on each side. He was probably right to take the path he did and create a new life. While that path brought him a reward, every reward still bears a price. He'd been paying it for forty years, but it was only now that he understood what that price had been.

In less than a week in this city, I have experienced more to change my world view than any week of my life. The more distinct experiences you have, the more hunger it builds within you. Coming to Paris has had me not only crave the idea of returning but has spiked my desire for similar experiences in other cities.

Getting to know John, more deeply than I could have ever imagined, has now filled me with the intrigue of getting to know people better. I don't mean random people, but the people I already think I know. How much do I know my family? There is so much to any person and we rarely do more than scratch the surface. Seeing the bluff and bravado of John in the first couple of days and then connecting to him once I saw what was lurking beneath was not just insightful, it was life altering. That may sound over dramatic, but I believe it has shown me the fears that have undermined so much of my life are normal. Everything I have sought to keep hidden from the world is no different to what lies within others. We all hide a certain amount of who we are.

I don't plan this to be goodbye. It may stem from a few days, but I now feel a closeness to John that I don't want to let go of. Paris is hardly a simple destination to drop-in on, but there is more to communication than being in the flesh. There is also an incredible city to serve as an excuse for a return visit, as soon as is practically possible. This has been Paris is in spring. Why not aim to see it in winter, summer and autumn too. You can only see an element of a city at any point in time, and this city is amazing enough that I want to see more.

Once again, I have a cab driver who doesn't speak English. In this instance I am more than happy with that. I know that he is aware of where I'm going, so there will be no need to communicate. Right now, I am far more in the mood for reflection than communication. Based on the way traffic is, I am feeling nervous. Although I have left more than enough time for the trip to Charles de Gaulle Airport, that was based on some degree of movement. Having spent ten minutes trying to get through one intersection, I'm less certain than I had been about how long the trip out there should take.

Every driver near the intersection is honking their horns. Not anyone in particular, for nobody can see the cause of the congestion, but it gives them a feeling that they are doing something. With the excessive noise and the frustration of not moving, I am getting a last look at the ugly side of Paris. It isn't the only example. From rude waiters to dog shit on the ground, there are constant reminders that this city of unparalleled beauty is also one of unparalleled flaws.

As much as I have loved Paris, I am happy to be leaving now. Maybe that was part of the paradox of Paris that John was so intent on writing about.

The protests are getting more frequent and more violent. From all reports, the president is going to use a clause in the constitution to pass the legislation without a vote in parliament. This is expected to see the turmoil in the streets to escalate significantly. More people striking was destined to make the city even more difficult. Many tourist sights and businesses will be forced to close, public transport will be interrupted, and the ongoing waste management issues look likely to continue.

None of this was behind my contentment in departure. It doesn't matter how exquisite a meal is, once you have significantly overeaten, the discomfort that follows renders the meal imperfect. When something is good, we always want more. The real paradox of Paris was that the city was built on an understanding that the best things only remain that way when experienced in the right quantities. Less truly can be more.

There is a balance to life. What is the point of learning if we don't get the opportunity to put those lessons into practice? If this week just blended into another, could it have continued to be as fulfilling? The most beautiful woman in the world had told me that perfection is fleeting. This experience had been perfect, and I'd carry that with me forever. Now it was time to use that perfection to make the rest of life the best it could be.

FROM THE AUTHOR

Like the character of Elliot, my first experience of being alone in a city where I didn't speak the language was in Paris. It was the day when I fell in love, not so much with the city itself, but with the magic of travel. Paris had lured me like nowhere else, mainly with the desire to see the sights that the city was famous for. Once I arrived it took little time for me to appreciate that the thrill of coming face to face with all you've looked forward to is secondary. The greatest joy of travel was not in seeing the known, but in the discovery of the unknown.

For me, the process of writing a travel novel varies greatly from city to city and book to book. Sometimes I've had a story ready, waiting for a city to fit around it. With Paris, I began writing this book without any semblance of the characters that would fill it, nor the story that would define it. Only once I'd reached the end of the initial manuscript did I find the theme that defined Paris for me. Paradoxes.

Paris is classic architecture, yet nowhere in the city is more admired than the more modern Eiffel Tower and Louvre Pyramid that the locals hated on construction. A city with a diet that should breed obesity, yet little is evident of this. A city that inspires more love than any other, yet also gives rise to Paris Syndrome, a psychiatric condition formed from the overwhelming disappointment that many tourists encounter when visiting the city. A city that values the common man so much that protests and strikes are constant, yet it is the common man who pays the price of this with gridlock and the stench of uncollected garbage. A city with beauty like nowhere else, but with so much of this beauty tarnished by filth.

Once the paradox theme emerged, it was on to the characters, and it was my late uncle, Martin John, who inspired John Martin. Although little of my uncle's life flowed into the fictional character, he had lived in Paris many years earlier, and it was his anecdotes that ran through my head while writing the story. Whenever I had to think of what this character would say or do in any situation, it was his voice I heard.

While writing is largely a solitary process, a book only gets to this stage with the help and impact of many people. Paradox in Paris never would have happened without the contribution of many people who impacted me across my numerous trips to the city. From the taxi driver who I could only communicate with through the mention of footballers, to the waiters who defied stereotypes, my experiences of Parisians have always been as positive as in any city I have ever visited.

My eternal gratitude to my wife Alison Page, for her constant support, for being at my side on several trips to Paris where the ideas behind this book festered, and for her contribution to the project through the design of the cover.

My sincere thanks to Olivia Fergusson, Ken Rose and Leonie Page for the provision of their feedback as the transformation from disjointed manuscript to final book took place.

Without doubt the greatest influence on my writing, and my life, has been my mother, Patricia. She travelled extensively, and whenever she did, she wrote the most detailed letters back to me. Not only did these inspire my travels, but they taught me the valuable lesson of documenting my experiences. As well as being incredible to look back on, the writing process helped to consolidate these experiences in my mind. Years later when it came to writing scenarios that my characters faced, this familiarity, and my notes,

Most importantly, thank YOU. To every person who has read the book, thank you for doing so. I believe that everyone enjoys reading, but some people don't realise it as they haven't found the right type of book for them. I was like that myself. I liked hearing stories, but the novels I read always seemed to fit into genres that never fully engaged me. I'd heard the adage, 'write the book that you'd want to read,' and began the journey of writing travel novels. Thank you for giving this a chance with *Paradox in Paris*. I hope you have enjoyed it, and I hope you will read further travel novels going forward.

I

HURDLES IN HOBART

Available 31 July 2023

First past the post isn't always the only winner.

Travelling in Australia with her family for a wedding, English journalism student Zaniya Fergusson fears six days in the small southern city of Hobart will leave her bored. A chance encounter in the hotel breakfast room with recent widow Helen O'Shaughnessy changes her mindset.

Lucky O'Shaughnessy was known as the world's worst jockey, falling in all forty-five jumping races he rode in. A figure of infamy and ridicule throughout his career, he'd been long forgotten until a newspaper article after his passing bestowed the title of Hobart's Greatest Loser upon him.

The Fergusson's experience the wonders of Hobart and its surrounds. The culture of MONA, the history of Port Arthur, the natural wonders of the Tasman Peninsula, the restaurants of North Hobart, the nightlife of Battery Point and the tranquillity of Bruny Island. Against these diverse experiences, they learn the fuller picture of the man Lucky had been.

Can Zaniya convert Lucky's legacy from loser to hero?

SURVIVAL IN SAINT PETERSBURG

Available 25 September 2023

Why does an 87-year-old woman spend hours each day in a dough-nut shop?

Saint Petersburg is arguably the world's most beautiful city, but beneath the beauty lies a city that has known trauma and tragedy like nowhere else.

Ekaterina Komarova has experienced it all. Born in the city in the 1930's, she lost her family through Stalin's Purge and the Siege of Leningrad. As an orphan, she was a victim of systematic rape and abuse. She escaped, finding happiness before tragedy again intervened.

When Australian tourists Adam and Louise visit a Soviet era dough-nut shop, they are amazed at the crowds and in awe of the authenticity of the step back in time. Before long, their intrigue turns to the mys-terious woman hobbling between tables. Neither a customer, nor an employee, they are desperate to gain an understanding of who she is, and what she is doing there.

Through interpreter Yuri, Ekaterina tells her life story. Intermingling with their experiences in the attractions of the city, Adam and Lousie discover what she and her city did to survive against all odds.

ABOUT THE AUTHOR

C.R. Page was born in Adelaide, South Australia. He graduated from the University of South Australia with a degree in business before working for many years in the South Australian public sector.

A love of travel led to him writing articles and short stories, planning to begin a travel blog, but in time the greatest elements he was seeing in places warranted a bigger canvas. The concept of the travel novel began to take shape.

In 2022 he won the Port Adelaide Writers Festival award for his short story, Sanctuary. This was followed by the release of his first novel, The Ride to Work, a story of mental health set on the morning commute to a workplace.

In 2023 he began his travel fiction series with the novel Bedside in Berlin.

Follow him on Facebook at CR Page - Travel Fiction.

www.ingramcontent.com/pod-product-compliance
Lightning Source LLC
Chambersburg PA
CBHW020359120726
47904CB00002B/627